MW01036992

The SPIRIT TREE

A *Tessa Lamar* NOVEL

KATHRYN M. HEARST

Kathryn M Hearst

THE SPIRIT TREE

Created in the United States of America

Cover Illustration: Marcela Bolívar
Cover Design & Interior Layout: Shawn T. King

Dedication

For my Great-Grandma Mae who taught me the value of a good story.

Acknowledgements

Special thanks to my crazy family for providing enough material to fill a thousand books, to Marcela Bolivar for the gorgeous cover art, to Shawn T. King for the cover design, to Tim Marquitz, Randall Andrews and Julia for whipping my work into shape, and to the folks at Kindle Scout for believing in this project.

One

SOME EVENTS LEAVE SCARS. THEY mark time, changing life as you know it into something unrecognizable. Death split my life into two periods—before Charlie and after Charlie.

That morning, I woke crying without knowing why. Dread followed me through the day. It needled my thoughts until I succumbed and acknowledged someone I loved would die before the sun set.

"Tessa Marie, we need you to come to the hospital. It's your uncle Charlie," my great-grandmother Mae said over the phone.

"Is he all right?" I knew the answer.

"No, child. He had a heart attack and is on life support. The doctors are talking about turning off the machines. Please hurry. We're at Florida Hospital on Rollins Street." The call disconnected. My great-grandmother must have lost cell service. Her impeccable southern manners wouldn't have allowed her to hang up without saying good-bye.

"I've got to go." I sprang from the bed, searching for my discarded clothing. Sex had been my last-ditch effort to shake the feeling that someone would die. It hadn't worked.

"I'll wait here until you get back."

"Ian, get up. You can't stay here." I pulled a T-shirt over my head.

Ian threw the blanket off and tugged on his jeans. "What's going on?"

"My uncle is on life support. This can't be happening. He can't die. I need him too much. I just talked to him this morning. He sounded fine. There has to be a mistake." I slipped on my flip-flops and headed for the door.

"Let me drive." Ian jangled his keys.

I wanted to tell him to stay put, but I didn't feel like driving.

We rode in silence for a while before Ian sighed and turned on the radio. A disembodied voice reported the murder of a young mother and the possible kidnapping of two small children. The victim's mother had found her daughter's body in the kitchen earlier that day. The children hadn't been located, and the police had yet to release any names. I drew my knees to my chest and prayed for both my own family and that of the murdered woman.

"Want me to come in?" Ian eased the car to a stop.

I studied him for the first time since the call had ruined our alone time. Wide-eyed, he rubbed his palm on his thigh and shifted in his seat. His expression puzzled me. I couldn't tell if he was worried about me or if he feared I would actually ask him to come inside. We'd dated about three weeks—if hanging out during happy hour and having sex at every opportunity counted as *dating*. Come to think of it, we'd never had a proper date.

"No, I'm fine. Thank you, though."

Ian exhaled and grasped the steering wheel. He started to pull away before the car door even shut. Actions spoke louder than words, and his actions screamed.

I stood on the sidewalk and gathered the courage to walk into the hospital's lobby. My skin prickled as I passed through the glass doors. I turned and found the woman behind the welcome desk glaring. Under the puff of cottony white hair, two dark, beady eyes fixed on me. The woman wore a blue vest with a colorful badge that proclaimed her status as a volunteer. Her lips twisted in disapproval. I wondered, *What have I done to offend her?* I resisted the urge to rush up the escalators in order to avoid the sour old woman.

Behind the welcome desk was the hospital gift shop, filled with flowers and balloons. The contrast between the not-so-welcome desk and the happy little gift shop made me grin. I squared my shoulders and walked to the desk.

"Can you tell me what room Charles Nokoseka is in?"

"Nokoseka? How do you spell that?" The old woman glared at me.

I spelled the last name for her, exaggerating the pronunciation of each letter. I knew the drill. It wasn't *my* last name, but I'd spelled *Nokoseka* a million times. The woman typed in the name, looking between me and the screen.

"He is in ICU Step Down. Only immediate family members are allowed to visit." For some unknown reason, the little old lady had an issue with me.

"I'm his niece, but he raised me . . ." What the hell? I didn't have time to argue. I needed to find my uncle.

"You've missed visiting hours."

"Considering they called me to pull the damned plug, I don't think visiting hours are going to be an issue. Tell me where he is." My outburst surprised us both. I didn't care.

I hurried to the escalators, then took the metal steps two at a time. The hairs on the back of my neck stood up. I needed to get to my family. Something was wrong—more wrong than the fact that the man who'd raised me was fighting for his life at this very moment. I rounded the corner to the Step Down unit and stopped.

Two large men stood in front of the elevators, blocking the hall. Their size didn't strike me as much as their ponytails and sharp features did. They could've been members of Charlie's tribe, coming to pay their last respects, had it not been for their tight expressions and stiff postures. They were angry, very angry.

I turned and went in the opposite direction until the elevator pinged. I counted to ten and doubled back toward Charlie's room, pausing in the hallway. At least twenty family members had gathered in the waiting room, including my mother. At that moment, I would rather have gone up against the two big guys in the hall than face down my family. I should've guessed my mother would be there. Even still, it struck me like a punch to the gut.

All eyes turned to me when I stepped into the waiting room. I scanned the faces, searching for my great-grandmother or great-aunt, but found neither. The television in the corner caught my attention. The newscast reported on the story of the murdered mother. Pictures of the young woman with two small children flashed across the screen. The police urged the public to call with any information regarding the whereabouts of the kids.

Hearing the story on the radio had tugged at my heartstrings. Seeing the children's faces yanked them out. "Shit."

"Now, darlin', that is something we do, not something we say." The sweet southern drawl and gentle chiding made me feel like I was eight years old. Gram Mae had told me the same thing while standing in her vegetable garden. The second time I cursed in front of her earned me Ivory soap for mouthwash.

I bent down to hug Mae's short, round body. Gram Mae had grown up in abject poverty but behaved like a southern lady. She grew her own tomatoes, drank her tea sweet as cane, and could drop a deer, or a whiskey, in one shot.

"How is he?" I cringed, wanting to believe Glinda the Good Witch would swoop down in her bubble and fix all the wrongs.

"Not good, darlin'."

"Can I see him?"

"He's waiting for you." Mae took a firm grip on my hand and led me away from the wide-eyed family members. Gram Mae didn't have that determined look in her eyes often. They all knew to get out of her way when she did—everyone, that is, except my mother.

Two

"TESSA! OH, I'M SO GLAD you came." Darlene rushed toward me with arms outstretched, her heavy makeup ruined with twin black streaks. A well-used tissue hung in her hand as she reached for me. *Sure, now she acknowledges my presence.* Long ago, I would have sold my soul for a few moments of my mother's attention. That ended around the time I turned ten.

Mae shook her head while Darlene pretended not to notice. I sidestepped the unwelcome hug and mouthed "Sorry" to my angry-faced mother as Gram Mae dragged me toward the door.

Darlene narrowed her eyes. "Tessa thinks she's too good for us."

A knot tightened in my stomach as family members surrounded my mother. They cooed and petted her, agreeing with everything she said. Little did they know how hard I'd fought to achieve a sense of self-worth. I'd struggled for years to overcome the pain of my childhood and to recreate myself. My family, like my southern accent, proved impossible to overcome.

"Trauma drama," Gram Mae whispered as she ushered me down the hall. "Don't let them shake you. They come out when there's blood or money on the line."

I forced myself to ignore my family. Truth be told, my real family consisted of the three people who weren't huddled in the waiting room. Gram Mae, Uncle Charlie, and Aunt Dottie had raised me. My mother came to collect me a few times, promising things would be different. The visits always ended sooner rather than later, and I found myself back on Dottie and Charlie's doorstep.

The second I entered his room, tears sprang to my eyes. I covered my mouth to stop the scream rising in my throat. I wanted to run away, to go home to Charlie's house and visit over sweet tea. I wanted him to tell me everything would be all right.

I hugged Aunt Dottie. When had my vivacious aunt grown old and frail? How long had it been since I'd sat with her, watching soap operas and eating macaroons? I turned toward my uncle, and my knees went out from under me. As they'd done my entire life, Dottie and Mae steadied me until I could stand on my own two feet.

"We're going to be right outside," Dottie whispered, and patted my shoulder.

My mouth fell open, and I shook my head. Before I could form a word of protest, they left me alone with my uncle and several large, noisy machines. Each step toward him felt like a monumental accomplishment. I sat on the edge of his bed, transfixed by the gentle rise and fall of his chest. His jet-black hair had grayed, and the smile lines on his cheeks had deepened. "I'm sorry I've been away so long. I promise I'll take care of Dottie and Gram Mae for you."

Memories flooded me as I placed my hand on top of my uncle's. I remembered being a tiny girl and setting my hand against his, measuring my small fingers against his larger ones, marveling over how pale my skin looked next to his.

My green eyes searching his dark brown eyes, I'd ask, "Am I Cherokee?"

"About half, I reckon," he'd reply.

I'd crinkle my nose and giggle. "Which half?"

"Your color is white, but your stubborn is all Indian." He'd laugh in his deep, good-hearted way and kiss the tip of my nose.

I would have given my life to hear that laugh again. "I need you. Please stay with us."

A soft sound filled the room—a whistled melody that reminded me of both nature and Uncle Charlie. I thought I was imagining it, until I recognized the tune. He whistled it while working in the yard, or when one of the tribe came for healing. I'd never asked about those visits, though I always knew he served as the tribe's medicine man.

The fluorescents overhead flickered and hummed, causing my temples to throb. I pulled back the heavy drapes, and sunlight flooded the room. I would have opened the window, but it was bolted shut. At least I'd given him sunlight. I knew Charlie appreciated the effort.

The whistling began again. I focused on breathing. *Inhale, one, two. Exhale, one, two, three. Inhale one* . . . I'd seen spirits before, but never the spirit of someone I loved.

A fresh breeze caressed my cheek, and my eyes flew open. I couldn't see the spirit as much as feel it. I closed my eyes again, and lips kissed the tip of my nose. "There you are."

"And here you are, little flame." Charlie's voice sounded distant, nothing solid to hold on to. Still, it moved with life and warmth. "Your aunt and great-grandmother are in danger. Crows will come for my notebook, to learn my secrets. Our secrets. Go get my cedar box and take it to Dr. Hicks in Gainesville. He will help you."

"I don't understand. Who would want your box? What secrets?" I stopped talking and focused on the more important issue. "Don't leave us. Please. You can't die."

"Some things cannot be changed; others can. Listen to me."

A cold sweat broke out across my brow, and I felt faint. Maybe my blood sugar had bottomed out. I'd skipped dinner in favor of having a flat tummy during the roll in the hay with Ian. The added stress was causing me to hallucinate.

"Tessa, tell Dr. Hicks you're my granddaughter." His voice drifted, lost to alarms and beeps.

"What? Great-niece. You meant great-niece, right?"

Doctors and nurses filed in. Dottie clung to the door frame with Mae.

"Dottie?" I couldn't move, let alone form a sentence.

A nurse ushered us into the hallway, directly into the crush of family. Someone shouted, "Tessa pulled the plug." Others spoke all at once. By far, Darlene's voice rang the loudest—my mother accusing me of killing my uncle.

"Come with me." My great-grandmother tried to shield me from the mob. Dottie wrapped her arms around me, whispering calming words. I couldn't breathe. I struggled free of the embrace and ran away from my mother's acrid voice. No matter how far I ran, the continuous monotone beep of the monitor echoed in my ears.

Three

I HIT THE GROUND FLOOR IN a blind panic. Ian dropped me off, I had no car, no way to get back to my apartment. In my rush to get to the hospital, I forgot my purse and cell phone. I needed to think. I needed to be still, but my brain refused to cooperate. I ran out the glass doors and dropped onto a bench.

In the corner of my consciousness, I sensed people watching me. *It's a hospital. People die here, and families cry and mourn. Big deal! Stare away.*

I tried to make sense of Charlie's warning. I remembered the heat rolling off the men waiting for the elevator. I bolted upright and surveyed my surroundings. Waiting outside didn't seem prudent, all things considered. I marched to the welcome desk. "I forgot my phone and need to make a call. Please."

The volunteer's attitude hadn't improved. The woman scowled and turned the phone toward me. The old woman made a point to watch as I dialed.

"Hailey, I'm at the hospital on Rollins Street. My uncle died, and I need a ride. Can you come get me, please?" I stopped listening after she said yes.

My gut told me to stay inside. The sane, educated side of me balked, craving sunshine. The entire ordeal had produced some sort of psychosomatic paranoia. Research showed that bereft loved ones often turned to magical thinking of ghosts and mediums in order to hold on to some part of their deceased loved ones. It seemed logical, but the textbooks didn't account for the scope of sensations and emotions rolling through me.

I wandered toward the windows, telling myself I should look out for Hailey. I scanned the front walkways and the line of shrubs on the other side of the road. Every small movement drew my attention and made the hairs on the back of my neck stand up. I waited for what felt like hours, preoccupied with looking for the boogeyman. I startled when Hailey waved from the other side of the window.

"Thanks for picking me up. Ian dropped me off, and I didn't think about how I was going to get home. I hope this wasn't too much trouble." My words came out too fast.

"Tessa, chill. It's not a problem." Hailey put the car in drive. "Are you sure you want to go home?"

"Yeah, I need my car. I have to go take care of some things at my uncle's." I sank into the seat.

"I can go with you. I don't have to be at work until morning." Hailey reached over to pat my thigh. "Hell, I can call off. It's not like they're going to fire me."

"No, I can't imagine your dad firing you. Who else would put up with counseling spoiled rich kids?"

"Certainly not you. Seriously, when are you going to grow a maternal instinct?"

"Maybe when I'm thirty."

Hailey grinned. "I'll come in. I miss staying up all night talking with you."

"Thanks, but I want to go alone. I think I need some quiet

time to process all of this."

"Right. Just don't isolate yourself, or spend too much time with that crazy-ass mother of yours. Neither are healthy options." Hailey shook her head.

"She was at the hospital. She accused me of pulling the plug."

Hailey's grip on the steering wheel tightened. "What the hell? That woman makes Mommie Dearest look tame. What happened? I mean, what happened to Charlie?"

I turned toward the window. "Gram Mae called and said he had a heart attack and was on life support. I didn't get any other details. The second I got there, they took me in to see him. Five minutes later, the machines started going crazy, and he was gone."

"I'm sorry." Hailey squeezed my hand.

"Something weird happened. I don't know how to explain it. I knew something bad was going to happen today, and at the hospital—"

"You've always been freakishly intuitive. Tell me what happened."

I admired Hailey. She was calm and even-keeled until she spat out a slew of curses that would've sent Gram Mae running for a bar of soap. Hailey gave the car in front of us the one-finger salute. The guy had almost run us off the road.

"Sorry, Tessa. Ever since I hit ten weeks, my hormones have been out of control." As soon as the words came out of her mouth, Hailey went wide-eyed. "I planned to tell you. Scott made me promise to wait until after the first trimester. Some ridiculous superstition."

I snapped my mouth shut. "So this is why you guys have been avoiding going to Fitzpatrick's with me and Ian for happy hour. I thought you were blowing us off."

"No, we've been avoiding going because we can't stand Ian."

Hailey smirked.

"Hormones got your tongue again?"

"No, just the truth. The guy is a complete douche."

"Seriously, Hailey, is that your professional diagnosis?" I snorted in laughter. "He is a douche, isn't he?"

"You can do much better. I mean look at you? You're like Jessica Rabbit, with your long red hair and curves. I'd kill for your figure."

"You have to say that because you're my friend. Try being five-two with D-cups." I crossed my arms. "Boobs aren't all their cracked up to be."

"I wouldn't know, but maybe mine will finally blossom now that I'm pregnant."

I lost myself in my thoughts for the remainder of the drive. When we arrived at my building, Hailey parked outside and cut the motor. "Now that I have that off my chest, tell me what happened that was so weird." She put on her professional face. "I can see it upset you."

"Are you going to charge me for this session? I can't afford your hourly rate."

"Out with it." Hailey grinned.

I debated telling her about the ghostly message from beyond, but Hailey never accepted anything except science. She would come up with some well-researched, clinical explanation. I needed to believe Charlie had reached out to me. Besides, if some sort of danger lurked about, I couldn't put Hailey in harm's way, pregnant or not.

"It's the same old family drama, Hailey. Nothing new." I smiled to cover my lie. "Thanks for the ride. I need to get going, and you need to get to home and put your feet up. Don't forget, you're growing a baby."

Four

AFTER TWO MINUTES ALONE IN my apartment, I wanted to call Hailey. The space felt too quiet, too dark, and too empty. Even after I turned on every light, I couldn't shake my unease. I turned on the television, and the screen filled with coverage of the murdered mother and missing children.

The place needed a good scrubbing. I had no one to blame but myself for the piles of dirty dishes, discarded clothes, and books. Maybe I should clean and get a couple of hours of sleep before retrieving the cedar box? A soft pillow and warm blanket sounded good, but even on a good night, sleep eluded me. Insomnia was a long-lasting side effect of my graduate-school days.

I decided to ignore the apartment and pack a bag. I would need my laptop if I had to track down this Hicks guy. The older generation of my family didn't waste their money on computers. They'd only recently broken down and ordered cable.

The picture of Charlie and Dottie on my nightstand caught my eye. I sat on the bed staring at their smiling faces, remembering the day I'd taken the photo. The entire family had gathered to celebrate Gram Mae's birthday. Charlie had unrolled a piece of Visqueen on the lawn and set the hose at one end. He was soaking wet after a turn on the homemade slip-n-slide, and had grabbed Dottie for a hug. Their smiles both warmed and broke my heart.

I buried my face in my pillow and willed myself to cry. The tears wouldn't come no matter how hard I tried. I closed my eyes and focused on my memories of that day. Ribs cooked on the grill and laughter in the air. Would we ever have another day like that—day of easy joy?

I woke in a panic but couldn't remember the nightmare. My heart raced and my head felt heavy. I had no idea how long I'd slept, but fatigue slowed my every movement. I had to go to Charlie's and find his cedar box, but my body begged for rest. On some level, I knew grief caused my exhaustion but refused to give in. There would be time to mourn later.

I drove in the dark early morning with the window down. The car reeked of cigarettes. Ian smoked, and though I hated the smell, I'd never bothered to ask him not to smoke in my car. Hailey's assessment was spot-on. He was a jerk.

I needed to break things off, but how? Calling him would cause too much drama. E-mail? Impersonal. Texting? Tacky. In the end, I decided to play the avoidance game and eliminate the chances of a confrontation. It might be cowardly, but I had enough on my plate without adding a wounded male ego to the mix.

My thoughts drifted from Ian to Charlie to my mother to the murdered stranger to Hailey's baby. Nothing stuck long enough to matter. My body knew the way to the house in the backwoods without the need to engage my brain.

The car crossed a set of rough railroad tracks and continued onto a dirt drive that ran parallel to the tracks. A patch of green grass grew down the middle of the drive. On each side of the grass, white sand dipped and rose like the hills of a roller coaster. One side rose while the other side dipped, so all four wheels sat at different levels. Gram Mae called them God's speed bumps.

As I stepped out of the car, a chill ran down the length of my spine. Several sets of tiny black eyes stared. My *snake sense*. No matter how many years I spent in the backwoods of Florida, I never got used to all the dang snakes. Using the light from my phone, I illuminated my feet in time to see a black racer slide under my car. Each step I took, the phone lit up more snakes. "What the fuck?" I glanced over my shoulder, thankful my great-grandmother wasn't around to hear me use the ultimate bad word.

I thought I'd jump out of my skin by the time I reached the front steps. The stairs consisted of concrete blocks stacked in neat rows. To my dismay, another snake rested on the second step. I shined the light on it, made shooing sounds, and stomped my feet. The dang thing refused to move. Its eyes reminded me of the old woman at the hospital: small, black, and mean.

I set my foot on the step above the snake, expecting it to slither toward my ankle. It didn't move, except to turn its head and watch me open the door. Once inside, I shook my arms and hopped around to shake the feeling of those beady eyes.

I left the porch light off to prevent attracting a battalion of bugs. Inside, I turned on every light to chase the shadows away. Pipe smoke and Old Spice—the scents of Uncle Charlie—lingered in the second bedroom. A twin bed and a desk sat against opposite walls, with a narrow walkway between the two. A cheap particleboard bookcase contained rows of old glass jelly jars, coffee cans, and the like. Charlie had labeled each container in a language I couldn't read.

I crawled under the desk to reach the bottom shelf where Charlie kept his cedar box. The hand-carved wood was as smooth as polished stone. I scrambled out from under the desk as a daddy longlegs crawled down the wall. Next to snakes, spiders were my least-favorite creatures.

I sat on the bed, feeling like a little girl getting into something forbidden. I said a quick prayer and opened the box. When nothing exploded and no one yelled, I peeked inside.

I smiled at a picture from my third birthday party. I was sitting on Uncle Charlie's lap beside a pink triple-layer cake. Charlie had a huge smile, and I crinkled my face to wink. Kool-Aid stained the front of my homemade smock dress, and my hair was a wild mess of red tangles.

My vision blurred, and I set the picture aside. "Okay, enough with the pity party."

The remaining contents included newspaper clippings from my high school and college graduations. a yellowed funeral notice for Charlie and Dottie's only child that read: "Nathaniel Nokoseka, 2," an envelope addressed to "Dr. Marvin Hicks, Univ. FL," and an old composition book held together by a thick rubber band.

I placed everything back inside and stuffed the entire box into my laptop bag. My stomach growled, sending me to the kitchen, where I proceeded to raid the refrigerator. Finding food in Dottie's refrigerator reminded me of a game of hide-and-seek. All sorts of good things hid inside old plastic containers. The Cool Whip container held some potato salad—a keeper. I set it on the counter. The small Country Crock bowl contained green beans; those went back. The large Country Crock container held . . . margarine.

I opened an orange container and found leftover meat loaf. "Jackpot."

I grabbed the ketchup, bread, American cheese, and mayo. By the time I sat down, I'd eaten half of the cold meat loaf. Outside, a dog growled something fierce—probably tangling with one of those darned snakes.

I rinsed my dishes, determined to ignore the dog. I didn't want to go out before the sun rose. The dog started to howl. Had the neighbors' hunting dogs cornered an opossum? I dried my hands and opened the front door.

At first I didn't see the animals, but they must have seen me because they darted for the porch. Three large black dogs. No, too big to be dogs. Wolves? Holy cow, three wolves stared from the bottom of the porch steps. I didn't know which freaked me out more—the huge wolves, or the gyrating pile of snakes now covering the porch. I ducked inside, slammed the door, locked the dead bolt, turned the useless lock on the knob, and set the chain for good measure.

My shaking fingers made it difficult to dial the phone.

"911. What is your emergency?"

"Snakes! Lots of snakes! I'm trapped inside. There are wolves, three. Big ones. Black, I think. Please help me. I'm trapped inside!"

"You need to call animal services after eight a.m." The woman on the other end of the phone paused. "Did you say wolves? Are you sure they aren't big dogs?"

My hand tightened around the phone. "No! Wolves! Listen." I went to the jalousie windows and opened one enough for the operator to hear the sounds of three huge-ass wolves howling. "Do you hear them?"

"That is going on outside your house?"

"Yes. Please send help to 2011 Sandy Lane, Apopka. This is my uncle's house. My name is Tessa Lamar. I'm alone and freaked the hell out. Send police, guns. Guns are good." One of the wolves slammed into the window. I screamed and dropped the phone.

The wolf clawed the slats of glass as I cranked the window closed. What kind of wolf tried to pry a window open? I hightailed it to the master bedroom and pulled out a single-barrel shotgun. A semiautomatic, camo-colored, brand-spankin'-new shotgun. Uncle Charlie used it for hunting, scaring off the Jehovah's Witnesses, and ensuring that the family from hell didn't get too rowdy. I checked for shells—one in the chamber, a full magazine, and a ghost round floating on the carrier. I had five rounds and three wolves. The odds were in my favor.

Could I shoot three moving targets from inside the house without breaking a window? I debated my options until I heard the glass break and claws begin to scratch against the metal. The darned thing had managed to get its paw inside the broken slat.

I stuffed the barrel into the broken slat and fired. Glass shattered, but only one slat broke. The kickback wasn't as bad as I expected. Unlike Charlie's old gun, it didn't knock me flat on my butt. The wolf fell back onto the wooden porch. My ears rang enough to block out sound.

The sun broke over the horizon as two wolves retreated across the yard. On the porch, the snakes moved over the large mass of the fallen wolf. Beneath the snakes, I swore I saw skin, not fur. "What the hell?"

I tried to get a better look, but couldn't through the various shades of snake. I grabbed the phone and rested the shotgun against my shoulder. "Hello?"

"I can't hear you. I shot one of the wolves." At least I hoped I'd shot a wolf. It looked like the snakes had moved off the body of a very naked and very dead man.

Five

FLASHING LIGHTS IN THE DISTANCE caused my heart to race. The first set of headlights bobbled and bumped along the dirt road. A second and third set followed close behind. Their arrival should have been a relief. Instead, I tried to remember the legalities of shooting people before they broke in. A few years ago, the Stand Your Ground laws were all over the news, if only I'd paid more attention.

Two uniformed police officers looked between the two houses. I flipped the porch light on and off until they moved in my direction. The male officer made a sound equivalent to an eight-year-old girl getting her ponytail tugged. The female officer shook her head and pretended to ignore the snakes. When she approached the door, the snakes moved out of her way, like Moses parting the Red Sea.

I opened the door and froze in place as the female police officer drew her pistol, shouting. The other officer noticed the dead guy on the porch and started screaming out more commands. By the time I realized what was happening, I had three guns trained on me, another cop yelling into the radio—more than likely calling for backup—and the snakes were rallying around me.

"Drop the weapon and get down on the floor," the female repeated.

"Oh. Sorry." I set the shotgun down on the porch, went to my knees, and thought better of it when the snakes moved over my calves. "Snakes! Please! Let me go inside."

No one knew what to do. They all stared at me with varying degrees of concern, pity, and rage. Having someone lie down in a pile of snakes had to be cruel-and-unusual punishment. I started to rise, when one of the male cops shouted to stay down.

The female shook her head. "Whooo-weee."

"I'm a licensed mental-health therapist. My name is Tessa Lamar. My uncle and aunt—Charles and Dottie Nokoseka—own this house. I'm going to stand and get away from these snakes before one of them bites me." I ignored the shouts and stood.

I eased into the house. No snakes lurked about the living room. I bent over to look under the couch, and pain tore through my calf. Had a snake bitten me? Was that a gunshot? My ears rang. The commotion from the porch confused me, and my vision swam as my brain slowly accepted the fact that I'd been shot.

I woke in the back of an ambulance. An IV tube stuck in my arm, and something smelled suspiciously like soured meat loaf and sweet pickles. I'd vomited down the front of my shirt.

"Now, you listen here, my granddaughter was in fear for her life. Some crazy, naked lunatic was breaking into the house. She said there were wolves, so there were wolves. There *are* large tracks near the porch. A few are still there, even after your people trampled all over the evidence. She has a severe fear of snakes and was in a state of shock. Leave her be, or I'll have the entire Cherokee Nation at the station before you can blink. They won't be happy to hear you shot her." Mae spoke loud enough to be heard two counties over.

"Gram Mae, it's okay. I'm fine." I tried to sit, but someone had handcuffed me to the gurney. "Am I under arrest?"

"They're sorting it out. You don't need to worry." Mae locked eyes with an officer.

"Ms. Lamar, would you mind answering a few questions?" The female peeked inside.

"No, it's fine." I tried to smile, but the slightest movement took too much effort. "If there are pain medications in the IV, my statement won't be legal."

The female officer appeared surprised by my reply. "We'll take a formal statement once we get you to the hospital. There are some things we need to know, if you wouldn't mind."

"Okeydokey."

"The emergency operator said you called in an animal attack. Other than snakes, we haven't found any stray dogs or wolves."

"There were three wolves, maybe dogs . . . the way they were howling and their size, I don't know. It was dark." I regretted consenting to answering questions.

"When did you see the male trying to enter the house?"

"Honestly, I thought it was one of the wolves. It was still dark outside, and I saw a black shape. I had all of the lights on inside, so I couldn't see clearly. Whatever it was had pried open the jalousie window near the door. I thought he was going to get inside the house."

I tried to wipe my face but couldn't. I started to shake and went on blubbering about snakes, Charlie, and the picture from my third birthday. The EMT must have taken pity on me, because he injected something into my IV.

Six

I WOKE IN THE HOSPITAL WITH Mae sleeping in the chair beside the bed. Dottie stared out the window. I lifted my arm, relieved someone had removed the handcuffs. Someone had changed me out of my vomit-covered T-shirt. The hospital gown wasn't much of an improvement, but it didn't smell. "Am I going to jail?"

"No. They're still investigating what happened. I called our attorney, and he assured me you acted within your legal rights. We're thinking about pressing charges against the dumbass who shot you." Mae blushed when she caught herself cuss.

I shook my head and regretted it. "It was chaos. I don't want to press charges. I didn't even realize I was holding a gun. I was freaked out by all the snakes."

"Hmmph. Well, you may feel differently if they charge you with murder." Mae fussed over the blanket.

"What was the deal with the snakes? I've never seen so many of them. It was like a scene from a movie or something."

"With all of the rain and construction for the new Walmart, they must have decided our place was safe. You know how your uncle feels about killing snakes; they're considered sacred," Mae said.

I hadn't paid attention to my leg until a nurse came in and messed with my calf. As soon as I thought about it, it throbbed. Kind of like a mosquito bite—they never itch until you see them, but then you can't stop scratching. "Is it bad?"

"The bullet grazed your calf. Lucky for you, it missed the bone."

My stomach lurched. The nurse must have seen it in my face, because she moved in front of me with a tiny bean-shaped container.

"False alarm." Even if I needed to puke, the idea of hitting such a small target made me swallow it back down.

On TV, reporters clamored for a statement as cops brought the estranged husband of the murdered woman into the police station. The anchorman said the father refused to cooperate with the investigation. To add drama to the story, they flashed pictures of the children, smiling with their mother and father. They made a beautiful family.

"Such a shame," Dottie said.

Mae nodded. "It's always the parents."

Before I could respond, a plainclothes detective and the female cop from the house came into the room. I remembered the female, Officer Smith.

"How are you feeling?" The detective looked me over.

The nurse gave him a weary look before leaving the room. Gram Mae stayed put in the chair, and Aunt Dottie stood. Neither woman gave off warm fuzzies.

"I'm okay, a little nauseous."

"The DA doesn't plan to file any charges against you. You appear to have acted in self-defense. We do have some questions that will help us close the case, though, if you don't mind." The detective hesitated at the death stares coming from the older women in the room.

"Sure. I guess that's fine. Do I need an attorney present?"

"It's your right to have an attorney present, although it's not necessary. You acted in self-defense." His reply came across rehearsed.

"Ask away." I questioned the wisdom of answering questions

without a lawyer present, but how much trouble could I cause with Mae and Dottie in the room?

"Did you know the perp?"

"No, I don't think so. I didn't see his face. Maybe?" Oh yeah, I regretted agreeing to questioning.

The detective pulled out a picture of the naked guy's face, along with a fair amount of blood, and the faded green stain of the porch. "Do you recognize him?"

Bile rose in my throat, and I shook my head. The guy in the picture might have been Native American. He reminded me of the guys getting into the elevator. "No, I don't think so. Maybe, when I'm out of here, I can come down to the station and look again?"

"Of course." The detective put the picture away. "We confirmed that the large animal prints outside the house were too big to be canine. Do you have any idea why the house was overrun with snakes?"

"No, but it has rained a lot lately. Maybe they were looking for dry ground?"

The detective made a grunting sound. "Is it common knowledge that you're afraid of snakes?"

"You think that guy brought the snakes to freak me out?"

"It's a possibility."

The room began to spin. "Wouldn't that mean he was out to get me, and this wasn't some random break-in?"

"Maybe. What time did you arrive at 2011 Sandy Lane?" The detective didn't have much inflection in his voice, but his jaw tensed.

"I don't know. Four thirty or five? I went home, took a nap, and drove over."

"Did you tell anyone where you were going?"

"Just my friend Hailey. She drove me home from the hospital. But please don't question her. She's pregnant and doesn't need the stress. Let me talk to her first." As soon as the words fell out of my mouth, I realized I sounded guilty. "Her name is Hailey Jenkins. She lives at

3220 North Haywood."

"We'll wait until you're released to contact her. Thank you for your time, and I'm sorry for all the trouble. It's not every day we encounter so much wildlife on a call." He turned to leave.

Officer Smith moved closer. "I apologize for the mix-up. The officer who shot you was aiming for a rattler on the concrete steps. The shot ricocheted off the block and hit you."

"It was a strange situation, to say the least." I hadn't noticed any rattlesnakes in the bunch. The story reeked of CYA by the Orange County Police Department, but if they didn't press charges, I'd let it go.

Seven

THE NURSE INFORMED ME that I'd be released later in the afternoon. Good news and bad. While I wanted to go home, my leg ached once they weaned me off the IV pain meds. Gram Mae and Dottie excused themselves to go to my apartment and pick up clean clothes, since the ones I'd worn to the hospital were covered in blood and vomit.

I woke from a nap to find a strange man sitting at the end of my bed—a Native American, judging by his dark skin and deep-brown eyes. Age and the sun had wrinkled his face. He met my eyes and tipped his white cowboy hat. A band of black fur and a fluffy black tail accented his hat. My pulse beat in my ears. I fumbled for the "Call" button, and the man disappeared.

The distorted voice of a nurse filled the room. "Yes?"

"Sorry, I was trying to turn on the television."

By force of will, and a healthy dose of fear, I managed to stay awake until the discharge nurse came. I partially listened as the nurse went over wound-care instructions and gave me a quick lesson on the proper use of crutches. Dottie and Mae returned with a change of clothes as the nurse removed the IV. Another hour passed while we waited for the orderly to come with the wheelchair.

Once in Dottie's car, I couldn't keep quiet. "I saw a man with a white cowboy hat in my room."

My aunt's eyes tensed in the rearview mirror. Gram Mae turned in her seat. "We'll talk once we get you home and resting."

Not what I wanted to hear. I wanted them to poke fun, laugh it off, and be done with the subject. I hadn't mentioned the conversation with Uncle Charlie's ghost or the wolf guy on the porch. No one asked, and I didn't want to get into it in the hospital. People had found themselves locked in the psych ward for less. Hell, I'd signed the orders to lock up a few of them.

The rocking of the car on the drive drew me from my thoughts. From the outside looking in, the piece of land appeared peaceful. Too bad the hairs on the back of my neck didn't feel the same way. A spike of fear made it difficult to breathe.

"Aunt Dottie, I need to get my phone and computer bag. I left them in your house last night."

"All right. We'll go with you."

I wondered how Dottie felt about walking into her house for the first time since her husband died. Heaven knows it had been nonstop drama since Charlie passed away. We walked to the porch in heavy silence. I hobbled along on crutches. No snakes were out and about in the afternoon sun, but the way my skin crawled told me they were watching.

Inside, the house looked the same as it had the night before, with the exception of a large bloodstain on the carpet. In the stillness, I heard my aunt's heart breaking all over again. She stood in her living room, looking around as if she'd never seen the room before.

"Well, I should get some dinner cooking. I have leftover meat loaf. I'll warm it up for us," Dottie said.

I cringed. "Um, I ate most of it last night. Sorry."

Dottie laughed. "It's all right. I wasn't looking forward to leftovers anyway. How about some pizza?"

"Pizza sounds great. I need to go to my apartment and get some work clothes. Want me to pick it up on my way back?"

"Are you sure it's a good idea to be driving?"

"I feel fine, don't worry. I'll be back before dark."

"Tessa Marie, you're not supposed to drive on pain pills. I've had my fill of hospitals. If you get in a wreck, don't look for me to come sit with you," Mae added.

"I'll take it easy. I promise."

Perhaps they were right, but I needed some time to myself. Once on the highway, I turned the radio volume up to an obscene level. Anything to drown out the noise in my head.

I entered my apartment, took a step back, and checked the number on the door. This couldn't be my place. Dottie and Mae had cleaned the place from floor to ceiling. Sparkling-clean dishes sat in the drainer, and the week-old pizza box had vanished, along with the mountain of dirty clothes and books. No wonder it had taken them so long to return to the hospital—they'd cleaned up my mess. Now, if only they could clean up my mess of a life.

I needed to do laundry. The only clean under things had holes, looked dingy, or were granny panties I kept in case I needed extra modesty, or a reason not to get naked with someone. In the end, I tossed the dirty clothes into a suitcase, to wash at my great-grandmother's place. I added a few pairs of shoes and zipped it. In the bathroom, I packed makeup and toiletries, careful to hide the pink packet of birth-control pills.

I smiled as I answered the phone. "Hi, Gram. I'm on my way back."

"Don't worry about pizza. Selma, from next door, brought over a casserole, and some of the ladies from the church showed up with more food. We'll be eating sympathy casseroles for weeks."

Neither my aunt nor my great-grandmother would willingly eat other people's cooking. Dinners would be like eating with a couple of food critics.

"All right. See you soon." I almost hung up, but added, "I love you, Gram."

"I love you, too, sweetheart. Don't be too long."

I dropped my phone into my purse, and it rang again. I wished I hadn't answered as soon as I hit the button. "Hi, Ian."

"Are you busy tonight? I have beer, and you have HBO." His voice grated on my frazzled nerves.

"My uncle died, thanks for asking. I was shot. I hate beer. Get your own damned HBO, and lose my number." I disconnected and mumbled, "Asshole." I hoped I'd disconnected before I said the last word.

GRAM MAE AND AUNT DOTTIE wwere waiting at Mae's kitchen table when I came through the door. "Is everything okay?"

"We were just visiting." Mae smiled.

I moved toward to my bedroom. "I'll be right back."

"Where are your crutches?" Dottie asked.

"In the car. They're more trouble than they're worth."

I dumped everything in the tiny bedroom and joined them. My leg had gone from a mild throb to full-blown pain, and Ian's call turned my already-gloomy mood into something worse.

"Your leg might be feeling better if you'd use the crutches, like the doctor said." Mae set dinner on the table.

"I couldn't carry my bags—"

Mae raised her brows.

"You're right. I'll use them." I eased my leg onto the chair beside me.

"We decided it's best if we all sleep here tonight." Mae poured a glass of sweet tea and set it in front of me.

"Thanks, Gram. Sounds good to me." I scooped myself a heaping serving of salmon salad. "I need to be up early. I have to work, and I should stop by the police station on my way in."

"You shouldn't talk to them without a lawyer, Tessa." Dottie served herself a helping.

"I need to look through some photos to see if I can identify the naked guy." I ignored the grunt of disapproval from Mae when I spoke with my mouth full.

Mae pulled a necklace from her pocket. "You need to put this on. Don't take it off, even in the tub."

I studied the turquoise-and-silver pendant. In the center, several snakes curled around a silhouette of a bird flying toward a tiny sun. "It's beautiful, but I thought it was forbidden to have the likeness of a snake in your home?"

"It is but Charlie revered snakes, and I think they revered him. This is a protection amulet."

"Thanks." I slid the necklace over my head, and the amulet heated against my skin. "What did you do to this thing? It's practically burning me."

"I didn't do anything."

"Please tell me what's going on."

Mae and Dottie exchanged looks. "Go take a bath. I left out the little rose soaps you love so much. We'll talk when you're done."

Mae's chin rose, and I knew better than to argue.

I ran a bath and sank into the tub, propping my injured leg on the outer edge. Being in the familiar space made me feel better.

Here, I could pretend the world made sense. I imagined myself at eight years old, soaking in the claw-foot tub. The water clouded from the quarter-size, rose-shaped soaps. I sang a song that sounded like gibberish, more sounds than words. Gram Mae baked oatmeal-raisin cookies in the kitchen. Uncle Charlie trimmed the hedges, whistling his private tune, while Dottie sunned herself nearby. If only I could go back to that time, I wouldn't take a second for granted.

I hummed the song from my childhood, trying to hold on to

the memories. The song still haunted my dreams, though I couldn't remember the words. Like so many childhood things, the lyrics were lost when I realized they weren't real.

A female figure appeared in the steamy bathroom: a beautiful woman with long red hair and pale skin. She was tall and willowy, with delicate features. This woman had appeared to me a few times over the years, always here in the rose-scented mist of my bath.

I whispered, "Are you real?"

"I was real once."

"Why can I see you?"

"You see much. But you can see more when you close your eyes." The woman laughed and disappeared.

"Wait. Come back. What does that mean?" I sat up too fast, my wounded leg slipping into the water. "Dammit."

Mae knocked on the door. "Tessa Marie? Are you all right in there?"

"Yes, ma'am. I must have fallen asleep. I got my bandages wet."

Mae and Dottie bustled into the bathroom to help me out of the tub. I loved them dearly, even though they had no sense of personal boundaries. In their eyes, I would always be a little girl.

"I saw the woman again—the one with the long red hair." I pulled a towel around my chest as Dottie bent over my calf with clean bandages.

"I figured she'd come to you soon enough. She always comes when you're having troubles." Mae glanced at Dottie.

I frowned at the silent exchange. "Okay, please tell me what's going on. I can tell you two are hiding something."

"Get dressed and we'll talk," Dottie said.

I limped into the kitchen, and Mae pulled the good whiskey down. She poured three glasses about three fingers full and left the bottle in the center of the table. A growing sense of doom filled me as my eighty-six year-old great-grandmother downed the shot.

"We aren't sure, but Charlie's death may not have been an accident." Mae watched Dottie finish her whiskey. "A healthy heart doesn't just go out like that."

I scratched the side of my head. The logical part of my brain screamed that they called heart disease "the silent killer" for a reason. Seemingly healthy hearts stopped all the time. Then again, I knew there were things in this world that defied logic.

"How does someone cause a heart attack?" I asked.

"A conjurer could do it, with black magic." Mae met my eyes. "Like the fellow you saw in your room, with the white cowboy hat."

I downed my whiskey. "Why was he in my room, then?"

"We aren't sure." Mae motioned to the necklace. "That will keep him from hurting you."

The amulet cooled to my touch, maybe because my chest burned from the liquor. "Uncle Charlie spoke to me, in the hospital."

This news drew both women's attention. Dottie's eyes filled with tears, and I regretted my words. "He told me you two were in danger. Do you have protection necklaces, too?"

Dottie shook her head. "We're safe, as long as we're here. The land is sacred and protected."

"The snakes."

"Yes, along with spells and such." Mae refilled her glass.

"Then why were the wolves able to get on the property? One almost got into the house last night."

"But he didn't get in. I bet they were trying to draw you out."

I sat back in my chair. None of this made sense. Then again, it didn't *not* make sense. A wolf turned into a man on the front porch. Anything could happen. "Who is the red-haired woman?"

Mae said, "I've never seen her, but I believe she's your uncle Charlie's daughter, Atsila. She died when you were small."

Dottie nodded. "Her mother was Cherokee."

My curiosity begged me to ask more questions, but my manners held the questions at bay. Did Charlie have a wife before Dottie, or had he cheated? I'd always believed they had an ideal marriage.

"It was before my time." Dottie squeezed Tessa's hand.

I poured myself another shot and debated telling them the rest of the conversation with Uncle Charlie. A call to Dr. Marvin Hicks at the University of Florida topped my to-do list.

Nine

I LIMPED TOWARD THE POLICE STATION on crutches. My hands hurt and my armpits ached, but I didn't dare get caught without them. Mae would tan my hide, though the idea of Gram Mae with a switch paled in comparison to jail cells.

Nervous tension knotted my stomach. I wondered if they'd arrest me on the spot. That detective said there wouldn't be any charges. Didn't cops lie? They did in the movies. I detoured into a coffee shop to rethink what I'd tell the police. I moved the strap of my laptop case higher on my shoulder and checked the time.

"It's always busy this time of morning," a male voice said from behind me.

I turned and met the most gorgeous set of blue eyes I'd ever seen. Not just blue, but a glassy shade of blue that reminded me of the Caribbean. He wore his dark hair short and tidy. I hadn't given much thought to my wardrobe. The plain gray maxi dress covered my bandages, and the old cardigan added modesty. The flat shoes made it easier to hobble around on crutches. A practical outfit, if not attractive. "Everyone's desperate for one cup of good coffee before they have to resort to the office swill." I smiled and turned. *Office swill? Who says that?*

The guy with the eyes laughed. I adjusted my bag again and took a step toward the counter. My back to him, I could feel him watching me. I tried to think of something clever to say. I hadn't gotten a look at his left hand. He looked too good, in his worn jeans and gray sports coat. He had to be married.

An image flashed through my mind. He sat on a worn brown-leather couch, his feet on a coffee table, beer in one hand and remote control in the other. I could smell steak cooking on a grill outside the sliding glass door. A large chocolate lab sprawled out beside him, taking up more couch space than he did. A poster or two on the walls, no feminine touches.

I drew a quick breath, unsure of what to make of the vision. I'd invaded his privacy. R*idiculous! My imagination is just playing tricks on me.* My mind had wandered where it shouldn't have.

"I'm Aaron, by the way."

The sound of his voice made me jump. "Huh?"

"Aaron. My name is Aaron."

"Tessa." I shook my head. "Sorry, I was in my own bubble there for a second. Nice to meet you, Aaron."

"What did you do to your leg?"

"Oh, it's nothing. A flesh wound." He took it as a joke. I had no desire to tell him a cop had shot me. What kind of person gets shot, anyway?

We took another step toward the counter. I angled myself so I could watch the line and him at the same time.

"What do you do for a living, Tessa?"

I liked the sound of my name on his lips. "I'm a mental-health therapist."

"Wow." He chuckled. "That isn't what I expected."

"What did you expect?"

"I don't know. Just not that."

People tended to react in one of two ways when I told them what I did for a living. They either closed up, or began spilling their deepest secrets. I bet he would clam up. I took another step toward the counter.

"An extra-large coffee, no cream or sugar. My name is Tessa." The barista behind the counter smirked. Most people ordered the fancy coffees and teas. I already had wide hips. No sense in tacking on five hundred additional calories in the form of fancy coffee.

"Extra-large coffee, black. Name's Aaron," the man said over my head as we moved to the edge of the counter to wait. "How about dinner sometime, Tessa, the mental-health therapist?"

I waited for the punch line, or for him to change his mind. Had he just asked me out? Our orders came up. I reached for my cup, and his hand brushed mine. He jerked his hand back, as if I'd shocked him with static electricity. I caught another flash of his life. This time he knelt with his arms around two dark-haired children.

"Sure. Dinner. I'd love to." I couldn't believe it when he scribbled his number on a napkin and stuffed it into my bag.

"Great." He held the door. We walked in the same direction, sipping our coffee. My heart sank when he turned to the entrance of the police station.

"Are you a police officer?"

"A detective."

"Oh." I waited while he opened the door. My inner voice told me to give his number back.

No one sat behind the Plexiglas window, but someone had taped a phone list to the window. I couldn't remember the name of the detective who'd come to the hospital. Had he given me a name? I could buzz for Officer Smith, though I doubted the woman would be happy to see me.

"Who are you here to see?" Aaron folded his arms across his chest.

"Officer Smith." I smiled and lifted the phone.

"All right, well, call me." He gave me an odd look and disappeared behind another door.

I drew a breath and dialed the phone. "Hi. This is Tessa Lamar. You came to talk to me in the hospital."

"I'll be right up." Officer Smith didn't sound happy.

I turned to a bulletin board and studied the faces of wanted criminals and missing children, including the two kids from the news story: Lilian and Jonas Rivera, ages four and eighteen months. I startled when the door buzzed behind me.

"I'm not on your case, but I'll walk you back to Detective Samuels." Officer Smith led me through rows of cubicles. Did my energy make her nervous, or was it something else? Something like me facing a murder charge.

Aaron leaned against a desk in an office as a small white-haired woman spoke to another detective. Officer Smith stopped in the open doorway and knocked. My heart fell to my feet. Detective Samuels, whom I'd met in the hospital, sat behind the desk. To add insult to injury, the old woman turned at the sound of the knock. The witch from the hospital. *Dang it.*

"That's her. That's the one I was telling you about. She said she was going to pull the plug, and she did." The wicked witch of the welcome desk pointed.

The room temperature spiked, and my leg started to throb. "I need to sit down."

Someone eased me into a chair. The woman spoke with the officers inside the office, but I couldn't make out her words. Not that I needed to hear to know what the old bat was telling them. So much for dinner with Detective Blue Eyes.

Ten

THE DOOR OPENED, AND AARON escorted the woman out. When he returned, he avoided my gaze. "Ms. Lamar, will you follow me, please?"

I placed a crutch under one shoulder and the laptop case on the other, following him inside the office. I couldn't believe my freakin' luck. When did my life turn into such a mess? I decided to ignore Aaron, and turned to the other detective. "Good morning, Detective Samuels."

"A suspect in two murder cases in one day. You've been a busy girl, Miss Lamar." He studied my face.

"I didn't kill my uncle."

"We will need to touch base with the ICU, but I doubt there's any truth to Mrs. Lipinski's allegations." He grew more serious. "I'm sorry for your loss. Please forgive my insensitive comment."

"I came to look at the pictures again. When you questioned me at the hospital, my aunt and great-grandmother were there. I didn't want to upset them."

"Of course." He opened a file and set a stack of pictures in front of me.

I ignored Aaron's presence and studied each picture. I maintained a poker face, determined not to let them see me blanch. Halfway through the stack, I knew I'd seen the would-be intruder before. "I saw him, at the hospital. Getting into an elevator, on the third floor, outside of the ICU."

Samuels glanced at Aaron, then back to me. "What time was that?"

"I'm not sure, maybe twenty minutes before my uncle died. He was with another man, and they seemed angry." I motioned with my hand. "Judging from their nonverbal cues, I mean."

"Did either of them see you?"

"No, I don't think so. I went the other way until I heard the elevator door close. If they saw me, it would've been from behind."

"What made you turn and go in the other direction?" Aaron crossed his ankles and unfolded his arms.

"As I said, they seemed angry. They were Native American. At first I thought it was some of my uncle's tribe coming to visit, only something was off. I don't know why, but I knew I needed to avoid them." I slowed down before I said something stupid. "If you check the hospital security cameras, you might be able to get video."

Aaron nodded.

"When you put the photos in front of my aunt and great-grandmother, please use the clean images. One lost a son, the other a husband. They don't need to see these." I sat straighter, emboldened after standing up for my family.

"Of course." Samuels eased back in his chair. "The report said you fired a semiautomatic shotgun through a jalousie window and broke only two panes."

"No. The guy broke one pane trying to get in. The hole was big enough to shove the barrel through. The second pane broke when I fired. It was a new gun, smooth, less kickback."

"How many shots did you fire?"

"One."

"Did you reload?"

"No."

"Who taught you to load a ghost round?" Samuels's grin returned.

Aaron exhaled a breath between his teeth.

"My uncle Charlie."

Samuels nodded. "Anything else that might help us solve this case?"

Both men perked up a bit when I hesitated, as if sensing I was holding something back. I bent and rubbed my calf above the ring of bandages. "Sorry, the gunshot wound is making me wish I'd followed doctor's orders and stayed off it."

Tension creased the corners of Samuels's eyes.

"I can't think of anything else, but I'll let you know if I do. Is that all?"

Samuels nodded.

I stood, making a show of holding on to the back of the chair. Aaron handed me the laptop bag. "Let me walk you out."

"Thank you." I wanted to run, or walk very fast, but I'd made such a point of my injury, I didn't dare.

Aaron turned to me. "Tessa, uh . . ."

"Dinner is off." I laughed.

"No, not off. Just postponed, until after the case is over." He glanced over the cubicles and leaned to whisper, "I'd like to get to know you. Any woman who can look at crime photos without blinking and fire a shotgun . . . Like I said, after the case is solved."

I nodded and hobbled toward the exit. Today sucked, almost as much as yesterday, and I had little hope for improvement.

Behind me, Samuels said, "Careful, Burns, you know what they say—your badge can get you pussy, but the pussy can get your badge."

Yep, being thrown in a jail cell would be a picnic compared to my morning.

Eleven

MY BAG BOUNCED AGAINST MY My bag bounced against my crutch as I walked into the counseling center. Mr. Owens, my first patient, rose when I entered the building. All eyes turned toward me, and I took a step back. *I shouldn't be here, couldn't be here. Lord in heaven, why had I come to work?*

My boss pushed toward me. "You're over an hour late. Why didn't you call?"

I lowered my voice. "My phone is dead. Can we speak in private, please?"

He drew his chin back, flattening his jowls. Did he expect me to discuss my personal issues in front of a lobby full of patients?

I limped toward the reception desk in the hopes of gaining a little privacy. "I apologize for not calling in. It took me forever to get here with these crutches. My uncle passed away this weekend, and I've been taking care of details."

"I see. Well, I suppose that is an acceptable excuse. I won't write you up, but we'll talk more after your session."

The receptionist squirmed, avoiding eye contact with the director. Once he returned to his office, the receptionist sighed. "Are you all right?"

"I've been better." I caught movement out of the corner of my eye. Mr. Owens stood beside me, fidgeting.

"Are you hurt?" he asked.

"I'm fine." I motioned toward the chairs. "Mr. Owens, please have a seat in the lobby. I'll be right with you."

I turned for the door, but he followed closely behind me, wringing his hands and mumbling. The door between the lobby and the offices remained locked until the receptionist pressed the button. The door buzzed, the lock turned, but I didn't catch it before it locked again. Once again, the receptionist hit the button and I missed it. "Hey, Mr. Owens, can you get the door?"

Once we sat, I decided to begin the session rather than unpack my bag. Mr. Owens's anxiety had spilled over to me. I squared my shoulders and drew a cleansing breath. "I apologize for running late. You seem anxious. Let's get started."

I eased back in my chair and waited for him to reply. He looked around the office, wringing and fidgeting. I'd treated him for severe anxiety over the previous year. Of all the patients to keep waiting, he was the worst.

"I went to the zoo with my son." Mr. Owens lowered his eyes.

"That is an impressive step. How was it for you, taking your son to the zoo?"

"We didn't stay. He wanted to look at the snakes."

"Mmm-hmm. Did you go into the snake exhibit?"

He shook his head. "No. I told him I had a headache. We left right after we got inside."

"A lot of people don't like snakes. What happened after you left?"

Mr. Owens's eyes locked onto my chest. I always dressed modestly for work to avoid potential sexual attraction on the part of my patients. My hand went to the turquoise amulet. "What happened after you left the zoo?"

Mr. Owens turned his head and his eyes went wide. He moved his lips but could only gasp for air. He clenched his chest as if his heart had ceased to beat. Spittle began to drip down his chin.

"Mr. Owens?" I stood, and his panic went from bad to worse. He leaped onto the chair and screamed. No words, just an ear-piercing sound that rivaled an air horn. I lunged for the phone, but he grabbed me before I reached the receiver. I was prepared for him to shove me down, but instead, he pulled me onto the chair by my arms. My calf scraped the edge of the desk, causing pain to burst through my leg.

The office door flew open, and two male therapists entered the room. Mr. Owens's racket set off emergency protocols.

Mr. Owens stopped screaming when the men stormed in. The fit ended, and I started to climb down from the chair. Mr. Owens held me in place and screamed one word that sent the ten-by-ten space into chaos. "Snake!"

My patient freaked out, and I held him in an effort to calm him. I knew I didn't have to worry. As much as I disdained the idea of snakes, they wouldn't hurt me.

A menacing-looking snake, about four feet long, crawled out of my computer bag. It appeared to have diamonds on its back. I didn't hear rattles. Certainly a rattlesnake would rattle. Then again, who could hear the rattling over all the commotion?

One of the male therapists backed out of the office, the other froze, crouched, arms wide—prepared to tackle something. Mr. Owens held on to me like a drowning man, and once again, became the human air horn.

People shouted down the hall—*snake, rattlesnake, 911, lockdown,* and various curses. I couldn't help but roll my eyes. We lived in Florida, home of more than fifty species of snakes. However, the fact that the slimy demon had hitched a ride in my bag did give me the willies. It might be my protector, but I'd rather not carry it around.

"Mr. Owens? Please. I can't breathe. We're safe on the chair." I struggled to get my hand beneath his arm to loosen his grip. I didn't want to have to use self-defense moves while standing on a comfy chair, with a potential rattlesnake on the floor.

Mr. Owens eased his grip but continued to howl. I managed one deep breath before the entire snake emerged from the laptop bag, and he gripped me even tighter. The other male returned with a push broom in one hand and a fire extinguisher in the other. Did he plan to light the broom on fire and burn the snake? The crouching orderly leaped back and took the broom. He wielded it like a sword, swishing this way and that.

"Cut it out. You're only going to make it mad!" I shouted over the screaming patient. How long could a human being continue to scream before his voice gave out?

My boss's voice rang out from the hall. "Close the damned door. The last thing we want is for it to get out."

One of the men glanced from me to the snake and up the hall. He shrugged and stepped into the hall. Even the croucher began to walk backward to the door. I, however, couldn't get the hysterical patient to the door without forcing him to step down off the chair. He could hurt himself, or me, if I forced him to move.

"Tessa. Out. Now!" My boss shouted, red-faced and angry.

I shook my head and motioned back toward Mr. Owens, trying to communicate my thoughts without words—it didn't work. My boss slammed the door. I couldn't believe he'd left me alone with a hysterical patient and a potentially poisonous snake. Mr. Owens's screams began to die down, only to return with vigor each time the snake moved.

Awhile later, the door to the office eased open, and Mr. Owens launched into a new series of screams. A man wearing hip waders came into the office. Others milled in the hall, but no one else came in. The hip wader guy followed Mr. Owens's wide gaze directly to the coiled snake and pulled out a long metal stick with a hook. As if the snake sensed a worthy adversary, its telltale rattle filled the office. Mr. Owens's nails dug into my arm, clawing me like a feral cat. The more the wrangler poked the snake, the more Mr. Owens clawed.

"Stop it!" I shouted. To my amazement, Mr. Owens stilled and quieted behind me.

The wrangler looked as if I'd sprouted a second head, and even the snake stopped rattling. "What the hell?"

"I have no idea." I needed to get down from the chair. My head throbbed.

The wrangler hooked the snake and pulled the loop closed. The snake wiggled as he dropped it into a heavy sack inside a five-gallon bucket.

Mr. Owens fainted. I tried to catch him before he hit the ground, and missed. "Could you check my bag for more hitchhikers?"

The wrangler poked the bag a couple of times and looked inside. "All clear."

"Thanks." I collapsed into the chair.

Twelve

TWO PARAMEDICS CAME INTO THE room. One tended to Mr. Owens, the other placed his hand on my shoulder. "Miss, are you injured?"

I wanted to yell, but the paramedic didn't deserve my anger. "My arm…"

Aaron and Detective Samuels crowded into my office. I frowned, and turned my attention to the stinging in my arm. The paramedic swabbed Betadine over the scratches.

"These are superficial. I'll clean and bandage them. You should follow up with your primary physician." The paramedic motioned to the blood on my foot. "Is your leg injured?"

I must have gone numb at some point, because I'd forgotten about my leg. "I have a superficial gunshot wound. I hit it against the desk pretty hard."

"Miss Lamar, are you up to giving us a statement?" Detective Samuels asked, a hint of humor in his voice.

"Why? Unless you're going to charge the snake with something, no crimes were committed here."

"Since there were snakes involved in the attempted break in, there may be a connection. We aren't ruling anything out." Aaron sounded almost apologetic.

"Sure, why not."

Samuels shut the door. "Who has access to this office?"

"The clinical staff and the director. My door was unlocked this morning when I came in. I lock it at night when I leave. I think the snake was already in my bag when I came in."

"What? The bag you were carrying around in the station?" Samuels paled.

"You know, we treat phobias here. If you're afraid of snakes…"

Samuels cleared his throat and Aaron raised his hand to cover his smile.

"Mind if I take a look?" Aaron motioned to the bag.

"Help yourself. The wrangler already looked."

Samuels took a step back as Aaron set my bag on the desk and removed Uncle Charlie's cedar box.

"No," I shouted before I could stop myself. "I mean, that's personal. It belonged to my uncle." My reaction drew out the cop in Samuels. He stepped closer to the desk to get a look. *Great, now they think I have something to hide.* I motioned to the bag. "Sorry. Go ahead and look inside."

I turned my head and wished my office had a window. Instead, I studied the pale green wall while the detectives rummaged through my uncle's personal items. It didn't take that long to check for snakes. Aaron had turned his back as Samuels studied the picture of me and Charlie. Samuels set it inside the box and closed the lid.

"Satisfied, Detectives?" My voice cracked.

Aaron asked, "Do you have security cameras in the building?"

"You will need to speak with the director." I stood as soon as the paramedic finished bandaging my leg. I slid my computer and the box back into my bag, and slung it over my shoulder. "Any more questions?"

"No." Aaron lowered his eyes.

I did my best to storm out, but with the heavy bag, a crutch, and fresh wounds, storming turned into skulking. Neither detective spoke as I moved past them.

My boss stood in the hall, with his arms folded across his chest. "Where are you going?"

"I'm going home. I'll be out for a few days on bereavement leave."

"Policy states bereavement leave can only be used in the death of immediate family members." He puffed his chest out like a rooster. A big, cheaply dressed, balding, rooster.

"Fine, then use a few days of the seven and a half weeks of unused vacation time as bereavement or my two-week notice, your choice." I needed to get out of the building before I imploded.

"Policy doesn't allow vacation time to be used in lieu of two-week notice." He snorted.

"I'm in no state to be seeing patients." I tried one last attempt at reason.

"If you quit without notice, you can be reported for patient abandonment."

I dropped the computer bag and the crutch, ignoring the other people in the hall. "Refer my patients to Jenkins and Associates. I'll be starting there as soon as I can bury my uncle." In my mind, that should have been enough. At least he couldn't accuse me of abandoning my patients. He behaved like a school yard bully, unhappy to lose his favorite target.

"Policy states that the therapist must notify—"

Something inside me snapped, causing me to suffer from stress induced insanity. Words bubbled up from my belly. I growled to keep them inside, to not give him the satisfaction of seeing me completely lose it. I failed. "You heartless son of a bitch, keep it up and I'll file a report with the board for sexual harassment. It's not only against policy, it's *illegal*, to grope your staff, or did they not teach you that in—"

A hand rested on the small of my back, and Aaron stepped between me and my boss. "Miss Lamar, I would be happy to take your statement regarding sexual harassment."

"Not today. I'll contact you when I'm ready." I took a few steps forward, and they allowed me to pass.

Thirteen

I SAT IN THE CAFÉ IN with Hailey in the midst of a full-blown pity party, barely holding back tears. If I cried, I'd never stop. I fought my more basic instincts to drink myself stupid, or to call Ian for a post-breakup booty call. I didn't want to explain the events of the morning to Dottie and Mae. I needed a few minutes to pull myself together. I needed lunch with my best friend.

"Hailey, how is this my life?" I pushed my salad around on my plate.

"It will get better. Look at this like cleaning house. You hated that job. You needed to dump Ian. Heck, you needed to clean your apartment. Maybe things aren't as bleak as you think?"

Hailey's advice should have helped, only I didn't want logic. I needed to wallow for a while before moving on. I told her, "I know you're right, but it sucks all the same." I picked at the bandage on my arm. "Your dad is okay with me coming to work for him? My current patients aren't exactly the paying type."

"He's thrilled. As soon as you're up for it, he wants you to carry half of my caseload. Scott wants me to cut my hours soon. I have months before the baby is born, but he worries." Hailey stuffed french fries into her mouth.

I hated dumping my crap on her.

"The adult half of your caseload?" I feared Hailey would attempt to bring out my maternal instincts by loading my caseload with kids.

"Yep, all adults. I can't have you scaring the kiddos with bags of snakes." Hailey laughed. "Tell me again about the hot detective."

"I don't know what else there is to tell. He's too hot to be a cop. We can't do dinner or anything until they close the case on the attempted break-in. I get the feeling there's something else going on. I mean, what if they change their minds and charge me with killing that guy?" The waiter overheard the wrong part of our conversation and sidestepped the table.

Hailey finished the last of her fries. "Stop borrowing trouble. You have enough on your plate right now without looking for more."

"You're right." I tossed my napkin on the table. "I should get going."

"Yeah, me, too. My boss is a jerk."

"Your dad is a saint."

"I know. Let's check out that junk shop down the block. They have some vintage Winnie-the-Pooh stuff in the window." Hailey's face brightened.

We walked into the dusty shop. Hailey rummaged through the vintage Pooh for her nursery, while I perused a shelf of antique bottles. I pulled a bottle down, turning it over to check the price.

"That one is seventy-five." The voice behind me caught me off guard. I almost dropped the bottle as I turned toward an elderly gentleman. "It's an old decanter from the late 1800s."

I smiled and returned the decanter to the shelf. "I'm looking for bottles for my great-grandmother's bottle tree."

"Bottle tree?"

"She hangs them from an old oak, on metal clothes hangers and twine. The clear ones are for wishes, and the colored ones trap evil spirits." I chuckled. "It's pretty, even if you don't believe in wishes or evil spirits."

The old man tilted his head. "I believe in both, and I think you do, too." His eyes fell to the amulet. "I have just the thing."

I followed him to the back of the store. Something about him set me at ease. He lifted a box, filled to the brim with bottles, and set it on the counter.

I inspected one of the bottles. "These are perfect. How much?"

"Oh, I don't know." He looked over the box, and I prepared myself for a hefty price tag. "Ten for the box? When I picked them up, I thought they might be antiques. They aren't anything special."

"Deal." I pulled out my wallet and handed him a ten-dollar bill.

Hailey carried a bag of Winnie-the-Pooh antiques. I followed behind, directing the shopkeeper to my car. Mae would love the bottles.

"See you next week. I'll drop off the case files when I visit Dottie. It's going to be like old times, working together." Hailey laughed as she embraced me.

"I can't wait." My eyes grew misty. The entire world hadn't gone to hell in a handbasket—just *my* world.

Fourteen

I STOPPED BY MY APARTMENT AND did a quick Google search for Marvin Hicks. I dialed the number and walked to the window. "Hello. My name is Tessa Lamar. I need to speak with Dr. Hicks. It's urgent."

The voice on the other end of the line said, "Dr. Hicks is out of the office."

"When is he expected to return?"

"Next week. May I take a message?"

I hoped his plans included a trip to Apopka. I had no desire to drive two hours to Gainesville. "Dr. Hicks is a close personal friend of my uncle, Charles Nokoseka. My uncle passed away two days ago. Do you know if Dr. Hicks is heading to the Orlando area?"

"I'm not privy to his travel plans, but let me get your contact information. I'll pass it along to his assistant in case he checks in."

Not the confirmation I'd hoped for. I relayed Dottie's and my contact information. I would have given my precise GPS location, blood type, and Social Security number if it would have gotten me in touch with Dr. Hicks more quickly.

I wandered around my apartment. Nothing else to do except go back to the little pink house and help plan a funeral. The idea made the knot in my stomach twist until it stole my breath.

In the parking lot, the hair on the back of my neck stood up. The amulet grew cold enough to send a chill through me. Something was wrong.

I hit the "Unlock" button and slid behind the wheel. Safe inside the locked car, I checked my mirrors. Something furry moved toward my car, and I hit the gas hard, making the tires scream against the fresh asphalt.

I broke several traffic rules on the way to Gram Mae's. I must have checked my rearview mirror a hundred times before I turned onto the bumpy drive. I waited a few minutes before opening the door, half expecting a giant wolf to come bounding out of the trees. When I'd psyched myself up enough to move, I grabbed my bag and headed for the house.

The door rattled in its frame when I closed it. Dottie and Mae sat in the living room watching their soaps. Where else would they be at two thirty in the afternoon on a weekday? Neither commented on my arrival, even though I'd slammed the door. I couldn't compete with *General Hospital.*

I dropped my bag and headed into the kitchen in the hopes of finding chocolate. The image of Aaron's muscular back danced, unwelcome, through my head, and I opted to eat watermelon instead. By the time Mae and Dottie entered the kitchen, I'd polished off half the melon.

"Commercial break?"

"They cut into the stories for a news conference about that murdered woman and her kids." Dottie eyed the watermelon. "The grandfather was on, asking for help finding the children. Breaks my heart to think of what might have happened to those babies."

"Detective Burns stopped by to see you. You just missed him." Mae surveyed the stack of rinds on my plate.

"Burns? You mean Samuels?"

"Left his card—it says Burns. He's a real looker, blue eyes." Gram Mae smiled. "No ring on his finger. Plus, he made a point to look at your pictures in the hall."

"What? Why was he in the hall?" Mortified that Aaron had seen every toothless, frizzy-haired picture of my childhood, I dropped my head to the table. "Why me?"

"I had him check out the leak in the spigot. I swear, I don't know how you can sleep with that dripping going on all night." Mae poured herself a glass of sweet tea.

"Gram, your doctor told you to stop drinking sugar in your tea."

"He isn't keen on the idea I drink whiskey or smoke, either. One shot and one cigarette a day never hurt nobody and neither will sweet tea."

Dottie glanced between Mae and me and bit her tongue. Smart woman. "You're home early."

"I had an incident. One of those snakes took a ride in my computer bag today. It crawled out in the middle of my session with a gentleman who's more terrified of snakes than I am." I held up my bandaged arm, expecting sympathy.

"Did it bite you?" Dottie cut herself a slice of watermelon.

"No, the guy scratched my arm up trying to get away from the snake," I answered, disappointed that neither had fawned over my newest boo-boo. Instead, they burst out laughing. I didn't see the humor, but laughed along with them. Given the stress over the last few days, we all needed a good belly buster.

"Are you going to call Detective Cutie-Patootie?" Mae had a wicked glint in her eye.

"Ugh, no. I'm done with cops for today." I plucked his card from Mae's hand. "I'm going to take a nap. It's been a long day, and my leg is killing me."

Fifteen

I THREW MYSELF ON THE TWIN bed and stared at the ceiling. I didn't bother to crawl under the faded rosebud quilt or remove the stuffed animals. The room hadn't changed much over the years, and I liked it that way. This was home—consistent and safe.

"Oh God."

The old house had an awkward floor plan. The bathroom door opened into my bedroom. If Gram Mae needed to use the bathroom in the middle of the night, she came through my room, which meant that Aaron had walked through my bedroom to get to that darned leaky spigot. He'd seen my room—pink ruffled drapes, stuffed animals, and all. Dinner was off. No coming back from pink ruffles and Bubba, the giant purple teddy bear.

My brain spun too fast to sleep. The new job with Hailey would work out, but I wouldn't stay more than a year. I still held out hope that I would land a position in criminal justice. Psychopathology has always intrigued me. I liked figuring out what made people do horrible things.

Memories of the last couple of days tumbled through my mind, causing me to rethink my plan. I'd seen a lot of horrible things. Perhaps working with the police department was a bad idea. Could I handle that level of stress on a daily basis? Maybe the job with Hailey wouldn't be so bad after all.

I needed to give Charlie's journal to Dr. Hicks. Maybe he could make sense of the break-in attempts. If nothing else, he could take the darned thing with him, and maybe the scary wolf guys would follow him to Gainesville. I couldn't shake the feeling that the naked guy had, in fact, started out as a wolf. I didn't have the energy to consider what that could mean.

Aaron's blue eyes crossed my mind. He frightened me almost as much as the wolf guy. My cell phone rang, but I couldn't get to it before it went to voice mail. Although the call came from a local area code, I didn't recognize the number. I waited a few moments to see if the caller would leave a voice mail. No such luck.

I dialed the number, and a familiar male voice answered. "Tessa, hey, it's Aaron. Detective Burns."

Several curse words danced through my head. "Hi. I was just about to call you. You came by?" And had a lovely visit with my great-grandmother and checked out my pink ruffled curtains.

"We checked the security tapes at the hospital and the clinic. We found the surveillance footage of the guys you described at the hospital. Looks a lot like the guy who tried to break in to your house. I'll be by in an hour with photos for your aunt and great-grandmother. I mean, if that's all right?" He paused.

"We'll be here." I gave him points for not referring to the dead guy as "that guy you killed."

"The only person who went into your office over the past twenty-four hours was your boss, former boss. He was in your office this morning. If he groped you, I think you should consider filing a report. I checked into it, and there have been a handful of complaints against the guy, but nothing stuck."

"I'll think about it. You don't think he put the snake in my office?"

"No, I don't. I think it came in the bag, which takes the case to a new level. Animal control confirmed it was a diamondback rattler. Whoever put it in your bag could be charged with attempted murder," Aaron said.

I counted to three. "Thank you for letting me know."

"Tessa, you need to be careful until we figure this all out and catch this guy."

I hung up, unsure of how to take the news. I doubted anyone planted the snake in my bag. According to the ladies, the snake served as protection, which terrified me on a different level. What if the bad guys had snake protectors, too? "I'm losing my mind."

"Tessa, is everything all right?" Mae's voice sounded as concerned as Aaron's had.

"No."

We returned to the kitchen table.

"That was Detective Burns. He thinks someone is trying to kill me by putting snakes in my bag. So now they're treating this like an attempted-murder case. He's going to come by later with some pictures. There were two scary-looking guys at the hospital outside of ICU. They could be tribe; he wants you two to look at their photos." I put my chin in my hand and stared at the tabletop.

"Maybe we should clean up before company arrives." Gram Mae looked pleased by the prospect of company—almost too pleased.

"Gram, please don't try to fix me up with the detective. It won't work. He'd get fired for dating me." I didn't like the twinkle in Mae's eye.

"Dottie, do you know a Marvin Hicks?"

If the name upset her, she didn't show it. Dottie, a serious card player, had a poker face that rivaled the masters. "I know Marvin. He's a friend of your uncle's. He's Cherokee. Why do you ask?"

I shrugged, regretting having asked the question. How could I explain this without telling them I'd stolen Uncle Charlie's journal? Not to mention that I'd held out on part of the conversation I'd had with Charlie's ghost. Unlike Dottie, I had a poker face only when in session with my clients. I couldn't lie to Dottie and Mae. "Remember, I told you I spoke with Uncle Charlie?"

They nodded.

"He told me to take his special box to Dr. Hicks."

Dottie sat back, and Mae leaned forward to take my hand. "Where is the box now?"

I recognized the sinking feeling growing in my gut immediately. I'd had the same feeling at six years old. Dressed for church, I'd grown bored and climbed an orange tree. When they asked if I'd climbed the tree, I said no. Mae had picked several twigs from my hair and wiped the sticky orange juice from my face. Charlie and I cried when the spanking ended. Now, I would have preferred a spanking to Mae's and Dottie's disappointed faces. I'd screwed up.

"In my computer bag," I mumbled.

"Marvin will be here Sunday. You can give it to him then. Don't take it out again," Mae said. "Dottie and I made the arrangements today. The funeral will be Sunday at the church. We will have the gathering of the elders on Wednesday at the sacred place in Geneva. They have to name a new elder to fill Charlie's position in the tribe."

"We will have folks come here after the services are finished, but don't mention anything about the gathering. It should be only us and the elders." Dottie nodded as if to confirm she understood.

"Some of the family won't be happy," I warned.

"Most of them wouldn't be happy if we stood them on a stack of gold bars. It will be difficult enough, without having them there. They're lucky we're inviting them to the damned funeral," Dottie said.

I said, "We'll ride over together Wednesday." I didn't want to say good-bye. In fact, I had a difficult time wrapping my heart around the loss, but we would do this—together. "Oh, I almost forgot. I have a box full of bottles for the bottle tree. We can hang them after we get home. Maybe plant a tree for Uncle Charlie?"

Dottie and Mae smiled, and Dottie put her hand over mine. "When did you grow so wise?"

I shrugged. "Yesterday?"

Sixteen

"TESSA MARIE, GO GET CLEANED up. Put on that pretty purple dress." Mae winked.

Mae loved to play matchmaker almost as much as she loved to entertain. She pulled the leftover Salisbury steak from the night before. Unless I missed my mark, Mae planned shepherd's pie for dinner. After the watermelon, my stomach groaned. I slunk off to my room to regroup.

I picked at the lavender sundress, feeling ridiculous. The dress came to just above my knees and accentuated the bandages on my arm and leg. I pulled my hair into a high ponytail and swiped on an extra layer of mascara. I couldn't justify more primping without looking too interested or needy.

The kitchen smelled like heaven—if heaven served beef gravy and chocolate-chip cookies. The older women buzzed around the space as if expecting a dignitary for dinner. I didn't have the heart to tell them it wasn't a social call. Poor Aaron. He didn't stand an ice-cube's chance in hell of getting out of the house without being stuffed with food.

"Do we have to have people over after the funeral?" My crankiness surprised me.

"Yes. How else are we going to get rid of all the sympathy casseroles?" Dottie winked as she pulled rolls out of the oven.

"I don't know why anyone would want to hurt me." I scanned the tree line on the other side of the railroad tracks.

Aaron followed my gaze. "We should get back inside. I need to show the ladies the pictures and get back to the office."

"You work around the clock, don't you?"

"When I'm on a big case."

I followed him back to the house. I understood his frustration, but couldn't betray my uncle or the tribe. Someone wanted Charlie's journal. I happened to be the one holding on to his secrets—it wasn't personal.

Aaron spread still shots of the hospital-security footage on the table. Although grainy, they captured both men's faces. Dottie and Mae studied each picture and shook their heads. "I don't recognize either of them," Dottie said.

Mae sat back. "Neither do I. Are these the men who tried to break in to the house?"

"Yes." Aaron pointed to one of the men. "This is the one Tessa shot."

We stared at the picture. I hated that I'd killed someone. Mae stood and wiped her hands on her apron as if she'd touched something dirty. She set a plate of cookies on the table and poured four cups of coffee without a word.

"I need to get back to work. Thank you for dinner." Aaron bowed his head and stood.

Dottie patted his hand. "Thank you for stopping by."

"Let me pack up your dessert." Mae packed several cookies, poured coffee into a travel mug, and showed Aaron to the door.

"Thank you, ladies. I will be in touch." Aaron met my eyes and dipped his chin.

"Have a good night, Aaron." Despite my embarrassment, I looked forward to our date.

"True." Someone knocked on the door.

I turned to answer, but Mae shooed me into the living room. "Wait till I open the door to come in. Make a grand entrance."

I frowned at the back of Mae's head. This would end in disaster. Aaron's voice filled the kitchen. I counted to ten before I walked into the room. Mae had him seated at the table while Dottie poured his sweet tea. Aaron looked way too comfortable, considering the two hens hovering over him. I mouthed, "Sorry."

Aaron grinned and stood. Someone had taught him manners. I motioned for him to sit as I plopped into my usual chair. Before I could get a word out, Mae filled the table with food.

"We were just about to sit down to dinner. You will join us, won't you?" She set a plate and silverware in front of him.

"Thank you. It smells great." Aaron set his napkin in his lap and waited for the women to sit. He took it in stride when we joined hands for grace, and because he was the only man at the table, Dottie and Mae expected him to say the blessing.

I frowned and bowed my head. It would never have occurred to Mae that Aaron wouldn't want to say grace. He said the blessing, and we dug in. Everything went well for about five minutes, until Mae said, "Tessa tells us you'd get fired for dating her. That doesn't seem fair."

Aaron almost choked on his mashed potatoes, smiling as I slumped in my chair. "We aren't allowed to date victims on the cases we're investigating. Though, I do plan to take your great-granddaughter out on a proper date after we solve this case."

"Tessa Marie isn't a victim," Mae insisted.

I wanted to crawl under the table. "Technically, no, but that's what they call it, Gram."

"I don't care what they call it. It's silly."

Aaron focused on his food, as if keeping his mouth full would save him from Mae's inquisition.

"Where are your people from?" Mae set her napkin beside her plate.

"North Carolina."

"Do you have any brothers or sisters?"

"No, ma'am." Aaron sipped his tea.

"How long—?"

I laughed, both at Mae's persistence and Aaron's willingness to play along. "Gram, how can he eat if he's busy answering all of your questions?"

Mae looked between me and Aaron. "Why don't you two go for a walk while Dottie and I clean up?"

Dottie grinned and began to clear away the plates, patting my shoulder as she passed.

"Sounds good to me." Aaron offered his hand. "Would you like to take a walk with me?"

"I'd love to get some fresh air." I took his hand as I stood.

He grabbed my crutches, and we slipped out the door.

Outside, Aaron chuckled, and I shook my head.

"I'm sorry," I said.

"Don't be. They're fantastic." He put his hands in his back pockets, rocking on his heels. "I like the dress. Was it Mae's idea?"

I nodded and covered my face. "Come on. Let's go sit on Dottie's porch swing. It's out of earshot. I'm sure they're spying on us."

We strolled through the yard hand in hand. After we settled on the swing, Aaron stretched his arm across the back, rocking it with one foot. "I meant what I said, about taking you out."

I gave him a little smile. "I was at my apartment this afternoon. I thought I saw someone following me. I'm going to stay here until things settle down."

He stopped the swing, giving me his full attention. "What's going on? There's something you aren't telling me."

Dottie stood. “We should get some rest. It’s going to be a long weekend.”

Seventeen

We drove to church in complete silence. Yesterday, we'd cleaned house and worked in the yard to prepare for company. Physical labor had kept my mind off my problems. Today, I couldn't escape.

Friends and family filled the building, but I stayed close to Dottie and Mae. We walked to the front of the chapel and sat in front of the wooden casket. To the side of the flower-draped box, a large picture of Charlie smiled at us. Soft music flowed over sniffles and whispered conversations behind us.

I'd taken the aisle seat and propped my crutch against the chair. I sent up a silent prayer of thanks when Darlene plopped down beside Mae. I needed to be as far away from my mother as possible.

Mae patted Darlene's hand, keeping her eyes forward. For once, Darlene remained quiet. Several others came forward and offered hugs and kind words to Mae and Dottie. Everyone ignored me, which was fine. I didn't want to hear how sorry they were, and if someone hugged me, I'd lose my thin grip on control and cry like a baby.

The fragrant flowers irritated my nose, and the sickly sweet scent clung to the back of my throat. The soft music grated on my nerves. I wanted to tell the flow of people to leave us the hell alone. I couldn't keep nodding at the same words, over and over again. The pastor took the podium, and I readied myself to leave. Had it not been for Dottie's hand wrapping around mine, I would've run.

A handful of people came forward and spoke about Charlie. They told humorous stories, recalled fond memories, and spoke of him in the past tense. I heard every third word or so, refusing to let my brain process any of what they said. My spine remained rigid and my chin firm until the final prayer. We remained in our seats as each person went up and said the same words as before the service.

We waited until the room emptied before Mae and I helped Dottie to the casket. She set her trembling hands on the soft wood and bowed her head. I did the same. The wood reminded me of Uncle Charlie's cedar box. My heart constricted, stealing my breath. Strong hands rested on my shoulders, and I turned to find Mae. We walked out the same way we'd come in, with quiet grace.

IT WAS A NICE SERVICE," Mae said.

Dottie and I nodded. Most of the others had already arrived when we pulled into the drive. People busied themselves by setting out food and catching up. The happy noise of children playing in the yard brought me to tears. No one should be happy today, yet life went on. Charlie always loved having a houseful of people and a yard full of kids, but it meant nothing without his laughter to punctuate the voices.

Dottie and I sat on the porch swing holding hands. We moved in slow motion while the world and people around us sped by. Cousins brought us food. We didn't eat more than a couple of bites. Someone else brought coffee, but it went cold in our hands. The metal chains squeaked and groaned above us, ignored like the voices around us.

"Is Dr. Hicks here?" I searched the yard for an unfamiliar face.

"No. He called, said he'd been delayed due to the elders making preparations for the gathering. He'll be here tomorrow for dinner."

"What happens at the gathering? This will be my first."

"They choose a new medicine man. The candidates have to prove their skills, then there's a vote." Dottie held my gaze.

I assumed whoever had tried to get Charlie's book would be there, likely one of the candidates for the position. "Is it safe for us to be there?"

"The elders won't let anything happen to us." Dottie's grip tightened on my hand and tensed. Darlene headed our way.

My mother squeezed between us on the swing and sighed. "It was a beautiful service."

Dottie nodded, and I turned my attention to a group of kids playing tag.

"Do you plan to sell the house now that Charlie's gone?" Darlene's saccharin-sweet voice turned my stomach. "This place is too much to take care of now that it's just you and Grandma."

"I haven't given it much thought," Dottie said.

"I could stay here in one house and you and Grandma could stay in the other. I mean, I would be happy to help take care of the place in exchange for rent." Darlene patted Dottie's arm.

I turned to my mother and narrowed my eyes. "You'd be willing to mow the grass and clean up after the chickens?"

"Well, no. They would need to get rid of the chickens, nasty things. I'd see to hiring a lawn service." Darlene smiled brighter.

"Thanks for the offer, Mom, but we have things under control."

All eyes turned to the swing when Darlene jumped up and started to shout, "You don't speak for Dottie. It's her decision to make, not yours, young lady!"

I steadied the rocking swing with my good foot. "Mom, let it go for right now. This isn't the time. We are all grieving and need time to process."

"Look at Miss College Degree talking all fancy."

Despite my education, I had hung onto my accent and poor white trash dialect to avoid appearing snobby around my family. Times like this I felt like a fraud as a professional and as a hick. I simply didn't belong. "You're upset. Let's take a little time and calm down. Would you like to talk about Charlie?"

"Don't you dare psychoanalyze me." Darlene played it up for the growing audience.

"I wouldn't even know where to start." I didn't see the slap coming until the sound rang out and my cheek stung.

"I birthed you, raised you, gave up my career. You're an ungrateful little bitch. Who do you think you are?" Droplets of spit landed on my face.

"Enough." Mae inserted herself between my mother and me, as she had so many times in the past. "Party's over. Time to get going."

People began to clean up paper plates and say their good-byes. Darlene stomped into the house. Mae kissed my cheek and walked to the bottom of the stairs. She accepted hugs and words of sympathy from the family. Mae stood watch like a four-foot-ten-inch guard, blocking anyone from getting too close until the last car pulled away.

Nineteen

"TESSA MARIE, GO GET THE big frying pan from Dottie's. I took out some chicken. We need to get dinner cooking before the boys come calling." Mae rubbed her hands together and took out flour, oil, and a dozen spices. Colonel Sanders didn't have a thing on Gram Mae.

Dottie took a chair. "Boys?"

"I invited Detective Burns." Mae grinned from ear to ear.

I grabbed my crutches and walked out the door. One day since we'd said good-bye to Charlie, and Mae was already playing matchmaker? I resolved to tell Aaron to stop accepting my great-grandmother's invitations.

I retrieved the bottles from my trunk and set them near Mae's porch steps. If the weather held out, I'd hang them in the tree later. I didn't bother looking for snakes on the path to Dottie's. I knew they were watching me; their eyes made the hair on the back of my neck stand upright. While I knew they were protecting me, I couldn't get past my apprehension.

Fear gripped me; no one had locked the front door. With people trying to break in, someone should have thought to lock it. A quick inspection told me that everything was in place. The bloodstain had faded, though still damp from scrubbing. The house seemed peaceful, but my heart continued to pound.

I half expected to see Uncle Charlie walk out of his office and ask about dinner. Several times a day, I had to remind myself he wouldn't be coming back. I didn't have time to follow that train of thought, though. Mae was expecting company.

A white sedan bounced its way up the drive. Our guests were arriving earlier than planned—good. I hurried to the kitchen, pulled the heavy cast-iron pan from the cabinet, and walked to the front porch to get a better look. The snakes had returned to the porch and walkway. *Perfect.*

A middle-aged man stepped from the car and glanced around. If he noticed the snakes, he didn't react. I couldn't decide if she admired him or thought him crazy. Snakes swirled in his path but managed to get out of the way before he stepped on them.

"Dr. Hicks?" I called from the porch and waved my free hand. The amulet around my neck grew cold.

"That's me." He smiled and walked in my direction.

I cradled the heavy skillet against my chest and limped toward him, mindful of the snakes at my feet. The amulet chilled me to the bone. I hesitated leaving the safety of the front porch, but the pan made as good a weapon as any. If Dr. Hicks set the amulet off, I could clock him with the skillet.

"I'm Tessa, Charlie's great-niece. My great-grandmother and aunt are—" I walked toward him and caught movement in the corner of my eye, a split second before a gun fired.

I would've bet my life that the cast-iron frying pan would stop a bullet—and I would've lost. The force of the shot knocked me to the ground, and the weight of the skillet made it difficult to breathe. I stared, half-blind, into the canopy of live oaks. In the distance someone yelled, "Stay inside."

Someone took pieces of the skillet from my hands. It dawned on me that I'd been shot. Panic and pain followed. Someone lifted me from the ground and ran, laying me on the ground near Mae's house. My body burned with a fire that started in my chest and ran out to my fingers, toes, and the top of my head, like lava in my veins.

"She's gone," a voice said from somewhere above me.

I'm not dead. I could see the sky, and hear Mae and Dottie wailing. My body burned as I tried to call out, but no sound came. Maybe I'd died and was on my way to hell. The little preacher in my head shook his Bible.

A black animal moved near me, but I couldn't turn my head to see. Had the wolves returned? I had to get inside, but I couldn't move, any more than I could call out. The animal sniffed near my ear, and I expected teeth to tear into my flesh. Instead, a huge bear filled my vision. The bear nudged the side of my face, grunted, and disappeared from view. It stayed close, but not close enough to see.

Snakes crawled over me, their cool skin slithering over my limbs. I wanted to scream, to flail and toss them off, but I lay helpless to their whims. When I thought my mind would break from the feel of them, they vanished.

Fire. I burned from the inside out. I screamed inside my head, and the earth shifted under my weight, as if to swallow me. My body changed so quickly I didn't understand what had happen until I caught a glimpse of feathers where skin should be. *Oh my God, I shifted?*

The pain threatened to consume me, until my body lifted, and a cool gust of wind replaced the burning sensation. I soared through clear-blue sky, still internally screaming. Sound filled my ears, alongside the sound of a bird screeching.

Brilliant red, orange, and yellow feathers moved in my peripheral vision. I cried out again, and the feathers shifted to flames. On the ground, three men crouched on the far side of the railroad tracks. I could make out the barrels on their rifles so clearly I could read the manufacturer's stamp. The men looked toward the heavens when I screamed. I locked onto my prey. Something inside me took over, a primal instinct. I descended, and my talons moved through flesh, until the only things that mattered were blood and flames.

Twenty

THE ENGINEER SIGNALED THREE QUICK blasts of the train's horn to get off the tracks. He hit the brakes but needed more time. The brakes squealed. The train smashed into a man on the tracks. When the train came to a complete stop, the carnage stretched for several hundred yards.

I sat in the tree, but I wasn't myself, I'd become some sort of strange bird. My feathers faded as I hid in the deep shadows of the tree. The train conductor went to his knees and sobbed. I wanted to tell him he hadn't killed the man on the tracks, only I couldn't speak. I could no longer see the two women holding each other, or the large black bear that guarded them. They'd gone inside the pink house; they were shouting.

I'm not dead. I stretched my right wing and groomed the coppery feathers. *I'm not dead.* I fluttered both wings and my head.

A man emerged from the house, went to a car, and pulled out a suitcase. He wore a towel around his waist and was barefoot. I edged forward on the branch until one of the rays of the sun touched my wing. It turned from dull copper to vibrant shades of red and orange. I screeched and pulled it out of the light.

The man in the towel turned his head and searched the tree, but I perched too high to be seen from below. He turned in the other direction as sirens screamed in the air. I jumped onto a higher branch to see five cars approach. The train conductor stood at the sound of the sirens. The man in the towel had changed into clothes and was walking toward the train.

The women came out of the house and walked toward the train as well. I worried that they'd see what I'd done. They would be disappointed in me; after all, I'd killed three men. Hadn't I killed before? I couldn't remember. Their tearstained faces drew another screech from my throat, and I leaped into the air. I soared high over the field until the trees ended and asphalt took their place. I circled back and flew over the house. One of the women looked up and pointed, and the other looked at me. They were yelling, angry.

Cars came to a stop on the sandy road; people spilled out and walked to the tracks. From the air, it looked like a beehive. Everyone focused on the dead man spread across yards of track—everyone except the two women. One shielded her eyes from the sun and smiled. The other waved her arm above her head, calling to me. I circled lower, trying to remember something I'd forgotten, something on the edge of my consciousness, just out of reach.

I alighted in the oak, and the women moved toward the tree. The closer they came, the farther back I went. Instinct told me to stay away from humans, but the women drew me to them. I fluttered my wings before settling. My predatory eyes turned to the uniformed men near the tracks, and I craned my neck to see if any were watching before easing from the shadows again.

"Tessa Marie, get down from that tree," the white-haired woman called to me.

Her voice woke something inside of me. The human part of my brain recognized my great-grandmother. I tried to call to her and shook my head in frustration. I landed beside her feet and looked up. Dottie ran toward the house and opened the front door, motioning for us to follow.

Mae nodded, and I flew toward the house, swooping down under the awning and through the front door. I landed on the kitchen table and waited. Mae and Dottie stood near the table, watching me. Neither seemed to know what to do or say.

"Change back, Tessa," Mae said.

I didn't understand. I knew the words and the meaning, but didn't know how I'd changed in the first place. How could I change back? I shook my head and stretched my wings.

"Tessa Marie, you have to change back or you'll be stuck," Mae cooed to me.

Fear tinged Mae's voice. I launched from the table and flew toward the window. The bird in me saw sky as a way out. I crashed into the window and fell to the dish drainer—glasses and plates falling, shattering.

"Dottie, go get Marvin," Mae said as she approached me.

The door opened, and I tried to make a break for it, but my wing hung limp. I paced the countertop, looking for a way to get down. The walls closed in like a cage. I needed to get out of the house. Panic threatened to choke the air from my lungs.

The door opened again, and a man and woman came inside. The door—I had to get to the door. The man smiled and reached for me. Humans were not to be trusted, but wasn't part of me human? I screeched and tried to fly away, only to land with a meaty thud.

I nipped his hand when he touched me. The moment blood hit my tongue, my feathers flared to life. Smoke filled the air as a dish towel caught fire. The flames licked at my feet but didn't burn.

"Tessa, you must stay calm and turn back," he whispered to me, and scratched the feathers on the top of my head.

I closed my eyes and tucked my head down to give him more room to scratch, hating myself for giving in to the affection. Humans, with their false smells and smiles. The animal in me hated him, but the girl loved the attention.

The older women began to hum a song. I'd heard the song before, but not hummed—whistled.

I opened my eyes. A strange man carried me in his arms. *Why am I naked?* Exhaustion made my head and limbs too heavy to move. He carried me into my bedroom and set me on the bed. Someone turned on the spigot, filling the tub. I touched my chest, and something crusty and sticky coated my fingers . . . blood.

Twenty-One

VOICES CARRIED FROM THE OTHER room. I made out Mae's voice among the lower tones of men. I tried to sit upright, and the room spun. The area between my breasts ached, and breathing hurt. It had to be one hell of a bruise.

"Gram?" I called from the bed. Bits and pieces of memories came uninvited, none of which made any sense.

"Gram Mae? Dottie?" The voices outside the door quieted, and Mae poked her head into the room.

"I need water." My throat burned. "Please."

Mae brought water and Detective Aaron Burns. He stayed by the door as if afraid to come into the room. I sipped the water, murmuring "Thanks."

Aaron smiled and dipped his chin. I must look like death eating a cracker. Only I couldn't bring myself to care.

"He wouldn't leave until he saw you for himself." Mae winked. She set the glass onto the nightstand, and grinned as she left the room.

"Hi?" I smiled.

"Hi, yourself. I hear you were saved by a cast-iron skillet?" He pulled the chair from my desk and sat beside the bed.

I winced and touched my chest. "Is that what happened? I can't remember."

Aaron watched me with concern. "Your aunt and great-grandmother refused to send you to the hospital. I tried to argue, but they're a formidable pair."

They must like him if he'd argued and come out of it in one piece. "I'm okay, but my chest is sore, and I have a headache. How long have you been here?"

Aaron made a show of checking his watch. "Four, five hours."

"Why did you stay so long?"

"Besides the fried chicken?" He laughed. "I wanted to tell you we have the man who tried to shoot you. His prints were on the gun."

I nodded and closed my eyes. He was holding something back. I remembered bits and pieces of what happened, and had some freaky dreams, but I couldn't put it all together. Aaron wasn't the one to ask. "Are you closing the case?"

"Not yet. There are still some unanswered questions. It'll be closed soon." He glanced out the window toward the field. "There'll be uniformed officers and inspectors from the railroad working near the house for the next day or two."

I tried to get a breath around the lump in my throat. "I'm not very good company right now."

Aaron stood and kissed my brow. "I shouldn't have done that when you aren't able to fight me off. I have to go. Get some rest."

I reached for his hand. "I wouldn't have fended you off, even if I could. Thanks for waiting for me to wake up."

The door opened and another man entered. I remembered him, only I'd forgotten his name. Aaron glanced between us. "I'll check on you in the morning."

Aaron clamped his hand on the other man's shoulder as he walked out and closed the door. The exchange made me curious. What in the world had gone on while I slept? Aaron acted like he and this guy were friends. I suspected Gram Mae had something to do with it.

"How are you feeling?" He stood near the foot of the bed.

"Tired and sore." I frowned. "I'm sorry. I forgot your name."

"Marvin. Dr. Marvin Hicks." He motioned to the chair. "May I?"

"Of course. I remember now. I called your office. They said you'd taken emergency leave. My uncle wanted me to give you something."

Marvin seated himself, his expression more serious. "Dottie gave me the cedar box, but I believe it was meant for you, my dear."

"My uncle told me to give the box to you."

Marvin tilted his head. "What else did he tell you?"

"Dottie and Mae were in danger and I should take the box to you. People would be looking for it . . ." I lowered my voice. "He said to tell you I was his granddaughter, which is wrong. I'm his grandniece."

Marvin turned his head toward the window. I didn't know this man from Adam, but I thought I could trust him. He reminded me of my uncle, but it was more than just a shared ancestry—he had the same kind eyes.

"Tessa, perhaps we should have this conversation when you're feeling better?"

"No, I need to understand what's going on. Wait. You were here? When I was shot? I remember that you'd just arrived."

Marvin nodded. "I helped Dottie and Mae take care of you."

I remembered him carrying me twice: once after I was shot, and once when I was naked. "What happened? Did that old skillet really take the bullet?"

He appeared to be in a silent debate. "No. The skillet didn't stop the bullet. It shattered on impact, slowing the bullet down. You were shot in the chest."

My head sank into the pillow. I couldn't have been shot. Aaron said they refused to take me to the hospital. People went to the hospital when they were shot.

"Tessa, you died. I carried you around the house, out of range of the shooter. You had no pulse. The bullet went into your heart."

"Then how am I still alive?" My heart pounded, proving him wrong.

"You rose. I wouldn't have believed it if I hadn't seen it myself. You are a firebird."

I laughed and shook my head. When I met his gaze, I stilled. "Like a phoenix?"

He shrugged. "Our people call it a firebird. To my knowledge, there hasn't been one here for centuries. You had to inherit it from your mother."

"Trust me, Dr. Hicks, my mother isn't anything special. Sometimes I wonder if she's even human."

He rested his hand on mine. "Tessa, your mother wasn't—she wasn't the woman you know to be your mother."

I'd always fantasized that I'd been switched at birth. I never fit with Darlene. As a child, I dreamed someone would tell me I belonged to a different family. Now that it had happened, I didn't want it to be true.

"Charlie had a daughter," he continued.

"Atsila," I whispered.

"Yes, her name was Atsila." He squeezed my hand. "She was Nunnehi."

"Nunnehi? Native American fairies?" My brain hurt. "I'm a firebird, and my real mother was a fairy?"

He nodded once. "They aren't the little folk who fly around visiting flowers. They are another race. They protected the Cherokee and tried to save the old ones from the relocation. It is believed that when the English settled in our lands, most of the Nunnehi died from Western diseases or war, and some may have gone underground—no one is sure. If any still live, they are hidden in the Appalachias. Some believe full-blooded Nunnehi are extinct."

"If she was Charlie's daughter, she would be half-blood." As soon as the words fell from my mouth, the truth clicked in my brain.

"Charlie?"

Marvin nodded and waited for it to sink in.

"How? I mean, why did Darlene raise me?"

"Her child was born a couple of weeks before you. Darlene's baby died of SIDS at three months old. Charlie worked a forgetting spell on Darlene. He made her believe that you were her daughter."

"That's so wrong."

"He did what he thought was best for you."

I pressed my fingers to my temples and closed my eyes. "Do you know who my father was?"

"Charlie never spoke of your father."

I nodded. I'd never had a real father. My jaw slacked as I stared at Dr. Hicks, unable to make sense of my thoughts. Then it hit me—hard. "Mae isn't . . . ?"

"She is human."

"She isn't Charlie's mother?" I croaked out the words.

"Not by birth, no, but she was a mother to him."

"She isn't my great-grandmother by blood. None of them are." I shook my head and laughed, not wanting to believe any of this. "I don't care. She is more family to me than anyone."

Dr. Hicks remained silent while I sorted it all out.

"She visits me. Atsila. Since I was a little girl, her spirit has come to me."

Marvin smiled. "I'm not surprised. Dottie tells me you can see spirits, and you're an intuitive, possibly a seer."

"I get feelings sometimes. Like the day Charlie died, I knew someone was going to die, just not who."

"Now that you have shifted, your other gifts will become stronger, much stronger."

"I'll see ghosts and be able to tell the future?" My intuition came in handy, but I didn't see an upside to seeing ghosts.

"Yes, but eventually it will be a part of you, and you will learn to control it." He stood.

"Wait. Please don't leave." I didn't want to be alone. I had more questions.

"Easy, little flame, I'll be right back." He smiled and walked out.

I cringed when Dr. Hicks used my uncle's pet name for me. *Charlie had to know I was part Nunnehi. Did he know I was a firebird? Had more than my red hair earned me the nickname? No, this couldn't be real, any of it.* Soon I'd wake up from this nightmare.

Dr. Hicks returned with Uncle Charlie's composition book and handed it to me. "I cannot read the pages."

I ran my hands over the cover. "Neither can I."

"Try." He insisted.

The change in his tone gave me pause. What difference did it make to him if I could read the book? I slid the rubber band off. The writing remained an unfamiliar mess of symbols and scribbles. As I stared at the page, the symbols began to make sense. "I can read it. It's a spell book."

Dr. Hicks's eyes darkened as he leaned forward. Something about him gave me the chills. I reached for the amulet, but it wasn't around my neck.

I closed the journal and set it between me and the wall.

Marvin frowned. "Do you remember what happened after you were shot?"

"No, just that you were carrying me. I had the most bizarre dreams, though."

"In your dreams, were you flying?" His voice lowered to a whisper.

"I saw a bear, and then I was flying. I saw three men with guns. Blood, a lot of blood."

"I'm the bear you saw. I'm a shifter, like you, only my animal spirit's a bear."

"Did I kill those men?"

"Your animal spirit did, yes, with my help."

"Is that the last of them? Who are they? Why do they want to hurt us?" My chest tightened, and my body burned from the inside out. "Oh no."

"Drink." He held a cup to my lips. It smelled like feet and tasted even worse.

Dr. Hicks sneered as the liquid slid down my throat.

Twenty-Two

I WOKE AND THE PINK RUFFLED curtains swaying in the breeze. It tasted like something had died in my mouth. I wandered into the bathroom and brushed my teeth, yet the taste persisted. A haggard reflection stared back from the mirror. My stomach loudly reminded me I hadn't eaten in days.

The cold fried chicken tasted like ashes on my tongue. The tea oozed, syrupy and thick. Even toast made my stomach clench as it turned to a paste. I gave up on food and searched for my cell phone.

Wednesday, I'd slept for almost two days. Twenty-four missed calls and twice as many missed text messages. I set the phone aside.

Someone had scratched out a note and secured it to the fridge. I didn't bother to read it. The thought of a bath enticed me, until the possibility of conjuring the spirit of my dead mother crossed my mind. I wanted to speak to her, to ask the questions that floated around in my mind, but I needed time to process everything I'd learned. Not to mention, my talks with her were cryptic at best.

"I need to get out of here," I mumbled.

Without any thought to the consequences, I stripped out of my night clothes and opened the window. Standing in the room bare as the day I was born, I wondered if I'd suffered from a psychotic break. I sat and put my head in my hands, trying to force myself to cry. I needed to let the emotions out, but none came.

The burning in my chest returned. Instead of letting it consume me with fear, I focused on the sensation. It didn't burn like an open flame, as it had before. It reminded me of sinking into a warm bath. My back bowed as my body tried to resist the change. I forced myself to relax, and the warmth filled me.

I launched skyward from the windowsill, faltered, and began to plummet. Each time I thought with my human brain, my innate ability to fly wavered. I couldn't allow the animal to take complete control.

As I understood how my new body worked, I ventured from my home. I soared high on the currents and dove toward the earth, only to spread my wings and drift high again.

For the first time since Gram Mae had called me to the hospital, my mind stilled. I had no cares, no worries of people trying to kill me, no grief or loss, no family drama, no job, no patients, no disappointments. I was free.

The gathering with the elders would happen on Wednesday—today. How had I forgotten? Better yet, how could they have let me sleep through the gathering? I couldn't miss the chance to make sure the people trying to kill me were dead.

I changed headings and flew east. Anger, hurt, and confusion whittled away at the fragile peace I'd found in the air. By the time I flew over the university, my wings glowed with an orange tint.

The sun had almost set when I reached the forest in Geneva, my tail feathers leaving a streak of red flames in my wake. The thick tree canopy made it difficult to see the ground, yet my predatory vision picked up the smallest movements. I tracked field mice as they scurried from my shadow. I approached the clearing. Several people stood in a circle around a fire pit. Some wore street clothes, while others wore ceremonial garb. The official change of leadership had begun. My heart beat with the cadence of the drums and stomping feet.

I tucked my wings and dove toward the fire in the center of the gathering. Circling once, I aimed for the sand surrounding the pit. Despite my efforts, I landed in the center of the flames. My initial instinct was panic, but the fire didn't burn. In fact, they energized me.

Shouts bellowed over the roar of the flames. People scattered away from the pit, wide-eyed and frightened. Dr. Hicks folded his arms over his chest and watched with a grim expression.

I spread my wings and rose until I hovered over the flames, quite pleased with my new skills. Had I been in human form, I would've laughed. Instead, the sound came out in a shrill caw. Those gathered there stared, and a few moved closer.

"Impossible." One of the elders reached forward but yanked his hand back when the flames licked his skin.

Gram Mae called my name—leave it to Mae to ruin all the fun. I tucked my head to my chest and focused on the sound of her voice. The shouts around me grew louder. My eyes watered from the smoke, clouding my vision. I stood in human form in the center of the fire pit, untouched by the flames.

The words that were being shouted surprised me. I'd been around these people my entire life and never heard them curse. Gram Mae needed a case of Ivory soap for this crowd. Dr. Hicks stepped forward and offered his hand. A little late to be self-conscious, I held my head high as I stepped out of the fire.

"It seems we have a challenger for the position of shaman." Dr. Hicks slanted his eyes to me. "Tessa of the Red Paint clan, daughter of Atsila, granddaughter of Cheasequah."

I hadn't heard Charlie's true name in a long time. I expected Mae and Dottie to give me the same disapproving look, but they smiled. Someone draped a heavy robe over my shoulders. I didn't know what they expected me to say, so I nodded. What had I gotten myself into?

Dr. Hicks spoke again. "I concede my claim." He ground my

knuckles hard enough to elicit a whimper. I pulled my hand back, resisting the urge to rub the throbbing joints. Any doubt I had about his disdain for me vanished.

Someone called from the crowd. "Does the girl have a tongue to speak?"

"I do." I searched the crowd for the person who'd spoken.

"Did Cheasequah train you?" Buck Oldham stepped forward.

"In his own way, he did. I have his book and can read the writings."

"Wait." Mae stepped forward. "Marvin Hicks has the book in his car. Tessa will need it back."

Dr. Hicks stiffened beside me. Several people began to speak in hushed tones, and Buck's voice rose. "There is no doubt you're a firebird, but how?"

Should I speak of my mother's heritage? The men had known my family since before I was born. They couldn't be the ones trying to hurt me. Could they? "My mother was Nunnehi."

Voices filled the air, and I waited for them to quiet. "Cheasequah worried that someone would try to steal his book. Since his passing, there have been attempts on my life. I stand before you now and ask the tribe's assistance in finding those who would dishonor my grandfather."

They all spoke at once. I knew I'd poked a skunk by bringing this up at a gathering. In the confusion, I lost sight of Dr. Hicks. "Where is Dr. Hicks?"

They continued to argue. I let the robe fall and embraced the heat in my gut. This time I shifted with ease. Before anyone could stop me, I took flight.

I flew over the parking area as a white sedan backed out. The car swung around and sped down the gravel drive, heading for the highway. I followed for a few miles, then turned back toward the gathering. My flying allowed me time to think. Obviously, Marvin had planned to take Charlie's position, but why? Charlie trusted him, and he'd helped me when I first shifted. He'd killed the men in the field . . . hadn't he? I couldn't remember seeing the bear after my change.

When I returned to the forest, the elders and my family had gathered beneath a pavilion. Food was set out, although no one had touched it. I shifted near the dying fire and slid the robe on. My skin prickled, as if someone was watching me from the trees. I wished I had my amulet, but I'd left it behind when I shifted. Whoever or whatever didn't seem to present a threat. I had no idea how I knew, but I trusted the feeling of peace flowing from the dark woods.

"Did you find him?" Buck met me on the path.

"No. He traveled north toward Highway 46. He has the book."

Buck set his arm around my shoulders and gave me a squeeze. "Don't worry, little flame, we will find him. Do you plan to claim the position of shaman?"

I stopped walking. I'd never considered the possibility. Did I want it? "May I have some time to grieve before I answer?"

"Of course, but we will need an answer before the next gathering. In the meantime, I'm going to keep you ladies safe."

"Good luck. Have you met my great-grandmother?"

Twenty-Three

RATHER THAN GOING INTO HIDING with Mae and Dottie, the tribal elders allowed me to leave under one condition—I had to agree to have a bodyguard with me at all times. Bryson, my new bodyguard, was the consolation prize.

Bryson was a shifter; specifically, he changed into a hawk. Nothing about him was hawklike, though. He looked more like a bull—a freaking hot bull with muscles, a strong jaw, and a long black ponytail.

I gripped the steering wheel. "Look, I don't need a bodyguard. The great thing about being a firebird is I can't die. I'll just rise from the ashes and fly away. You can just drop me off." I smiled.

"There are ways to kill a firebird."

"Right." I pulled the car up the drive and cut a hard left onto the grass.

"Pull up closer to the door."

"Mae will pitch a fit if I park on her grass."

"Do it."

I eased the car forward. A thick arm crossed my chest before I could open the door. "What now?"

"Wait until I come around," he said.

"Oh, for Pete's sake."

Bryson took his time checking the perimeter before unlocking

Mae's front door. By the time he opened my door, I wanted to punch him in the face. I hopped out and took my time walking around the car. The box of bottles sat on the bottom step, and it smelled like rain was coming. "Would you bring that box inside for me?"

My phone rang as I walked inside, giving me an excuse to leave Bryson in the kitchen. "Hello?"

"Tessa, it's Aaron. Detective Burns. I've been trying to reach you. Is everything all right?"

"Yeah, we had a tribal meeting. It's been a long few days. I left my phone at the house."

"Do you remember seeing any wild animals around the house the day you were shot?"

I reached for the doorjamb. "Which time? I've been shot twice in two weeks."

"The second time."

I decided to lie. "No, nothing since the attempted break-in. Why?"

"We found two men mauled and burned in the field by the house the day you were shot."

Oh God, had I really killed people? My heart slammed against my chest. "Weird."

The line went quiet. I pulled the phone from my ear and glanced at the screen. "Are you still there?"

"Yes. Mind if I stop by? A personal visit. Uh, what I mean is, they'll be closing the case soon. I would like to see you, personally."

I laughed. "Personally, sure."

"Great, be there in ten." Aaron disconnected before I had time to change my mind. How in the hell would I explain 250 pounds of Native American muscle in my living room?

"Hey, Bryson?" I found him fiddling with his cell phone. "I'm expecting company, a cop friend. Let's not get into the whole bodyguard thing, okay?"

He shrugged. "Cousin Bryson, in for the funeral. Don't even think about leaving with him."

I turned and headed for my room. I needed a quick shower and to change out of the robe. My hair smelled like smoke and bird feathers. I'd moved as fast as I could, but someone knocked on the door before I could rinse the conditioner out of my hair. "Crap."

Male voices drifted into the room as I stepped out of the shower. Aaron could have a conversation with anyone, including a Neanderthal. I combed out the tangles and slid into a pair of jeans. He'd seen me look worse, but I still wished I had more prep time. I wiped the steam off the mirror for one last check. In the reflection, a woman stood behind me . . . my birth mother.

How had I not noticed the resemblance? We shared the same hair and eye colors, and the shape of our faces was similar, though our builds couldn't have been more different. I reached forward and touched the spirit woman. I'd never tried. Even as a child I'd assumed my hand would pass through her. Her skin was solid beneath my fingers.

"You're my mother?"

"Yes." Atsila brushed my hair from my face.

"I have so many questions."

"Tessa? Who are you talking to? Is someone in there with you?" Bryson banged on the bedroom door.

"I'm on the phone." I turned and Atsila vanished. "Dammit. Seriously, would a little privacy kill you?"

I went into the kitchen, and Aaron cleared his throat. "Hi, Aaron, sorry to keep you waiting. I had to shower. I smelled like a bonfire."

Bryson laughed and went back into the living room, shaking his head.

"You met my cousin?" I tried to make light of the situation, but I was thinking of ways to cook hawk stew.

Aaron folded his arms across his chest. His eyes moved to the phone on the table.

I leaned in to whisper, "I was giving myself a pep talk. I do that sometimes when I'm nervous."

"Why are you nervous?" He grinned. "I'm kidding. I'm nervous, too. You look good for someone who's been shot twice."

I couldn't exactly tell Aaron that my wounds had healed when I shifted into a firebird. I shrugged. "Gram Mae is a miracle worker."

Aaron gave me a dubious look.

I debated sitting at the kitchen table. Mae would approve, but it left Bryson within earshot. I motioned for him to follow me into my bedroom, making sure to limp and grimace every so often. Aaron closed the door behind him. If Bryson needed to pee, he'd have to go outside.

"This isn't what it looks like. It's a small house, and with him here, there will be no privacy."

"As long as you know I don't put out on the first date."

I sat on the bed. "My Gram Mae would pitch a fit if she knew I had you in here with the door closed."

"She didn't mind me being in here when you were shot." Aaron ran his hand over his chin. "Where did the nickname 'Gram Mae' come from? I'm betting there's a story behind it."

"Great-Grandmother Mae was a mouthful when I was little." I grinned at his socked feet.

"We were never allowed to wear shoes in the house. Old habits." He sat beside me.

"Where did you grow up?"

"Montreat, North Carolina. Took me forever to lose the accent."

"I've been there. My family is Cherokee. We spent a lot of time in the mountains when I was a kid." I frowned at the bathroom door, wondering when I'd have the chance to talk to my mother. "Oh, I'm rude. Do you want something to drink? We have beer, water, or tea."

"Sure. Mae filled me to the gills with sweet tea the other day. How about a beer?"

I stood and limped to the kitchen. Before I returned to Aaron, I looked in on Bryson. "There's beer in the fridge and some leftovers. Help yourself."

He nodded without taking his eyes off the television.

I snatched a beer from the fridge and returned to my bedroom. "How long have you lived in Florida?"

"I went to UCF right out of high school, been here ever since." He took the beer and smiled. "You don't drink beer?"

"Naw, tastes like it's been through someone once already."

He nearly spit beer on the quilt. "Never thought about it like that. How about you? I assume you were born in Florida?"

"My great-grandmother was born in the green house next door. I went to college at FSU, then grad school at UCF. I've traveled quite a bit but always lived in Florida." I settled against the headboard and drew my legs beneath me.

Aaron followed my lead and leaned his back against the wall. "They transferred Samuels and me to the Rivera case. With all of the media coverage, the chief is under a lot of pressure to find those kids."

"He put the best detectives on it?"

Aaron ran his hand over the back of his neck. "Yeah, I guess."

"Are you allowed to talk about it? I've seen some of the news coverage. It's awful." I couldn't take my eyes off him.

"The father isn't giving us any information. He's our only suspect. It feels off." Aaron shrugged. "Let's not talk shop. I want to know about you."

"What do you want to know?"

"Let's see. You know how to shoot a gun. Do you hunt?"

"If you count tin cans as hunting." I laughed. "Do you?"

"I used to with my dad. We'd camp out in the mountains and

bring home enough deer to last months. I haven't gone since I moved to Florida." His eyes lost their sparkle.

"When did your dad pass away?"

Aaron tilted his head. "My senior year of high school. Both of my folks were killed in a car accident. How did you know?"

"I read people for a living. What they say with their words is only half of what they actually say."

"You should have been a police officer." He laughed. "You'd make a good one. You've had a rough go of it the last few days, and you're still standing."

I smiled and touched his cheek. "That's because I was raised by two genuine southern ladies, sweet as honey and tough as nails."

He leaned forward and brushed his lips across mine. The angle made the kiss awkward. I pulled back as the image of him hugging two young children flashed through my mind for the second time.

"Do you have kids?"

"Uh, no. Why do you ask?"

"I don't know. It just occurred to me you might have kids."

He leaned forward to put his beer on the nightstand and kissed me again. This time his mouth pressed more firmly to mine. He traced a slow line across my lower lip with his tongue as he pulled away. His eyes locked on mine, and I kissed him again. I'd imagined kissing him since we'd first met. The real thing was better than I thought it would be.

I ran my hand to his chest as he slid his arm around my shoulder. He eased me closer and tangled his fingers in my hair. We held each other, lingering in the kiss. When we parted, he nuzzled his face against mine. I melted.

He whispered into my ear, "Who takes care of you, Tessa?"

My breath hitched in my throat, and I shook my head. Any other time I would've said I could take care of myself. Lately, my life had

had more twists than Mae's soap operas. The idea of someone taking care of me sounded pretty darned good.

He pulled back and brushed his fingers over my cheek. "You look tired. I should go?"

"Stay."

Twenty-Four

I SMELLED BACON AND SNUGGLED INTO the pillow. Aaron's cologne lingered, reminding me of the night before. I threw the blankets off and slid into my jeans. Where had Aaron gone?

I had to give myself props for keeping my hands to myself—well, mostly to myself. My lips ached from too much kissing. I brushed my teeth and splashed some water on my face. I pulled my hair into a ponytail and limped into the kitchen. The limp purely for Aaron's benefit.

Aaron and Bryson sat at Mae's table eating a mountain of eggs, bacon, and grits. Both men turned and smiled. They seemed too friendly with each other. I went for the coffeepot and stumbled over the box of old bottles.

"Are you okay?" Aaron stood to help.

"Yes, just not used to having a box in the middle of the kitchen." I slanted my eyes at Bryson, and he shrugged.

"When do you have to be in the office?" I sat and sipped my coffee.

"I'm off, unless they call me in." Aaron motioned to the food. "You should eat some breakfast. We didn't do a half-bad job."

"We?" I filled my plate. "Would you two mind helping me with a project this morning? I need to hang those bottles in the oak out front."

Bryson said, "Do you think it's a good idea to be outside? I mean you're so white. You'll will burn in the sun."

I choked on my coffee. "I'll be fine."

"Why do you want to hang bottles in a tree?" Aaron had watched the exchange between Bryson and me with an amused grin.

"Gram says the clear ones are for wishes, and the blue ones trap evil spirits."

They grinned and remained quiet, finishing their breakfast. It surprised me when they each took their plates to the sink. I debated offering to do the dishes, but decided to enjoy watching someone else do them. I sat on the floor and sorted through the dusty old bottles. "Mae would wash these before she hung them. It's supposed to rain later. I say we just—"

"Hose them down in the yard," Aaron said.

Pain bloomed in my finger, and I yanked my hand back. "Ouch, dang it."

"What did you do?" Bryson blanched when I stuck my bleeding finger in my mouth.

"Cut my finger on a broken bottle."

Aaron offered me his hand. "Stand up. Let me take a look."

I reached for his hand and allowed him to hoist me to my feet. As I pulled my hand free, my fingertips brushed across his watch. My mind flooded with images of a man and woman riding in a car. "What in the world?"

"Are you all right?" Aaron put his hand on my shoulder to steady me.

"May I see your watch?" I held out my hand.

He looked at me as if I were nuts, slid the watch off, and dropped it into my hand. I closed my hand around the watch, and more images came to me. I saw the couple in the car, laughing. The man had the same crystal-blue eyes as Aaron; they had to be his parents. The warmth of the moment ended when another vehicle slammed into the side of the car. Aaron's father stared at his wife. Blood coated her face. He tried to call her name, to reach for her hand, but the car exploded before he could touch her.

My screams rang in my ears. I startled when Aaron touched my arms, and I dropped the watch. The vision stopped, but the terror took longer to shake. I sank to the floor, sobbing.

"Tessa, what is it?" Aaron sat on the floor beside me. He looked up at Bryson. "Does she have seizures?"

Bryson shook his head and picked up the watch.

"What's happening to her? Has she done this before?"

Bryson folded his arms across his chest. "I don't know."

I raised my head and swallowed the bile in my throat. "I saw your parents. That was his watch. He was wearing it when he died."

Aaron stared as if I'd punched him.

"I see things sometimes. I saw the accident."

Aaron let out a nervous laugh. "Come on, Tessa, be serious. This isn't funny."

"I'm not joking. They were broadsided. The car exploded after impact."

Aaron's mouth fell open. "How did you know that?"

"I told you. I see things sometimes." I stood and went to the cupboard for Mae's whiskey.

Aaron watched me as I drank straight from the bottle. "You're right, that's how they died."

I wrapped my arms around myself. "I'm sorry."

"Can you do that with a murder weapon?"

"No. That isn't a good idea," Bryson chimed in. "If she comes forward as a seer, both Tessa and the department will be ridiculed."

Aaron and I stared at Bryson. "He's right, Aaron. I'm sorry."

"What if we do it on the down low? Maybe you can point us

in the right direction? You said you didn't believe it was the father."

"You're talking about the Rivera case, the missing kids?"

"Yes." Aaron reached for my hand but stopped short.

Bryson said, "Tessa, you can't get involved in this."

I turned to Bryson. "And if an innocent man goes to jail?"

"You'll help?" Aaron stared at me.

"Yes, as long as we keep it between us."

Bryson shook his head. "If you're going, I'm going."

"Great. I'll call you when I get to the station." Aaron hurried out the door.

Twenty-Five

"YOU LIKE HIM?" BRYSON LEANED against the counter.

I scowled. "Not that it's any of your business, but yeah, I do."

Bryson turned to the sink of dishes. "He seems like a straight-up guy . . ."

"Why do I feel like there's a 'but' in there?"

"Using magic around outsiders isn't a good idea."

"I didn't use magic. I don't even know what I used. It just happened."

"Your relationship with Aaron—it can't work," Bryson said.

"Why not?"

"It's forbidden to expose your animal self to normal folk. Most of the tribe doesn't know about us, let alone outsiders."

"I didn't expose anything to Aaron."

Bryson shrugged. "The more he's around, the more risk you run of him finding out."

"My uncle—I mean, my grandfather—married an outsider. It didn't cause them any problems." I didn't want to hear it, especially from someone I barely knew.

"Dottie was exposed to shifters before she met your grandfather. She survived an attack, and he healed her. She was permitted to live, if he took an oath to keep her silent." Bryson set a pot in the dish drainer.

"How do you know about this and I don't?"

"I was there when he took the oath." He turned and dried his hands.

"What? When you were two? Bull."

"I was in my late sixties when they were married." He tossed the towel on the counter. "We don't age like others."

I sat down and put my head in my hands. "My grandfather was a shifter?"

Bryson nodded.

"He aged like a normal man."

"Are you certain?" Bryson's chin rose. "He was Nunnehi. There's no telling how old he was. Purebloods can live forever."

I tried to process the information and the wash of emotions surging over me. "Are you a half-breed like me?"

He nodded. "My mother was full Nunnehi. The elders thought I was the last of the blood, until last night."

"It was no accident they sent you to guard me, was it?" I had a sneaking suspicion this was like Gram Mae inviting eligible men from church to dinner.

"No, it wasn't. I had my mother to show me the ways. You have no one."

"So you're my bodyguard and magic teacher?" I laughed. "As long as they aren't playing matchmaker."

"Oh, they're doing that, too." He chuckled. "I volunteered."

I shook my head and stood with both hands up. "I'm going to hang the bottles. Alone."

I threw a roll of twine into the box and grabbed wire hangers from the closet, along with wire cutters. When I came back into the kitchen, Bryson held the box. "Ready?"

"I don't need help. I can do it myself."

"Are you forgetting someone shot you in the yard? You aren't going out there until I have a chance to check the fields." He pushed the screen door open. "Wait here."

How much protection could a screen door provide from a bullet? I shook my head.

Bryson set the box on the ground and pulled his T-shirt over his head. He kicked his boots off and dropped his jeans. I would have enjoyed the view more if he weren't so annoying.

Bryson ran and leaped into the air. One second he was a man, the next a large bird. "Impressive," I remarked. I envied the ease of his transition. I turned and went into my bedroom. My frown disappeared when I caught a whiff of Aaron's cologne in the air.

I checked my phone—no messages. He'd just left, too soon for a call. What if he didn't call after the weirdness this morning? Maybe Bryson was right. Bringing in an outsider would only complicate matters. Would the elders kill Aaron if he knew the truth? Better question: Would Aaron believe me if I told him?

The screen door opened and Bryson walked in, naked. "Are you coming?"

I covered my eyes and turned my head. "Yes, but put some clothes on."

"I'm going to shift again in a minute. Easier to fly with the twine than haul a ladder or toss it up."

"Fine, then shift. We don't know each other well enough to be walking around naked."

"Whatever you say, miss 'naked in the middle of the fire.'"

I pushed past him and walked out the door. He shifted, and landed in the tree. I ignored him and sat in the grass, wrapping a piece of wire around the neck of a bottle. Once I had the bottles wired, I cut long pieces of twine. Bryson flew down and watched me. I knew it was Bryson, yet I felt silly talking to a bird.

"Can you knot it around a branch?"

Bryson dipped his beak and flew into the tree with a piece of twine. He cawed, and I fastened a bottle to the hanging twine. He hopped down and took a second piece of twine, returning to the same branch.

"No, do a different branch." I shook my head. "Now you're too high. I can't reach to tie it off."

Bryson screeched, and it sounded way too close to annoyance. After a few attempts, we found a rhythm. The entire project took less than an hour. I admired our handiwork. "Looks good."

He flew down and landed beside my feet, chirping.

"What?"

He flew in a circle above my head, landed, and nudged my leg.

"You want me to fly with you?" I hoped against hope that no one was watching the strange conversation. "Turn around."

Bryson turned his back. I entertained the idea of kicking him while I had the advantage of height and weight, but thought better of it. In human form, he outweighed me by a hundred pounds. I stripped down, focused, and managed to change forms. Even after I'd fully changed, I was disoriented. The hawk nudged me until I shook out my wings and took flight.

Bryson blew past me, creating a change in the air current. I glided into his wake, riding his draft. He cut to the side sharply and flew higher, his wings stretched to their full span as he circled above me. I followed his lead and circled with him, until he turned and came head-on.

The human part of my brain panicked as he barreled toward me. I twisted to change course, and his talons locked with mine. Before I could free myself, he took us into a steep dive. He released me before we hit the tree line, and soared back into the sky. I followed.

The play felt intimate somehow. Instinct took over, and I hung back as he showed off with spins and dives. He flew higher than I dared, then dove toward me. This time I used my wings to stop my flight, which sent my talons and tail feathers to the front. Once again, we locked talons and spun in a dizzying dive.

We played in the sky until the sun sat directly overhead. He circled over the pink house and landed on a branch of the bottle tree. I landed beside him, grooming my feathers. I didn't let them blaze, though the heat burned below the surface. Two birds in the morning sky wasn't anything unusual; a bird with wings of fire would draw unwanted attention.

Bryson watched as I groomed my feathers. When I finished, he rubbed his head against mine and nipped me. I ignored him, stretching my wings before I flew to the ground.

He followed and shifted back before he touched the grass. I shifted a moment later. We stood staring at each other. He ran his fingers across my cheek with half-lidded eyes. I huffed and marched to my clothes, scooped them up, and headed toward the house.

"Tessa?"

"What?"

"You may not want me, but your spirit animal does. Otherwise, she wouldn't have allowed you to do the mating dance with me." He chuckled.

I wasn't amused. I snapped my mouth closed and walked into the house, slamming the screen door behind me.

Twenty-Six

THE NERVE OF THAT MAN. Since when did bodyguards try to pick fights with the people they guarded? My phone rang, distracting me. "Yeah?"

"Hello, Tessa?" A male voice came across the line.

"Speaking."

"This is Dr. Hicks. I need to see you."

"Are you serious?" I frowned as Bryson walked through the door. "Why?"

"I have some things that belong to you."

"Yeah, I guess you do." I turned my back to Bryson. "When?"

"I can be there in half an hour."

"Sure, fine, whatever."

The call disconnected. Determined to ignore Bryson, I walked into my bedroom and closed the door. I was acting like a child, but I didn't care. Screw him and his mating dance.

"Tessa, open the door," Bryson called from the kitchen.

I went into the bathroom and turned on the spigot. Water poured into the tub as I sat on the toilet lid. A bath sounded great, but I didn't have time. Nor did I want to be naked and alone in the house with that jerk.

Bryson knocked on the bathroom door. "Tessa?"

"I'm in the tub."

"Bullshit." He opened the door and folded his arms across his chest. "Look, I'm sorry if I offended you, but I need to know what's going on. Who called?"

"I can take care of myself."

"Dammit, Tessa, listen to me." He turned the water off and knelt in front of me. "Like it or not, we may be stuck together for a long time. Not because I'm guarding you, but because we may be the last of our kind."

"Are you seriously giving me the 'We're the last people on earth,' argument?"

"Yeah, I guess I am."

I hung my head. "Fine."

"Fine what?" He took my chin between his thumb and forefinger and turned my face toward his.

I wanted to yell or slap his hand away. Whatever anger I had melted away and left nothing except an empty hole in my chest. He must have seen it in my eyes, because he pulled me against his chest.

"Tell me what's going on." He brushed my hair back. I exhaled the tension from my shoulders and closed my eyes.

"Everything is changing, and I don't like it."

"Let me help you."

"Help me what? You *are* part of the changes, remember?"

He slid his arms around me, pressing my head to his chest. I wanted to argue, but I couldn't find the strength. When I relaxed against him, he ran his hand over my back. For the first time in days, my brain slowed and I relaxed.

"I'm so tired," I said.

"Grief will do that to you."

"I haven't had time to grieve."

"Maybe not outright, but your spirit grieves, Tessa." He pulled back and looked at me.

I turned my face toward his and held my breath. Would he kiss me? Did I want him to? My heart raced as my eyes closed, just as Bryson released me and moved toward the door. His apparent rejection stung, and I didn't want him to leave me—not yet.

"Marvin Hicks is on his way over," I called after him.

He stiffened, drew a breath, and nodded. "I'll answer the door when he arrives." Bryson gave me a dirty look and left me alone in the bathroom.

I sat on the toilet lid, trying to decipher my emotions. I must have been more tangled up than I realized, because I came out of my skin when someone knocked on the front door. Two males exchanged words in the front room; from the sound of it, neither was happy.

I splashed water on my face and walked into the kitchen to find Marvin. Bryson stood, resting against the counter. His cold, impassive expression made me nervous.

"Thanks for seeing me." Marvin smiled as I took a seat across from him.

"Do you have Charlie's book?"

Marvin nodded and reached down into his case. Bryson unfolded his arms and took a step forward, ready to disarm the man if he did anything unfortunate. Marvin's eyes went wide as he pulled the book from the case and set it on the table. "I didn't know you and Bryson were friends?"

I handed the book to Bryson, ignoring Marvin's question. "You can go now."

"Tessa, we need to talk." He pulled my amulet over his head and set it on the table.

"Where did you get that?" I snatched it up and handed it to Bryson.

"I found it in the yard after you shifted. I hoped it would protect me. It did for a while, but stopped." He glanced between me and Bryson.

"Protect you from what? Yourself?" I sat back.

"I'm in serious trouble. I owe a debt to a conjurer. If it isn't paid, he'll kill me." Dr. Hicks ran his hand through his hair. "I was hoping I could use the book to find a way to break the deal, but I can't read the pages."

"Is that why you're here?" Bryson moved closer to the table. His energy ratcheted up several notches.

"Yes, and to explain." He swallowed hard. "I didn't know you were Nunnehi until I read Charlie's letter. Though, I'm not surprised."

I didn't care what he had to say. I'd liked this guy, trusted him, and he betrayed me. "What deal did you make?"

He frowned and shook his head. "It was made a long time ago."

"Does this have anything to do with a guy in a white cowboy hat, trimmed in wolf fur?" I knew the answer before he spoke. I could see the fear in his eyes and feel the emotions rolling off him.

"How?" He shifted in his chair. "Did you have a vision?"

"No. He visited me in the hospital. Did he kill Charlie?"

Bryson set his hand on my shoulder.

"Maybe. I don't know for sure." Marvin glanced over my shoulder to Bryson. "Yes. He is responsible for Charlie's death."

I breathed deeply to control my emotions. "Why?"

"He wanted to take his power and gain influence over the tribe." Marvin's eyes darted around the kitchen. "He thought Charlie's power would flow to him when he died, but the spell didn't work. The power went someplace else."

I eased my chair back. "Wouldn't the power die with him?"

"Unless someone was able to steal it, or if Charlie had an heir." Marvin met my eyes. "I didn't know you were his granddaughter. As soon as I found out, I tried to break the deal."

Bryson asked, "What deal?"

"I agreed to get the spell book in exchange for a position among the elders—Charlie's position."

I stood. "You sold my grandfather's life in exchange for power?"

Marvin glanced around the room again. "No. No, you don't understand. My wife was dying. I went to Charlie to help her, and he refused. I had no choice."

"What do you want?" Bryson tucked me behind him.

"I want her to break the hold the conjurer has on me." Marvin tried to see around Bryson. "When he finds me, he'll kill me."

"Because you returned the book?" I tried to step from behind Bryson, but he held me in place.

"I'll break the bond, for a price." Bryson reached behind him and pressed his hand to my side. The message was clear: stay behind him, out of sight.

"Anything. Name it." Marvin's chair scratched across the floor, as if he was going to rise. Bryson shook his head, and Marvin stilled.

Marvin tried to crane his neck to me. The longer I was out of his view, the more agitated he became. He fidgeted, and the chair scraped against the floor again. I pressed closer to Bryson and held as still as I could.

"Tell me his true name, his spirit name," Bryson commanded.

Marvin made a strange noise, and I peeked at him. Bryson tightened his grip on me. Marvin pounded on the table and laughed. The sound that came from his mouth wasn't his voice.

"Outside—now!" Bryson edged me toward the hall. I grabbed Charlie's book and held it tightly against my chest.

"I want to see the girl." Marvin's voice sent a chill down my spine.

As soon as Bryson stepped in front of the hall, I turned and ran into Mae's bedroom. I locked the door and pulled a pistol from under my great-grandmother's pillow. I put my back against the wall and listened.

Sounds of a struggle drifted down the hall. I would put my money on Bryson winning the fight. Marvin cried out in pain in his own voice, not the strange one from moments before. The front door creaked on its hinges, followed by the screen door smacking against the side of the house. The doors slammed shut. I sank into a crouch below the window.

Time passed and everything remained quiet. I held my position and waited for Bryson. I needed to know what had happened before I dared leave the room. A flash of headlights shone through the window, and a car moved up the drive, bottoming out a few times. Tires squealed and the front door opened again.

Bryson called out, "Tessa?"

"Yeah?" I lowered the gun.

"Are you armed?" His voice sounded strange, but I couldn't tell if pain or something else was the cause.

"Yeah."

"Good girl. I'm going to take a bath and use some of those pretty little soaps of yours. You need to stay put until I tell you to come out. Understand?"

"Yes." I didn't need to understand to do as I was told.

"If I do anything unusual, shoot me." The spigot came on and water poured into the tub.

"Bryson, what is going on?" I quieted and listened. He didn't reply. A few minutes passed. I sat on the floor and removed the rubber bands from Charlie's book, said a small prayer, and flipped through the pages.

Most of the spells had to do with healings, but one drew my attention. "Sending one on its way." Cryptic, but it sounded right. Then again, it could mean sending someone anywhere, maybe death? The only reason Bryson would tell me to shoot him was if he lost control of his body. Marvin had channeled something, or someone.

If the conjurer were in Bryson . . .

I read the lines to myself until I knew the simple rhyme. I tiptoed down the hall with the spell book in one hand and the gun in the other. Rose-scented steam poured from the bathroom as I opened the door. In my panic, I nearly dropped the book. The rhyme flowed through my memory and out my mouth: "*Someone has to move, they have to go. They will go in the dark, they will hide in the day. I send someone away, back to where they were. Through paths not walked, with eyes not seeing. I send someone away. This is written. This will be.*" I repeated the spell three times.

Bryson's sigh drew my attention. He wore nothing except a grin in the milky water. "Do you have any idea what you just did?"

My fingers tensed around the gun. "No."

"You sent him away." Bryson looked at the gun, and his grin faded.

"How do I know it worked?"

He hesitated too long and I raised the gun.

"Hold up. Your spirit animal is going to be pretty pissed off if you shoot me after we danced together."

I lowered the gun. "Was he really inside you?"

Bryson shuddered and nodded. "I'm stronger than he is, so he couldn't get control. Though he sure as hell tried. The soap helped, but your spell sent him away."

I sat on the toilet lid and set the gun in the sink. "The soap?"

"It's charmed. You didn't know?" He rested a wet hand on my thigh.

"I've never felt so ignorant. I don't know anything." I wiped my eyes.

Bryson stepped from the tub and embraced me. It struck me as humorous that we were back where we'd started, before Marvin knocked on the door. Of course, Bryson hadn't been dripping wet the first time. I pulled away, but he held me tighter, and for one heart-stopping moment, I thought he might kiss me.

I froze in place. Part of me wanted him to kiss me until I forgot my pain and loss, but another part of me resisted him. Aaron and I had started something promising. But how could it go further with so many secrets between us? If I cared about Aaron, why did it feel so natural to stand here with Bryson?

He nuzzled against my cheek and buried his face in my hair. The intimacy of those few precious moments tore down a wall I'd built the night Charlie died. I struggled to hold in the parts of myself that were threatening to spill out.

"Baby, let it go," Bryson whispered.

I pulled away. "I can't."

He pressed his lips into a thin line and turned his head. I brushed my fingers across his jaw. A need welled up inside me—a need to take away his sad expression, to make him smile. "Kiss me."

Bryson shook his head. "I would love to, but not now, not like this." His eyes followed his hand as he brushed my hair from my face. "There will be no sadness when I kiss you for the first time."

Twenty-Seven

"TESSA, ARE YOU DECENT?" BRYSON Bryson knocked and turned the knob. He slipped inside, hurrying to the bathroom.

I burrowed deeper into layers of quilts, unwilling to move from my cocoon. Living with a man, even on a temporary basis, had its share of strange moments. Could he pee any louder? I had a hard time sleeping the night before; my brain refused to turn off. When I managed to fall asleep, I woke with nightmares.

"Good morning, sunshine." Bryson plopped down beside me.

"God, please tell me you're not a morning person." I peeked out from under the pillow, and he smiled. I groaned and covered my head.

"Mae called and said they're coming home. They'll be here soon. You might want to get out of bed and get some coffee in you." He pulled the pillow from my head.

"What? It's not safe."

"Mae sounded resolute." Bryson shrugged. "It sounded like you had a rough night. Want to talk about it?"

I grabbed for the pillow. "Which part? Do you mean the part where some mystic bad guy tried to possess you, or the part when you sent me to bed like a child?"

"I didn't send you to bed." Bryson chuckled.

"Whatever."

"Tessa, I—"

My cell phone rang. "Hi, Aaron."

Bryson left the room, closing the door behind him.

"Can I drop by? I need to bring you that thing we talked about," Aaron said.

"You're bringing it here?"

"I thought it best to do it there, in case you freak out again."

"Yep, I'm here. Come on over." I frowned at the phone.

Aaron was all business. No niceties. Just the facts, ma'am. I missed straightforward, uncomplicated men. I'd never emotionally invested myself in a relationship before. I never saw the need, or perhaps I'd never met someone worth the trouble. Aaron, and now Bryson, presented a danger because I reacted to them on an emotional level—but they were worth it.

Aaron knocked on the door before I finished my first cup of coffee. I'd managed to French-braid my hair and throw on a pair of cutoffs and an old Soundgarden T-shirt. Anything more would have to wait until I had caffeinated. He smiled when I opened the door. *Oh no, not another morning person.*

"Coffee?" I turned to refill my cup.

"No, thanks." He pulled an evidence bag from his briefcase and set it on the table. "Whenever you're ready."

Bryson came into the kitchen and leaned against the wall.

"Sure, I guess." I shrugged.

Aaron pulled a knife from an evidence bag and offered it to me. "Be careful. It's sharp."

"What if I leave fingerprints?"

"Don't worry about that. It's already been processed."

The moment I wrapped my hand around the handle, visions exploded behind my eyes.

A young woman stood in a crisp white kitchen, with two kids hiding behind her legs. She had one hand on each of their heads. Her eyes widened in terror as she took a step away from something. A flash of a distorted face and blond hair reflected in the blade.

The first blow took her by surprise, but she didn't scream as the butcher knife sank into the middle of her stomach. The second stab came fast, a few inches from the first. This time she screamed and stumbled forward.

"Run." Her hands went to her middle and blood coated her fingers and palms. "Lilly, run." Desperation filled her.

The children didn't understand. They were too young, so young that they clung to their mother as she was stabbed seventeen more times. They held to her arms as she lay dead on the floor. The little boy wailed the way toddlers do, mouth wide open, face wet with tears and drool. The girl hadn't shed any tears; she only whimpered and begged her mother to get up. The assailant changed the angle of the knife and hit the screaming boy between the eyes with the blunt end of the handle. He stopped crying. The intruder set the bloody knife on the countertop. The vision went white, but someone shook a trash bag.

I dropped the knife on the table and backed away. "You have the wrong guy. It wasn't the dad."

"What did you see?" Aaron set his hand over mine. "Tessa? What did you see?"

"She was stabbed in the stomach and chest, twenty times, give or take. She was wearing an orange tank top and running shorts. Her glasses broke when she fell." I went to the sink to wash my hands. I couldn't stop shaking any more than I could stop the tears from rolling down my face. "The father didn't do it."

Aaron wrapped his arms around me. "Did you see the kids?"

"Yes, they saw their mother being murdered. He hit the boy with the butt of the knife. I think he was still alive. They were both alive. I heard the rustle of a trash bag and couldn't see anything else."

"Did you see the killer?"

I curled against him. "I saw blond hair. I couldn't make out the face. It was quick."

Aaron pulled away. "Can you try again? I mean, touch the knife and see if you can get anything else?"

Bryson said, "No."

At the same time, I said, "Yes. I have to try." I placed my index finger on the flat side of the blade and closed my eyes, focusing on the feel of the metal. "Nothing."

Aaron nodded and kissed my cheek. "I have an idea, but I'll have to bring Samuels in on this."

"He's not my biggest fan, but sure. I guess." I wrapped my hands around my coffee mug, soaking in the warmth.

"You said you didn't want to explain your psychosis to anyone."

I choked on my coffee. "It's not psychosis, it's psychic abilities. I've had a rough go of it, but I haven't descended into psychotic episodes—yet."

"Yeah, right. Sorry." He ran his hand over the back of his neck. Dark circles shadowed his eyes. I wasn't the only one who hadn't had much sleep.

"If I can arrange it, would you be willing to go to the house where the murder happened?"

Bryson made a sound somewhere between a grunt and a groan. I ignored him. "Yes, but I can't promise it will work."

Aaron stood. "I need a couple of hours sleep, and then I'll see what I can work out. Can I call you later?"

"Sure." I walked him to the door. The two men shared a silent nod, and Aaron left.

I turned and gave Bryson a hard look. "I have to help."

"I know." He frowned. "Let's go get some food. I have a craving for a greasy burger. Do you know Chet's Diner?"

"Yes, I love that place, but we can't leave until Dottie and Mae get here." As soon as I said the words, I changed my mind. "Actually, let's go. I don't feel like answering a bunch of questions. I'll leave them a note."

I drove slowly up the drive and hit the gas on the hard road. Bryson held on to the handle as if in fear for his life. I ignored him and sped up.

"You need to be careful. The more involved you get with this case, the more risk you run of being outed." He gritted his teeth.

"Does my driving scare you?" I chuckled when he squinted his eyes. "I know the risks. I could lose my new job or even my license. But, I'm not sure the board has rules against psychic powers. It's common for police departments to hire psychologists to do profiling and evaluations."

"You need to lie low until we're sure Marvin's conjurer is taken care of."

"Maybe helping someone else is exactly what I need to distract myself, until I can get my life back in some sort of order."

"Or maybe you need to focus on *you* right now?"

I whipped into the fast lane and pushed the gas pedal until the force pushed me against the seat. "Did Marvin tell you the conjurer's name or how to find him?"

"No. After I broke the connection, he didn't feel much like talking."

I turned toward Bryson. "You hurt him badly enough that he couldn't talk? How are we going to end this if we don't know his name or where he is?"

"Eyes on the road." Bryson stepped on his imaginary brake. "I didn't hurt him any more than I had to. When people are spelled as deeply as Dr. Hicks, their memories are fuzzy when the connection is broken. It might come back to him, or he may never remember the details of the guy."

I slowed and merged right toward the exit. "Is this ever going to end?"

Bryson squeezed my thigh. "It will end. We just have to wait for him to make a mistake."

I removed his hand from my thigh. "So until he screws up, I'll have shifters shooting me in the yard? I'm supposed to start work on Monday."

Bryson glanced out the window. "It's not a good idea to work until this is over. Everyone around you will become a target. This guy is a skinwalker. He can change forms and take control of the humans he possesses."

"Skinwalker? Never mind, I don't want to know."

"He's a conjurer who can change into animal or human forms. He isn't a shifter. He needs spells to change, and can't stay in the form for long."

I gripped the wheel. "Well, great. We don't know what he looks like, and even if we did, he could just poof into something else?"

"I can spot a skinwalker. He got by me last night, but now that I've felt his magic, it will *not* happen again. I'll teach you to see magic."

I remembered Atsila's words: *"You will see more when you close your eyes."* I pulled in to the restaurant.

"What are you thinking?"

"Nothing, let's go."

Twenty-Eight

"Hi, I'll have a cheeseburger, fries, and a glass of tea." I smiled at the waitress and wished I'd dressed properly.

She looked at me like I'd annoyed her, and turned to Bryson. "What'll you have, handsome?"

"I'll have the same as her. Is Scarlett working today?"

"Yeah, she's in back. Want me to get her for you?"

"Please."

The waitress winked and walked away.

I leaned across the table. "Who's Scarlett?"

"An old friend. She might be able to lend some assistance."

Bryson stood when an elderly woman approached the table. He motioned for her to sit. "Scarlett, this is Tessa. Tessa, Scarlett."

"Nice to meet you." I offered my hand.

Scarlett slid into the booth and shook my hand. The moment our skin touched, I felt her power wash over me. She shook her head. "Nice to meet you, too. I heard about Charlie. Such a shame. He was a good man."

I pulled my hand away. "Have we met?"

"No, child."

"How did you—?"

"You and I, we have some things in common." She watched my

reaction.

"You read me?"

Bryson wrapped his arm around her shoulder. "Scarlett is a seer. She can read anyone she touches."

"Oh, wow. That must make life interesting." I sat back in my chair.

"I *can* read anyone, doesn't mean I do."

"You knew Charlie?"

"Everyone knew Charlie." She chuckled and turned to Bryson. "How can I help?"

"Tessa is able to read objects. I thought you might be able to give her some pointers."

Scarlett pursed her lips as she nodded. "What sort of objects?"

"The first time was a watch, the second, a knife," I said.

"Could be metal, could be another quality. Hard to say. It takes time for the gift to reveal itself."

"I saw a vision once when I touched someone's hand. It might have been the future. I don't know, just a hunch."

"Trust your gut, but don't pick the visions apart. You see what you need to see. It takes time and practice."

"I'll work on it."

She titled her head. "It will come when it comes. I saw you getting shot in the leg. Was it recently?"

My mouth fell open before I could stop it. Knowing she was a seer and experiencing it were two different things. "Yes, ma'am."

"But you're healed?"

"It was just a flesh wound. I'm feeling much better." I hadn't given much thought to my gunshot wound.

She looked at Bryson. "She's more like you than like me, no?"

Bryson smiled. "Tessa and I have a lot in common."

The bell jingled and Scarlet turned toward the door. "I need to get back to work."

"Thank you," Bryson and I spoke in unison.

"You two make a nice couple."

"Uh no, we aren't a couple." My cheeks heated.

She titled her head and looked between us. "I know a good match when I see one." She winked at Bryson. "Don't let this one get away."

Scarlett walked to the front of the restaurant. The look in Bryson's eyes made me pause. He didn't seem surprised by her words. He took my hand and smiled. "Don't let her rattle you. She likes to speak her mind."

"I like her."

"She's right. You should try to read different things, see what works."

"Miss Lamar." Detective Samuels took in the two of us.

I released Bryson's hand. "Detective Samuels, long time no see."

The detective appraised Bryson and turned his attention back to me.

"No crutches? Are you feeling better?"

"Much thanks for asking." I stood. "Excuse me, I need to use the washroom."

"No bandages?" Samuels bent to get a better look at my calf. "Son of a bitch, you don't even have a scar."

Once again, I'd screwed up. I should have wrapped my leg where the wound had been. "Mederma. Great stuff."

Samuels's expression went from unfriendly to downright hostile. He grabbed my arm. "I don't know what games you're playing, but leave Aaron out of them."

Bryson tensed beside me, and I felt his energy change. I pulled my arm away from Samuels. "I'm not playing games."

"The hell you aren't. I know he slept at your place the other night, and here you are with *him*." He hitched his thumb at Bryson. "Then he comes in saying something about a murder weapon and a mystery informant, and suggests we take you to the murder scene. Two deaths. Six, if you count the carnage beside your family's property. This is beyond coincidence."

"Let's go." Bryson stood beside me.

"But we haven't had lunch."

"No, you two stay. I've lost my appetite." Samuels turned and left.

I returned to my chair and rested my head on the table.

"Didn't you need to go to the ladies' room?" His voice softened, though he still oozed anger.

"Not really. I just wanted him to leave me alone. He didn't hurt me."

"It's not that." Bryson glanced over his shoulder.

"Then, what is it?"

"You have enough to deal with, without getting involved with this case."

The waitress brought our food. My stomach roiled. Samuels wasn't the only one who had no appetite.

"You should steer clear of the cops for a while." Bryson shoved food into his mouth.

I picked at my fries, thinking about Aaron and the case. I couldn't stay away from him, not with two kids missing. "Are you angry with me?"

He shook his head. "He had no right to put his hands on you."

"Who? Aaron didn't. I mean, we didn't have sex."

Bryson turned his head and stared until I wanted to crawl out of my skin. "I meant Samuels. He shouldn't have grabbed your arm. But thanks for the information."

"Sorry, I was trying to figure out how to explain this to Aaron."

"Explain what? His partner ran into us and jumped to the wrong conclusions?"

"That, and why people around me keep dying."

"You shouldn't try to explain. It only makes you look guilty."

"I know, but he has to be thinking the same thing as Samuels."

"This is why you shouldn't involve outsiders. How will you explain the parade of folks coming for your help once you officially become a shaman?"

"I'm not sure I want to become a medicine woman."

"That's the stupidest thing I've ever heard, and the most selfish." His mood went from bad to worse.

"I had a life before all this happened, a life I want to get back to. Why don't *you* take the position?"

"You don't think I have a life to return to?"

I frowned and bowed my head. I'd never considered that Bryson might have something else to do. I knew nothing about him, other than the fact that his spirit animal was a hawk, he was a half-breed, and he was a serious pain in the butt. "Of course you do, but you're better suited for it than I am. I don't know anything about magic."

"That's bullshit, Tessa. Stop making excuses and feeling sorry for yourself."

Is that what I'm doing, feeling sorry for myself? Don't I have the right to?

I said, "You don't know me or what I'm thinking."

Bryson leaned closer and whispered, "I know you're more concerned about what Aaron thinks than the legacy your grandfather left you. I know you would have used me last night to keep from being alone with your pain. I know you have a huge heart, and you're a spoiled brat."

I took some time to let his words sink in. Other people had called me a brat, but this time it stung. "You really think I care more about Aaron than I do about my family?"

"No. I think you have your head up your ass, and you're using him as a distraction to avoid dealing with other issues." Bryson turned and motioned to the waitress. "We need our check."

I thought of a few things I'd like to say to Bryson, none of which were nice. Mae always said, "If you didn't have anything nice to say, keep your mouth shut." but darn it I wanted to lay into him.

My phone buzzed, startling me. "Hi, Gram."

"Hi, honey, we're home. Where are you?" Was Mae angry or worried?

"Bryson and I went out for a little bit."

"The bottle tree looks really pretty. You did a good job." Her voice softened.

"Bryson and I did it. He was a big help." I looked anywhere except at Bryson.

"I know. He called to check in a few times. He told me you'd finished it. Will you two be home for dinner?"

"Um, hang on." I pulled the phone away and turned to Bryson. "Will we be home for dinner?"

He nodded.

"Yes, ma'am. But we won't be staying tonight."

"Oh?"

"I have a sleeper sofa at my apartment. We can't all four share one bathroom, Gram."

Mae laughed. "We're having chicken-fried steak, mashed potatoes, and green beans. I have a hankering for some strawberry pie."

"Sounds good. Do you need us to pick up anything at the store?"

"No, darling, but thank you."

"Love you, Gram."

"Love you, too, Tessa Marie."

I put the phone in my purse. "You didn't tell me you were calling my great-grandmother."

"You didn't ask." He led me out of the restaurant.

Bryson held his hand out. "Keys."

"What?"

"Give me the keys."

I handed him the keys and sat in the passenger's seat. He stood outside the car talking on the phone. I tried to listen but couldn't hear him. He'd notice if I cracked the window to eavesdrop. He slid into the driver's seat and started the car while I scrolled through my e-mail, doing my best to ignore him.

Bryson shrugged and put the car in gear. He seemed to know his way around, so I returned to my e-mail. I clicked through the messages without reading them, unable to stop thinking about what he'd said in the diner. My first reaction was anger, but there was some truth to his words. Maybe too much truth.

"We're staying at your place?" His words came out of nowhere, and it took me a minute to figure out what he'd asked.

"That or we'll get a hotel room. I thought you might not fit on Mae's couch, and I'm tired of people coming into my room to use the bathroom. It worked great when I was eight, but now, not so much." My attempt at humor fell flat. "I think they'll be safer if I'm not there."

"Good thinking."

"Would you mind taking me to the store? I'd like to pick up some ice cream for dessert."

"No problem. Tell me where to go."

I turned my head to hide my grin. I'd tell him where to go, all right.

Twenty-Nine

BRYSON PARKED NEXT TO AN unfamiliar car, glancing between me and the car.

"Could be anybody." I frowned at my cutoffs and baggy T-shirt. I hadn't dressed for company.

"Stay put." Bryson did the bodyguard thing, looking for monsters hiding in the yard.

"The ice cream is melting."

He ignored me.

By the time he opened my door, I wanted to tell him to just take me to my apartment. One look at his face and I decided not to test his patience.

We walked through the front door, and I stopped short, causing Bryson to bump into me. Aaron sat at the kitchen table enjoying a sandwich. I needed to tell him to stop dropping by unannounced. I had enough on my plate without worrying about him. "Aaron? What are you doing here?"

"Hey. Sorry to come by without calling, but I want to talk to you." He stood.

I shoved the ice cream into the freezer and turned. Mae, Dottie, and Bryson's constant presence crowded the room. If Aaron planned to discuss my conversation with Samuels, I wanted privacy. "Outside?"

"No." Bryson stood in front of the door. Would he stop us from leaving?

"Bryson." I'd had about all I could take of him for one day.

"She's safe with me," Aaron said.

Bryson bowed his head and moved from the door. Thankfully, he remained quiet. Mae and Dottie exchanged a look; neither seemed happy. I resolved to return to my apartment as soon as possible. I had no idea what had crawled into their tea, but the last thing I needed was another lecture.

I marched out the door with Aaron on my heels. "There's a reason people leave home when they're grown."

Aaron nodded, his face as unreadable as Bryson's. "We need to talk."

We settled onto the porch swing at Dottie's—close enough to the house to appease Bryson, and far enough away for privacy. Aaron wasted no time in getting to the point. "Why were you holding hands with Bryson in the diner?"

"I don't remember holding his hand." Samuels had tattled.

"What's the scoop with Bryson? Why is he so protective?"

I took a second to get my words in order before answering. "The elders of the tribe asked him to keep me safe. Word about the break-in and the shooting got back to them, and they were worried."

"He isn't your cousin?" Aaron leaned back.

"Not by blood. We're connected through the tribe and share a similar lineage. *Cousin* was the closest word I could think of to explain it."

"Okay." His jaw tensed.

"Samuels saw us and got the wrong idea. He told me to stay away from you."

Aaron turned toward me. "I know. He thinks you were involved with the Rivera murder. Somehow both cases are tied together. I told him you were a psychic."

My jaw dropped. "Oh God."

"He took it better than I thought he would. He says he believes in mediums, but he still doesn't trust you."

"Samuels believes in mediums?" The idea of the detective having his cards read made me grin.

"He's not as bad as he seems, Tessa. He's seen a lot. Not much surprises him anymore."

"Okeydokey. Now what?" I relaxed against the swing.

"He agreed to take you to the crime scene." He watched me, as if gauging my reaction.

"Sure. I can do that, if you're there, and Bryson. He'll flip if I go without him. He's taking the whole bodyguard thing pretty seriously."

"Bodyguard." Aaron said the word as if it were something foul.

"It's important to him."

"What's the deal with your leg? Samuels said you didn't have a scratch."

"I used a home remedy of Mae's, fixed me up." I'd planned to put a bandage where the wound had been, but didn't have time. "I heal fast, I guess."

"Not like you could fake the injury in the hospital. Hell, I saw how badly it was bleeding after you banged it on the desk." He leaned forward and looked over my calves, then shook his head. "Damn."

"It was just a flesh wound."

Aaron stared for a beat. "I'll let Samuels know you agreed to come."

"I'm sure he'll be thrilled."

"He's a good guy, once you get to know him." Aaron's shoulders relaxed as he leaned back.

"Does Samuels ever use his first name?" I wrinkled my nose. Richard was fine, but the nickname that went along with it suited him much better.

"Only his wife gets away with it." Aaron kissed the tip of my nose.

The sweet gesture reminded me of Charlie. Here, sitting on his porch swing, it hit me like a punch to the stomach. I pulled away and closed my eyes, trying desperately to keep my emotions under control.

"Tessa?" Aaron took my hand. "What's the matter?"

I swallowed the lump in my throat and shook my head. "Charlie used to kiss my nose like that."

Aaron draped his arm around me. "I wish I could tell you it will get better. Just the other day a woman walked by me at the grocery store, and she was wearing the same perfume my mother wore. I had to go splash water on my face, it hit me so hard."

"When do you want to go to the house?" As soon as I changed the subject, I wished I could console him. He deserved someone who cared that his mother's death still hurt him. Normally, I was that kind of person, but right now I needed the emotional wall between us.

Aaron pulled his arm back. "We could go now. I just need to check in with Samuels."

"Sorry I changed the subject so fast. I'm not ready to talk about it. If I start crying, I'll never be able to stop."

"I get it, but sooner or later, you're going to have to let it out."

"I know. Maybe when my life gets back to some semblance of normal." I'd spent enough years in psychology classes to know that my preferred coping mechanism was denial. Hell, I'd counseled countless clients to face their feelings. Perhaps that old saying about doctors making the worst patients was true for more than physical health.

Aaron started to speak, but stopped and looked away. He pulled his phone from his pocket and called Samuels. I walked inside Charlie's house to give Aaron some privacy. It was peaceful inside, and smelled like home.

I wandered into the office and sat behind the desk. For the first time, I could read the handwritten labels on the glass jars and old coffee cans. Herbs, plants, and a few things that made my stomach churn filled the jars. If being a medicine woman meant I'd have to collect bits and pieces from snakes and frogs, I didn't want the job.

"Tessa?" Aaron stood in the doorway with a tentative look.

"Come on in." I rested my head against the leather chair. "This is Charlie's office."

Aaron nodded and stepped inside. His eyes changed from normal to detective as he looked over the shelves. I didn't worry about explaining the jars—he couldn't read them, yet something about the way he looked around made me nervous. Maybe in detective school they taught students how to make perpetrators nervous so they would spill their secrets.

"Is he going to meet us?"

"Yeah, he's wrapping up some stuff at home. We'll meet at the house in a couple of hours."

I turned my head. I'd agreed to go, but my nerves kicked in. "All righty, then. I hope this works."

"If it does, it does." Aaron moved to my side of the desk and captured my chin between his thumb and forefinger.

I met his eyes. He smiled and brushed his lips across mine. Another of my less-than-healthy coping mechanisms kicked in: distraction. I wrapped my arms around his neck and drew him down until he deepened the kiss. One minute it was sweet and innocent, the next it was a hot mess of tongues and urgency.

Aaron gripped my sides, half lifting me from the chair. I stood, and we swapped places. I climbed into his lap, facing him. He moved his hands under my T-shirt while my hands tangled in his hair. I rolled my hips forward as he drew my lower lip between his teeth. Aaron lifted my shirt until we had to break the kiss for him to pull it off. Before the shirt hit the floor, he dipped his face to my shoulder and kissed a line from my collarbone to my breast. He met my eyes, as if asking permission. I nodded my consent.

I needed this. I needed to lose myself in him and forget. My bra came off. I closed my eyes and focused on his hands moving over my body. He cupped my bottom as he ran his tongue over my breast. I deserved to feel something other than pain. I pushed my chest forward, and he closed his lips over my nipple. I tugged on his shirt until he eased back and pulled it over his head. *Oh my God, he is gorgeous.* He wrapped his arms around me and pulled my body against his. I knew he was built, but seeing him shirtless beat my expectations.

Aaron kissed me before I had time to second-guess myself. I was batting above my average with Aaron, and I knew it. He slid his hands over my butt again, only this time he lifted me as he stood. I wanted to protest that he'd throw his back out from lifting me. Instead, I wrapped my legs around him and ignored my heart slamming against my chest.

"Aaron."

"I got you." He carried me to the bed and eased me down. "You're so beautiful. You remind me of that cartoon character. What's her name?"

"You mean Jessica Rabbit?" Why did everyone equate me to a freaking cartoon?

"Yeah, that's the one."

I turned toward him as he stretched out alongside of me. I wished he'd crawled on top of me, or had turned the bed down so I could hide under the quilt. He grinned when I reached for the button of his jeans.

"You sure?" Aaron ran his hand down my chest.

"Yeah, are you?" I felt his certainty when fumbling with his zipper.

"Absolutely, but hang on." He pulled back, hopped up, and locked the door. On the way back to bed, he slid out of his jeans.

"Wow." I couldn't turn away.

Aaron chuckled and made quick work of my cutoffs, slowing his pace as he ran his hands from my ankles to my hips. He looked me over as if trying to decide where to touch.

I blushed from my chest to my forehead. I hated feeling exposed and vulnerable. Aaron leaned in to kiss me, but I slid under the quilt.

"Never figured you for a shy one."

"Only in the bedroom." I pulled my panties off and dangled them on one finger.

"Uh-huh." He chuckled and buried his face into my neck. My breath hitched as he drew my skin between his teeth. "Careful, I mark easily."

He nodded slightly and dropped his head lower. "But you heal fast." He murmured, "You're so hot."

One word struck me: *hot*. I was hot. Not the sexy, beautiful kind of hot—temperature hot. My body kicked off an abnormal amount of heat. Talk about a mood killer.

He couldn't see my frown with his face in my breasts. "Aaron, wait. I can't do this."

I groaned and sat upright. We had to slow things down. No, I needed to run from the room into a cold shower. Would that raise too many questions or potential hurt feelings?

"What? Wow, okay." He sat up and ran a hand through his short hair.

"I'm sorry. It's just—"

"You don't need to explain. It's too soon, in the wrong place, at the wrong time." He turned his head and smiled.

I didn't feel like smiling or talking. "Thanks."

He pulled his pants on. "Tessa, it's okay."

I nodded, sending up a silent prayer of thanks that I hadn't shifted and burned the bed to ashes with Aaron in it.

Thirty

AARON AND I WALKED INTO Mae's house, hand in hand. Bryson glared, and Mae gave us a hard look. She liked Aaron, but something upset her. Did she know what we'd done? My guilt got the better of me. I dropped his hand and moved to the stove to check on the beef stew. I felt like a coward, leaving Aaron by the door, but when it came to my great-grandmother, it was every man for himself.

Mae eased beside me. "Best be careful, Tessa Marie. There are one too many roosters in the henhouse."

I turned to the two men sitting at the kitchen table. Of course, they'd heard the whisper. Mae couldn't speak quietly. Tension visibly rose between Bryson and Aaron. I chewed on my lip, trying to think of something to say to smooth things over. In the end, I decided to go with distraction.

"Hope ya'll are hungry." I immediately regretted speaking. I didn't mean to poke the skunk, but Aaron sighed and Bryson glared.

I turned and pulled dishes from the cupboard. Aaron stood and set the table. Not to be outdone, Bryson pulled the bread from the oven. He took his aggression out on the unsuspecting loaf, hacking it into chunks.

I moved to Bryson's side. "Samuels is meeting us at the victim's house in about an hour."

"Us?"

"I need you to come along. I, um, I need to talk to you." I set my hand on his forearm, and he turned toward me. Although the look he gave me made me shrink back, it didn't take a PhD to see a healthy dose of hurt beneath his anger.

"Right." Bryson scooted past me and took the soup kettle from Mae. "Let me help with that. It looks heavy."

No one spoke during dinner. I picked at my food and pretended not to notice that it tasted like ashes. Dottie and Mae shared a couple of knowing looks but kept their opinions to themselves. Sooner or later they would share those opinions with me. Not a conversation I looked forward to. The men focused their attention on the food. It seemed as though they were competing to see who could eat the most. I hadn't liked it when they were friendly with each other, but I would have welcomed their teasing.

Mae and Dottie abandoned me in favor of catching the early news. For a couple of soap-opera fans, they sure headed for the hills when drama landed in their kitchen. I filled the sink as Aaron and Bryson cleared the dishes.

"Tessa, you should try to calm down before we see Samuels." Aaron set his hand on the small of my back. "We'll clean up."

Anger rolled off Bryson like heat rising from fresh asphalt. I had to put an end to this, though I didn't know how. A shower sounded pretty darned good—a few minutes away from the testosterone to clear my mind, but I didn't want to leave them alone.

"Thanks. I'll just go change clothes." I dried my hands and went into my room. The wind picked up outside, and the bottles in the tree clinked together, adding to the melody of the wind chimes. I sat on the bed and stared at my reflection in the mirror. A set of dark eyes stared back from under the brim of a white cowboy hat.

"Bryson!" Paralyzed, I couldn't tell if it was shock or something more sinister. I couldn't move. The amulet on my neck cooled, and I remembered the words from Charlie's book: *"Someone has to move, you have to go. You will go in the dark. You will hide in the day. I send you away, back to where you were. Through paths not walked, with eyes not seeing. I send you. This is said. This will be."*

I continued chanting at the face in the mirror until a hand touched on my shoulder. My words faltered, and I began again. Bryson slid his hand from my shoulder to my neck. The second his skin touched mine, power flared between us. The conjurer's eyes widened a fraction.

A burning in my gut caused me to stumble over the words. I closed my eyes and began the spell for the third time. Bryson said the words along with me, only in his native tongue. The face in the mirror faded, and I thought it had worked. The mirror shattered, sending glass flying.

"What the hell was that?" Aaron came into the room and took a step forward. "Tessa?"

"I'm all right." The tone of my voice betrayed me. I trembled as Bryson pressed me against his chest, putting his body between me and the ruined mirror.

"She's bleeding." Bryson carefully moved the larger glass shards from my lap and turned them facedown on the bed.

Aaron asked again, "What was that?"

Mae and Dottie stood behind Aaron, both peeking around him to see me. Dottie ducked into the bathroom and returned with a first-aid kit. Mae guided Aaron from the room. Dazed, he followed her to the kitchen.

I met Bryson's eyes and motioned to the other room. His jaw tensed, and he shook his head. His eyes held an unspoken warning. I frowned and called to Aaron, "It was a ghost, and a pretty angry one."

"I saw it," Aaron called from the kitchen.

Bryson nodded his approval and took the first-aid kit from Dottie.

"Go rinse off. None of the cuts are deep enough for stitches. I'll clean up."

"Aunt Dottie? Will you sit with me in the bathroom?" I felt foolish for asking. "Could you cover the mirror?"

Dottie smiled and smoothed my hair back from my forehead. "Of course."

I stepped into the shower, with Dottie sitting on the toilet beside me. The quietness between us unsettled me for two reasons. First, I couldn't help but feel I'd disappointed my aunt. Second, I needed reassurance that the woman on the other side of the curtain was still my aunt and not possessed by a skinwalker.

"Dottie?"

"I'm here, darlin'."

"Bryson told me it is forbidden for a shifter to date a regular human. Is that true?" I lathered a rose-shaped soap.

"It is."

I peeked from behind the curtain. "Because of situations like just now?"

Dottie nodded. "I was allowed to marry Charlie because I already knew about shifters. It wasn't easy being around all that magic. Sometimes I wished I didn't know what I knew."

"It's a lot to take in, human or not."

"Yes, but you have no choice. It is part of you. He doesn't have to carry your burden. If you share it with him, he might resent you for it later."

"I know you're right, but it doesn't make it any easier to swallow." I ducked behind the curtain.

"Tessa, your life will always be filled with danger and secrets. Aaron is a police officer. He won't be easy to lie to. It's not easy being a liability to the one you love. I imagine it will be harder for a man like Aaron to accept."

I wrapped a towel around myself and pulled the curtain back. "You weren't a liability. Charlie loved you."

Dottie gave me the same patient smile she had when I was young. She wouldn't tell me how to live my life directly. Unlike Mae, Dottie offered softer advice. She gave just enough nuggets of wisdom to make me think, and to allow me to sort it out on my own. In times like these, I wanted a more direct approach.

Bryson knocked and called my name. "Tessa, I need to talk to you."

"Come in."

Bryson nodded to Dottie before turning to me. "We need to work a spell of forgetting on Aaron. He's pretty shaken up and asking too many questions."

"We can do that? Make him forget?" I squeezed my hair in the towel.

"Yup, an hour or two at the most. Any more than that and it gets more complicated."

An hour or two meant I could erase more than just his memories of the mirror. Was that what Bryson suggested? Could I make Aaron forget about the almost sex? Should I? "I don't want to mess with his mind."

"You may not want to, but that is exactly what you're doing."

I pressed my lips into a thin line, more frustrated than angry. Once again, I didn't know what to do.

"The spell book is on your bed, open to the page." Bryson turned to leave, as if we'd settled the matter.

"Wait. Is it permanent? We do this and he wakes up in my room with no idea how he got there?" I shook my head. "That seems wrong on so many levels."

Bryson narrowed his eyes and lowered his voice to a growl. "What is wrong is involving an outsider in this battle. You have made him a target."

"How will taking his memory make him less of a target?"

Dottie cleared her throat. "Bryson is right, Tessa. Take away everything after you stepped into the bedroom."

"Not earlier?" I spoke before I thought the better of it.

Bryson gave me an unfriendly look. "If there's something you regret doing, by all means."

"I'll give ya'll some privacy." Dottie slipped out of the bathroom.

I tightened the towel around my chest and stepped out of the tub. I had to turn sideways to get past Bryson, but still I brushed against him. He hung his head and muttered something under his breath.

I ignored him and threw some clothes on. I pulled my suitcase from under the bed and threw my clothes inside. Once packed, I peeked at myself in a shard of mirrored glass. I had a small cut above my brow. Half an inch lower and I would have needed a trip to the emergency room—I was lucky.

"I'm not okay with messing with his memories. I know it's a risk, but I'm not going to do it."

Bryson frowned. "It's your call."

"Let me talk to him. If he freaks out, then we'll do the spell."

Bryson opened the door and Aaron stepped inside the room. He looked at the ruins of the mirror and tensed. I reached for his hand. "Aaron, it was just a ghost. It happens to me sometimes."

Aaron asked, "Will that happen at the victim's house?"

"I don't know."

Aaron nodded and looked between me and Bryson. "Were you two speaking Cherokee?"

Were we? I didn't know I spoke Cherokee. I quirked a brow at Bryson, and he nodded. "It happens when we're stressed out. Are you feeling better, Aaron?"

"Yeah, sorry about that. It's not every day you see a ghost."

Bryson moved to my side and touched my arm, and power flared between us. "We should go."

Thirty-One

THE DRIVE OVER WAS BY far the most uncomfortable fifteen minutes of my life. Aaron followed in his own car, leaving Bryson and me alone.

"You should have done the forgetting spell," Bryson said.

"He's fine."

"We'll see. If you get excited and shift—"

"I have it under control." I didn't believe for a second I had it under control, but I didn't want to talk about it.

"Deep breathing helps. If you feel yourself slipping, take my hand. I can help."

"I said I have it under control."

"I felt your energy change when you and Aaron were at Dottie's."

I turned to face him. "What do you mean you *felt* my energy change?"

"You almost lost it." He pulled into the driveway behind Aaron.

"But I didn't. I reined it in before I lost control."

"Try to keep your clothes on around Aaron until you get used to your new powers." Bryson opened the door.

Samuels stepped out of an unmarked police cruiser when Bryson got out of the car. Aaron grasped Samuels's shoulder and smiled. Aaron and Samuels had an easy friendship, like mine and Hailey's. I climbed from the car beside Bryson, and the mood changed. Samuels hooked his thumbs around his front pockets and rocked back on his heels. I expected Bryson to glare. Instead, he grinned. Samuels must have taken the grin as a challenge, because he took a step toward Bryson. Aaron turned and strode to the front door, breaking the tension, but not before Samuels gave me a dirty look.

I whispered to Bryson, "Stop it."

"I didn't do anything." Bryson chuckled under his breath. Evidently, he'd won the standoff. I'd never understand men. All the psychology classes in the world couldn't explain their behavior.

The entire exchange irritated me. I marched into the house and stopped inside the foyer. To my left was a family room, and to my right was the kitchen. I turned to leave, when Bryson whispered into my ear, "Breathe and focus."

I nodded and caught Aaron and Samuels staring at us. "Am I allowed to touch things?"

Samuels made a sweeping motion. "Have at it."

Aaron added, "The scene has been processed. Touch whatever you want."

Samuels coughed and pulled Aaron into the hall. The two whispered back and forth, their voices too low to make out what they were saying. I guessed I was the topic of conversation.

I took a centering breath and stepped into the kitchen. When nothing happened, I tried to relax. Unsure of how to go about this, I ran my fingertips over the granite countertops and caught bits and pieces of images of the technicians dusting for prints.

I touched the refrigerator door—nothing. From the vision, I knew the killer had opened the cabinet under the sink. I caught a flash of black leather when I touched the knob.

I called to the detectives, "Did he wear gloves?" Their conversation had grown louder, but I'd tuned them out. "Aaron, did you find prints here?"

"No. Not in the kitchen."

I wrapped my hand around the knob and opened the cabinet door. I saw the killer reach for a garbage bag. I set a box of black heavy-duty trash bags on the counter. The earlier vision had fizzled out after the killer pulled out a trash bag. I turned and touched the hot-water spigot. The reflection in the faucet shifted, and I saw blond hair. With my eyes closed, a distorted face came into my mind. When I reached for the soap, I knew he'd touched it, but I couldn't read anything more.

"This is frustrating," I whispered to Bryson as my fingers trailed over the stainless-steel sink. "I keep catching blurry images. Like here, in the sink. I see hair color but can't make out the features."

I remembered the mirror in my bedroom, and the nearly perfect reflection in the knife. On a whim, I placed my hand flat against the window above the sink. Images flashed through my mind at a dizzying speed. I grabbed the countertop to keep from losing my balance. "Whoa."

"Are you all right?" Bryson put his hand on the small of my back.

"I think it has to do with reflective surfaces." I rose to my tiptoes and touched the pots and pans hanging from a rack above the stove. The moment I touched them, I saw the murder scene from a higher angle. Still blurry, but it was there. I ran to the kitchen door and placed both hands on the small window. I closed my eyes and watched the young mother die. Everything in me screamed to remove my hands from the window, but I held on until the murderer left the kitchen. Something wasn't right. The little girl was still there, beside her mother.

"Oh my God!" I staggered back and pressed my back against the refrigerator.

Samuels and Aaron came into the kitchen. While Aaron looked hopeful, Samuels was still hostile. At least I had their attention.

"He wore black-leather gloves. He killed her there." I pointed to the floor. "He hit the boy, because he was screaming. Took a garbage bag out of the cabinet, there." I pointed to the open cabinet under the sink. "He took his gloves off and washed his hands."

I paused to collect my thoughts.

"Is that all you got?" Samuels sounded irritated.

"No. He took his shoes off, stuck them in the bag, and went down the hall." I followed the path the murderer had taken. "What did he do in here?"

I pressed my hand to the hallway mirror. It gave me a good profile shot, and I knew I could pick the killer out of a crowd. I found nothing in the guest bedroom or hall bath. In the pink bedroom I caught more images. "He took clothes from this dresser."

The nursery didn't have any reflective surfaces, other than the window. I pressed my hand to the window and caught glimpses of the murderer taking clothes from the drawers. "Here, too. He took clothes and a blanket."

I walked into the hall and hesitated. Where did he go next? I turned right and went into the master bedroom. I touched the mirror above the dresser. "Did you guys take a computer from the desk?"

Samuels shook his head. "There was no computer."

I frowned and closed my eyes. "He did something on the computer. I can't see if he took it, but someone did."

The men followed me to the master bath and crowded the doorway. "He, uh, I think he stole a pair of shoes. I can't see what he's carrying from this angle. Was anything missing?"

I turned to see three stunned faces. Aaron's jaw hung open, Samuels stared dumbfounded, and even Bryson was wide-eyed.

"I bet it was shoes," I said.

I knew I shouldn't enjoy their discomfort, but for the first time since Charlie had died, I felt useful. Maybe being different wasn't so bad—maybe. I pushed past them and walked downstairs. "He wrapped the boy in a blanket and left through this door carrying a trash bag and the boy. The little girl followed him out. She knew him."

I put my hands on my hips and smiled. Sure, I gloated, but I'd earned it. My cockiness didn't last long. I caught movement from the corner of my eye and turned. I stood face-to-face with Mrs. Rivera's spirit. Stunned, I didn't notice the anger in the spirit's expression until she landed a punch in the center of my face.

Before that moment, I didn't believe a ghost could break someone's nose. The sickening crunch and fountain of blood changed my mind. "I'm so sorry. Please, I'm trying to help."

I leaned forward to keep the blood from running down the back of my throat. "Tell us his name so we can find your kids."

Samuels drew his gun and moved from one window to the next in search of something tangible that could have caused the injury. Bryson on one side, Aaron on the other, the two men shielded me from the invisible attacker. I craned my neck to see the spirit, but she was gone.

Aaron eased me to the floor while Bryson searched the drawers for a dishrag. It was probably against the rules, stealing dishrags from a victim's house. Then again, a so-called psychic getting punched in the nose by the victim's ghost wasn't likely to be listed in the police policies-and-procedures manual.

"I blew it. I could've gotten a name." My voice sounded ridiculous. My nose throbbed, but my injured pride hurt much more.

"You made contact. She may reach out to you again." Bryson held the towels in place until I winced and held them myself.

"Are you all right?" Aaron shook his head. "That was crazy."

"No shit. Even the ghosts don't like your girlfriend." Samuels burst out laughing. I bristled until Aaron and Bryson laughed. Being the butt of a joke wasn't the worst thing that could happen, not when it took the haunted look from Aaron's eyes.

Thirty-Two

I WOKE IN MY OWN BED. For a few precious moments, I forgot the wreck my life had become since Charlie died. His absence had left a hole inside me that I couldn't face. I nuzzled into my pillow and winced. My face hurt like hell.

I walked into the hall and paused. Bryson slept on the foldout couch, snoring. Thankfully, I didn't have to deal with him before I had coffee. I splashed water on my face and patted my nose. My reflection made me gasp—with a broken nose and two black eyes, I resembled one of the walking dead.

"You should shift and heal your face." Bryson's voice startled me. For such a big guy, his stealth unnerved me.

"I don't want to shift."

"Why?"

"I just don't."

"Shift for a few minutes, then change back." He shrugged.

He used my toothpaste but had brought his own toothbrush. The intimacy of sharing personal things made me cranky. "I don't want to burn my apartment down."

He spit, rinsed, and spit again. "So don't light up."

"Right. Why didn't I think of that?"

"Tessa, stop being pigheaded and shift."

"I'm afraid to, okay? I'm not in control of myself when I shift."

"The more you practice, the more control you'll have."

I made a face and walked out. He stayed in the bathroom, doing God knows what. I wanted to smack him upside his head.

I went back to my room and locked the door, checking it twice before I stripped out of my pajamas. I tried to find the tiny ball of fire in my gut, but the more I tried to shift, the more it frustrated me. It was like trying to pick a piece of fruit from a tree just out of reach. No matter how far I stretched, I couldn't get a grip on it.

"This is ridiculous," I said out loud. "He's supposed to be teaching me how to do this crap." I threw on my bathrobe and marched into the living room. "I can't do it."

Bryson emptied the contents of my coffeepot into his mug. "Do what?"

"Did you just take all the coffee?"

"Yeah, it's only two cups. I'll make more."

"Forget it." I turned and stormed back into my room, slamming the door hard enough that something fell off a shelf in the living room. It occurred to me that my passive-aggressiveness was out of control, but who wouldn't be, given my situation? My life was upside down. I had powers I didn't understand, and I was in so much danger that I had a bodyguard.

I gave in to my frustration and crawled back into bed, pulling the comforter over my head and curling into a ball. Hailey and Scott expected me for our usual after-church brunch date. I thought, *I should start reviewing case files for my new job. I need to follow up with Aaron about the investigation. I can't stand the thought of that innocent father spending another night in jail. I should pick up Mae's medications and check in with the ladies.* My to-do list had no end, but none of that mattered. I closed my eyes and let the weight of Charlie's death crush me.

My cell phone vibrated on the nightstand. The voice inside my head told me to check to see who was calling. I ignored it. A few minutes later it buzzed again. I reached for it and frowned at Aaron's number on the screen. "Nope, not ready for that."

I sent Hailey a quick text, excusing myself from brunch, and turned the phone off. "I can't do this without you," I whispered into my pillow. No one answered. Had I expected Charlie to answer? Why couldn't I see him, if I could see other spirits? "I'm so angry with you. How could you lie to me and leave us in so much danger?"

I wanted to scream and break something, to throw a fit like a toddler. More than anything, I wanted to cry—only the tears wouldn't come, even though my throat felt like it had swollen shut, and my eyes burned. I closed my eyes and hugged my knees. Even with all my newfound powers, I was defenseless.

I woke to knocking on my bedroom door. "Please, leave me alone."

"Someone is here to see you," Bryson said.

"Tell whoever it is that I'm not well." I pulled the covers tighter around me.

It sounded like a minor scuffle on the other side of the door. The doorknob jiggled and metal scraped metal. Was that pretentious son of a bitch picking my lock? My anger flared, only to be lost to despair. I couldn't bring myself to care.

The door opened. "Tessa? Honey, are you all right?" Hailey lifted the comforter from my head.

"How did you get in?"

"Resourcefulness." She held up a screwdriver. "Don't change the subject. What's going on?"

"I'm fine. I'm exhausted. Need to sleep." I hugged my pillow tighter.

"Holy smokes, what happened to your face?" Hailey crawled in beside me and pulled the covers over our heads.

"I got punched by a ticked-off ghost."

She pulled the pillow away from my face and smiled. "What's going on?"

"I think I hit stage four of the grieving process. Skipped over the first two, dabbled in the anger stage, and landed squarely in depression." I wiped my nose, and my eyes watered from the quick jolt of pain.

"Oh, honey." Hailey scooted closer and carefully drew me into an embrace. "I got your message and tried to call you back. I got worried. You never turn your phone off."

"I'm sorry."

"Do you want to talk?"

"Nothing much to say. Life sucks."

"I know, but it will get easier. Give yourself a break. You've been through a lot in the last few days."

"I feel alone. I keep screwing up, and I need Charlie. He would know what to do." My voice cracked, and my chest hurt so much that I had a difficult time catching my breath.

"It may seem that way, but you have Mae and Dottie and me. Plus, that hunky guy out there is worried about you." Hailey went from counselor to nosy-friend mode in the blink of an eye.

I frowned. "He is an ass."

Hailey grinned. "A step up—from a douche to an ass. Why do you think you're screwing up?"

I debated how much of the disaster I could safely share with Hailey. "I almost slept with the detective."

"Not the guy in your living room?"

I shook my head. "No, not him. Bryson turned me down. The thing is, I didn't care about the sex. I just wanted to forget everything else. It was awful."

"The almost sex was awful, or you felt awful?"

"Both, I guess."

"You used the detective to help you deal with your loss. There are better ways to cope, but I don't think that's screwing up. You're being too hard on yourself."

"You don't understand. He's a good guy, too good, but he's a cop and was asking questions I didn't want to answer, so we ended up half-naked in bed. Then it seemed like Dottie and Mae knew, but they didn't. I was paranoid, I guess, because we almost did it in Charlie's office. Then Bryson was so angry. He gets on my nerves, but he doesn't deserve the way I've been treating him. He's trying to help, and I hate it. I think I might care about him, maybe?"

I needed to blow my nose but knew how much it would hurt. "Aaron's partner is a jerk, and he hates me. He's undermining my relationship with Aaron, which is a good thing. It would never work with us, but I care about him, too. Now I don't know what the hell to do, because Bryson and Aaron are at each other's throats, and it's my fault, because Samuels saw me and Bryson holding hands at the diner."

Hailey did her best to keep her expression neutral and pretend to understand. I knew I'd overwhelmed her with too much information, too quickly.

"Was it a date?" Hailey asked.

"No, it wasn't a date." I sighed. "My 'intuition' is off the charts lately. Bryson took me to lunch to introduce me to another 'seer.' That mom who was killed? I saw her and the kids in a vision. I'm helping the police find the killer. Helping Aaron, he's—"

"Whoa, hon." Hailey held her hand up and tried to sort through the layers of verbal vomit. "Okay. Let me see if I got it all. You have feelings for two guys, and they're aware of each other. You believe you had a vision of the murdered woman and are working with the police. Like a psychic?"

"Yes."

Hailey laughed. "You've always wanted to be a criminal

psychologist."

"Yeah, but this is different."

"You know how I feel about the metaphysical mumbo jumbo, but it could lead to something else. Which is a good thing, right?"

"I guess."

"As for these guys, you need to take time to grieve before you make any promises to anyone. If they care for you, they'll understand that you need friends right now, not fuck buddies."

"Hailey!" I giggled, despite my foul mood. Hailey laughed along with me, and the world didn't seem like such a scary place.

"Ready to get up?" Hailey grabbed the corner of the comforter.

I nodded, and Hailey threw the covers back.

Thirty-Three

"THANK YOU." I SAT UP and took in my surroundings. It was after six. I'd slept most of the day.

"I'll mail you my bill." Hailey stood and waited for me to follow her into the living room. Bryson and Hailey's husband, Scott, sat on the couch, watching a high-speed-chase movie.

Hailey grinned at them. "Ready, Scott?"

"Yeah." He winced when he noticed my face, then stood and gave me a tight hug. "Call if you need anything."

"Thanks for letting me borrow your wife."

"No problem. I'm sure you'll have plenty of opportunities to talk her off the ledge before the baby's born." Scott hugged me again and turned to Bryson. "Nice meeting you, man."

Hailey took Scott's hand. I wanted to crawl back in bed. I felt out of place in my own living room. Scott and Bryson acted like they were old friends. Hailey and her hubby were always sweet together. The small gesture of holding hands reminded me how much I wanted a real relationship.

"Tessa, take another week. Dad will understand. Plus, we can't have you seeing clients when you look like you lost the featherweight championship." Hailey hugged me one more time, and the happy couple left.

I stared at the front door. My bedroom called to me. Whatever ground I'd gained with Hailey quickly retreated now that I was alone with Bryson.

Bryson asked, "Did you mean what you said?"

"When?"

"We could hear most of the conversation. That's why we turned on the television."

"You eavesdropped on a private conversation?"

Bryson's shoulders slumped. "Forget it."

"Yes, I meant it." I lowered my head. Bryson stared with a skeptical expression. The silence between us stretched out until I couldn't take another second. As a counselor, I prided myself on my ability to wait out a patient. I was comfortable with silence, unless of course it was *my* personal life under discussion. "I need time. I had a life before this happened to me, and I want it back. At least some of it, anyway."

"You made that perfectly clear." He sounded tired.

"That's not what I meant." I walked to the couch and plopped down, drawing my feet under my body. "As much as you drive me crazy, I feel comfortable with you."

He sat on the other side of the couch, facing me.

"I'm not used to leaning on people, especially not someone I've only just met. I know I need to lean on you, though, and it's making me nuts." I hoped he understood what I was trying to say.

"I can see that." He held his emotions so close to the vest, I couldn't read him.

"I'll stop being such a jerk. You don't deserve it." I chewed the skin on the edge of my fingernail and frowned. A nervous habit I thought I'd kicked a few years ago—wrong again.

"I'd appreciate that." He leaned forward and took my hand. I blushed. Did he take my hand to keep me from chewing my cuticle, or because he wanted to hold it?

Bryson stood and drew me to my feet. "Take off the robe."

"What? No. I don't think we should fool around, Bryson."

"I wasn't propositioning you." He shook his head. "You need to shift."

"Oh." The heat in my gut, the small coil of my power, flared to life. I closed my eyes and focused. The room grew brighter, and my vision changed from human to something more precise. I stepped from the robe and opened my wings.

I stretched my neck and rolled my head. Bryson's smile lit up his eyes. In that moment, I felt strong and beautiful. The instinct to fly rose up, but closed windows and a ceiling fan presented new dangers.

"Stay focused. Shift back," Bryson urged.

I struggled to push aside the needs of my spirit animal. I dipped my head and closed my eyes. When I opened them again, I was human. The horror movies had it all wrong. My bones didn't morph, and I didn't produce supernatural goo when I changed forms. It felt like putting on, or taking off, a well-worn coat.

"Your face is fixed." Bryson didn't drop his eyes to my bare chest. He maintained eye contact, unaffected by my nudity.

"My headache is gone." I bent down and picked up my robe. Smoke rose from the sleeves and hem. "And this is ruined."

Thirty-Four

BRYSON LOOKED OVER THE MENU as if studying for a final exam. He flipped back and forth between three pages in complete concentration. He'd taken nearly five minutes to decide on a beer, partly because the drink menu was twice as long as the dinner menu. The Willow Tree Café had the best German food for miles, and a fun, laid-back atmosphere.

"Can I make a suggestion?" I grinned and pointed at a sampler platter. "The menu says it's for two, but it's enough food for four people."

Bryson read over the description and flipped the page one last time. "That works, as long as we can get an order of sauerbraten to go."

I sat back in my chair. "Sure. We'll be eating leftovers for a week, but I'm game."

"Pssht. I'm starving. I could eat it all right now." He took a gulp from his mug. "I love German food. It was one of the perks of being stationed in Germany."

"You were in the military?"

"Twenty years in the army, four stationed in Heidelberg." He smiled at the waitress as she set a breadbasket on the table. I chuckled when he placed the order in German. The waitress seemed surprised but fell into a conversation. The only word I caught was *Heidelberg*, which he'd just told me was a place.

"What do you do now?" I sipped my gummi-bear martini.

"This and that. I haven't had a day job in years." He finished his beer and motioned for the waitress to bring another. "What made you go into psychology?"

I missed his question, surprised by his casual attitude toward being unemployed. No wonder he hadn't complained about sleeping on the couch, or in Mae's bed. Maybe he lived at the tribal house.

"Tessa?"

"Hmm?"

"Why did you choose psychology?" Bryson nodded to the barmaid as she set his mug on the table. The woman tried to make eye contact with Bryson, hanging around the table. Heck, she even glanced over her shoulder to see if he was watching her departure.

"I like figuring out what makes people do the things they do." I smiled. "For instance, the barmaid was trying to flirt with you. You, on the other hand, were clueless."

Bryson laughed and leaned across the table. "Not clueless. She's five three, greenish-blue eyes, has a tattoo on the side of her neck, and her earrings are in the shape of crescent moons. I didn't encourage her because I'm here with you."

My mouth fell open. "Wow. I'm embarrassed."

Bryson shook his head, his smile brightening his eyes. "No, you aren't. You blush when you're embarrassed."

"I don't know if I'm flattered or freaked out that you notice so much about me."

He grinned and leaned back in his chair. "It's part of the job."

Was I just part of the job? I sipped my martini, considering his words. The elders had ordered him to guard me. From previous conversations, I knew they'd spoken to him about the two of us collaborating to ensure the survival of our race. That couldn't be all there was to it, but I didn't know how much he cared about me as a person versus me as a Nunnehi mate.

"Excuse me, I need to visit the ladies' room."

Bryson stood when I did. "Something wrong?"

"Not at all." I smiled and walked away.

When I returned, the waitress brought the food to the table. Perfect timing, because I didn't want to discuss his job duties. Bryson surveyed the enormous platter of food. He reminded me of a kid at Christmas, trying to decide which present to open first.

"Ladies first." He motioned to my plate. I served myself a little of each of the items.

Bryson filled his plate and put a different flavor of mustard on each of the sausages. He made an art out of eating—each bite a mixture of meat, mustard, and sauerkraut.

He said, "Man, you weren't kidding. This is really good."

Something about watching a guy stuff his face made me happy. Maybe it was because I was raised in a house where dinner was an event, and nothing ever came out of a box unless it was pizza. "Save room for dessert," I told him.

"No worries there. I have a separate stomach for sweets." He winked and took another bite.

I mulled over his words. "Do birds have two stomachs?"

Bryson laughed, deep and loud. His smile softened the hard lines of his face as he wiped his mouth with his napkin. "I didn't mean it literally."

"Have you ever been married?" My curiosity got the better of me. I hadn't seen this side of Bryson, though in all fairness, I hadn't given him the chance.

"Once, but it was a while ago. She was a shifter, a fox." Bryson must have seen the question on my face, because he quickly added, "Literally. Her spirit animal was a fox."

I grinned. "Thanks for clarifying. What happened?"

"She died." His smile dimmed, and he turned his attention back to his plate. "She was coming home from work. The roads were icy. She died at the scene."

"I'm sorry." I reached for his hand. "Do you have children?"

"No kids. Just dogs. They're easier, and no one complains if you leave them in a crate while you're working."

"I love animals. I'd love to have a pet, but I'm allergic to cats, and I'm not home enough to take care of a dog."

"What do you like to do for fun?" He crossed his fork and knife over his empty plate and sat back in his chair.

"I love the beach, camping, hiking, movies, and concerts. Anything, I guess. How about you?"

He titled his head. "With your skin, I imagine you burn easily."

"Burn, freckle, peel. But I lather on the sunscreen and suck it up." I debated opening the button on my jeans to make more room.

"I like to be outdoors, but I have been known to attend the ballet and theater now and then."

"I was in theater all through school, at least when I was with Mae. I wanted to go to Florida State and major in fine arts, but I bombed the audition."

"There's this great community theater about an hour from here. I'll get us tickets, if you want to go next weekend."

"That sounds like fun." We smiled at each other across the table.

The polka band started, and our conversation slowed. Music filled the restaurant, and several patrons danced. Bryson scooted his chair close to mine and leaned close. "I'd ask you to dance, but I'm no good at the polka."

"I can do the chicken dance, but that's about it." I watched the band, distracted by how close he sat. I hadn't noticed how good he smelled. I hadn't noticed a lot of things about Bryson.

Two rounds of drinks and an apple strudel later, we wandered onto the street. Bryson took my hand and led me toward the parking lot, his to-go order dangling in one hand. "Want to walk a bit?"

"Sure. The lake is a block that way." I pointed north, trying to think of something to say. I had so many questions, yet nothing sounded right. I stumbled on the uneven sidewalk, and Bryson put his arm around my shoulder.

"You're a little tipsy?"

"No, I'm a little drunk." I laughed, enjoying the comfort and safety of being tucked close beside him. We walked along the lakeshore. Moonlight was dancing across the water.

Bryson stopped walking and pulled me close. I turned my face up toward his. He brushed his hand across my cheek, cupped the back of my head. "May I kiss you?"

"Yes." My stomach did a somersault and landed in my feet. Bryson slid his arm around me. The plastic bag made crinkling sounds as it brushed against my back. It distracted me, until he pressed his lips to mine. He teased my lips with his tongue, urging me to open my mouth. Bryson kissed me both gently and fiercely. He held my head firmly in place as he explored my mouth. When he pulled back, he ran his thumb over my lower lip, kissed the top of my head, and held me close.

"We should get you home," he whispered into my hair.

"Uh-huh." My head spun, but not from the alcohol. I couldn't help but wonder if he had plans for me at home. The last thing I needed was to do something we might regret. Just because he said we should go home didn't mean we would fall into bed. Did it? Did I want to?

"Tessa, relax. I can hear the gears turning in your head." He turned toward me and smiled. "Stop thinking so much, and be here. With me. Right now."

I laughed. "You and Hailey are going to get along great."

Bryson drove back to my apartment and parked. I waited for him to check the surroundings without complaint. For the first time A.C.—"after Charlie," as I began to think of it—I felt normal.

"Thanks for dinner. I didn't expect you to pay." I smiled when he took my hand.

"I don't feel right letting a woman pay. I know it's old-fashioned, but so am I." He put my key in the door and motioned for me to stay in the hall while he went inside. "All clear."

"Still, it was my suggestion, and it was expensive."

He was unemployed. Besides, I owed him a huge debt for everything he'd done for me. "I mean, I don't know if the elders are paying you for being my bodyguard, but you're unemployed. I feel bad."

"Unemployed?" He looked as if I'd lost my mind. "Why do you think I'm unemployed?"

"You said you hadn't had a day job in years. I assumed."

"I'm a sculptor. I do well for myself. Well enough that I don't have to punch a clock." He grinned. "Now you're embarrassed."

My cheeks burned. I wanted to crawl under a rock and hide. "I'm usually better at figuring people out. You have me all out of sorts."

"Don't worry about it." He plopped down on the sofa. "Want to watch a movie?"

"Sure. Just let me change first." I went into my bedroom and pulled on a pair of boxers and an old concert T-shirt.

When I returned to the living room, Bryson was laughing at the screen. "I love *The Princess Bride*," he said. I sat beside him. He pulled me close.

The next morning I woke in my bed and smiled, listening to Bryson snore from the other room.

Thirty-Five

"TESSA? IT'S AARON. WE HAVE a lead on the missing kids. Can you come to the station around ten?"

Bryson watched me out of the corner of his eye. It wouldn't have surprised me if he'd overheard Aaron. The volume of his voice made my hangover worse. I turned my back to Bryson. "Yeah, sure. Be there in an hour."

"Great. See you then."

The call disconnected, and I set the cell phone on the counter. "There's a lead in the case. Aaron needs me at the station."

"I'll come with you." Bryson flipped the eggs he was cooking and put two pieces of bread in the toaster. The only salvageable food in my fridge: eggs and bread.

"I was hoping you'd say that." I sipped my coffee. "I need to shower."

"Eat first. It'll help your hangover." Bryson dumped half the eggs onto a plate, along with toast. "Or you could shift, and cure it in a few minutes."

"That would be cheating. Hangovers are God's way of making us not drink so much next time."

"If you say so."

I ate standing at the kitchen counter. My mind raced, distracted only by the pounding in my head. Bryson finished his food and moved to the sink. When we'd first met, I'd thought he was a Neanderthal, but the more I learned about him, the more he intrigued me.

"What's on your mind?" He put his plate in the dishwasher.

"Thinking about the case." I set my plate beside his, my shoulder brushing his arm as I turned.

"As soon as we're done at the station, we need to go speak to the elders. We need to find the conjurer before he finds another puppet."

"How are we going to find him? We don't even know his name."

"You've seen his face. Besides, how many conjurers out there are powerful enough to pull off half the crap he has? I'm sure it's a short list. Once we know who he is, we can track him down and finish this." Bryson sounded sure of himself.

"Then we can get back to our normal lives." My stomach sank. I didn't know what normal looked like anymore.

"Somehow I doubt life will ever be the same, Tessa. Like it or not, we're bound together."

I held his gaze, unsure if he liked the idea of being stuck with me. Had I read him wrong? We'd had a great night, between the conversation and that kiss. Was he making the best of a bad situation? I repeated, "I need to shower."

I showered and dressed. Despite my hangover and the jumble of emotions, I wanted to get to work. I couldn't do much about my life, but I could help solve this murder case and find the missing kids.

I came out into the living room and said, "The bathroom is yours." I sat at my desk and turned on the computer. Bryson headed for the shower. Hailey was right. I shouldn't get involved with anyone until things settled. I needed to focus on finding two murderers before I worried about getting a date.

It took some digging to find Buck's e-mail address, and I rewrote the e-mail three times before I had it right. I didn't want to tell him too much, but I needed to grab his attention.

Bryson emerged, wearing only a towel. "We need to talk."

I hit "Send" on the e-mail and stood. "I sent Buck an e-mail catching him up on the situation. I requested a council meeting this afternoon."

"I wish you would have let me read it before you'd sent it."

I said, "I didn't mention anything personal. I told him about Marvin, and the conjurer being a skinwalker, and that you've stopped two attacks on my life." I went to the kitchen for more coffee. "I'm not stupid."

"Tessa." Bryson paused, likely counting to ten to calm his temper. "Buck has a secretary who reads his e-mails. Not to mention, whoever is doing this is vying for power within the tribe, which leads me to believe it's someone who already has a position."

I stared at him, my eyes burning. I wouldn't let him see me cry. I wouldn't. "I'm sorry."

"What's done is done."

"What did you want to talk about?" I turned and filled my cup.

"Last night."

I hung my head. "There's nothing to say. We had dinner, got a little drunk, and kissed. It was stupid, but it won't happen again."

He moved behind me and took my mug from my hand. "Is that how you feel?"

I turned to face him. "I don't know how I feel."

"Tessa, I enjoyed last night and hope we have many more together, but you've been through a lot. I don't want to push you."

"Maybe I want you to push me."

He slid his arms around my waist and kissed me. My hands played over his bare back as I returned the kiss. Any rational thought fled when he lifted me to the counter. He pulled back and took my face in his hands. "I should get dressed."

I cupped the back of his neck and pulled his head down to mine, brushing my lips across his. "We have time. Aaron said to meet him at ten."

"Tessa . . ." He stepped between my knees and kissed a line from my ear to my collarbone.

I draped my arms over his shoulders as his fingers pressed into my hips, pulling me forward. I wanted to pull his towel loose, to explore his muscular chest with my tongue, to wrap myself around him like a vine.

Bryson lifted his head and held me to his chest. His heart raced against my ear. "We can't do this."

I didn't know what to think. On the surface, his hesitation felt like rejection, but I knew better. He was stopping to keep me from getting hurt, or perhaps to keep himself from getting hurt. Then again, he had a job to do—he was supposed to keep me safe. Did he have an issue mixing business with pleasure? "Why?"

He smiled and brushed my hair back from my face. "Because you need time to heal your heart before you can give it to me."

"It wasn't my heart I was offering."

He bowed his head and nodded.

The hurt look in his eyes gave me pause. "Bad joke. I'm sorry."

"I haven't dated in years. I don't know the rules anymore." He took a step back and leaned against the opposite counter.

"How long has it been?"

"Since my wife."

"Oh."

"I've been busy." He folded his arms across his chest.

I never thought I would see Bryson actually pout. I grinned and hopped off the counter. "You should get dressed," I told him.

He grabbed my arm and spun me against his body. "Don't sleep with Aaron until we part ways."

I wanted to tell him I would sleep with whomever I chose, but the words wouldn't come out. He kissed me again, and I couldn't imagine kissing anyone else. "Okay."

Thirty-Six

BRYSON AND I DROVE TO the police station in silence, hand in hand. He focused on the road, but I stole a few glances in his direction. I'd never met someone who could frustrate me one minute and melt me the next.

Aaron met us in the lobby and ushered us into a small conference room. A palpable tension simmered in the room. Aaron sat and pounded on the keyboard, while Bryson hung close to me. Samuels leaned against the wall, watching us with a disapproving look. The guys seemed to suck all the oxygen from the air.

Samuels pressed his lips into a tight line. "Miss Lamar, I see your nose has healed."

"Thanks for noticing." I took a chair and waited for someone to tell me about this lead. I had enough to deal with without taking Samuels's bait. Aaron glanced between Bryson and me, then back to the laptop. After a moment, he turned the screen toward me.

"Do you know this guy?" The satisfied smile on his face told me he fully expected me to recognize the face on the computer.

I studied the face and shook my head. "No."

Aaron winked at Samuels and clicked to the next picture. I knew the face. The blond man staring back at me was the same man I'd watched stab the woman twenty-some-odd times. "That's him."

"Miss Lamar, can you be more specific?" Samuels leaned in as Aaron pulled up another photo. This one showed the killer and the murder victim arm in arm and smiling.

"Yes. That's the man I saw stabbing Mrs. Rivera in her kitchen. And that is Mrs. Rivera." I sat back to put more distance between myself and the image.

"Great." Aaron stood, grinning from ear to ear. Even Detective Samuels seemed pleased as he turned for the door.

"Who is he?" I wasn't going to let them walk out without an explanation.

"We don't know yet. Once we got her e-mail address from her mother, we were able to get a court order to access her e-mail history. Someone deleted everything from this guy, but nothing ever truly vanishes from cyberspace. We have his e-mail address now. It shouldn't take long to figure out who he is. With any luck, we'll find something incriminating enough to get a search warrant." Aaron clamped a hand on my shoulder. "Thanks, Tessa. I'll call you soon."

I stayed in the cold metal chair after the detectives left the room. I hung my head and took some deep breaths. Bryson ran his hand over my shoulders. I whispered, "Give me a minute, please."

"Babe, just let it out." He kissed the top of my head.

I made a sound somewhere between a sob and a cough, and wiped my eyes. "We need to get to Geneva and talk to Buck."

Thirty-Seven

BRYSON AND I SAT IN aa different conference room. Unlike the sterile metal table and chairs at the police station, this room contained heavy wooden furniture covered in handwoven blankets. Buck Oldham sat across from us, his hands gripping the chair.

"You should have brought Dr. Hicks here. I do not understand why you allowed him to go free. Your purpose was to keep Tessa safe, and he's obviously a threat. Even if you broke the bond, he is susceptible to being possessed again, and he is a criminal." Buck's voice boomed through the room.

"You're right. I should have brought him here. I allowed my concern for Tessa to get in the way of my better judgment." Bryson sounded so contrite that I found myself fidgeting.

"No, that's not what happened." I wanted to pull the words back in as soon as they came out. The warning Bryson gave me would have made a grizzly bear cower.

"Go on, Tessa." Buck cast Bryson a look of his own.

"Um. The conjurer appeared in my mirror. I screamed and started the banishment spell. Bryson heard me and came to help. If he hadn't come when he did, I don't know what would have happened. Dr. Hicks got away when Bryson came to help me," I stammered as I lied through my teeth. It wasn't a total lie; the conjurer had appeared in the mirror, and Bryson *had* helped me—only not when Dr. Hicks was there.

"How did he help you?" Buck leaned forward, giving me his undivided attention. When Bryson tried to speak, Buck raised his hand.

I would have given anything for a time-out. I needed to talk to Bryson alone. "I wasn't strong enough to banish him. Bryson said the chant with me, and we were able to force him to go."

"Is that all? He spoke the words with you?" Buck's voice had a curious lilt, as if he knew the answer before I spoke.

"No. He touched my skin and the mirror shattered."

Bryson sucked in air and hung his head.

Buck glanced between us and smiled. "Tla'nuwa, why do you look so defeated? You have found your flaming arrow."

"So it appears." Bryson glanced between Buck and me. "Do you know who this man is?"

"I have my suspicions but can't be certain. You will need to catch him through one he possesses. It is the only way to prove what you say is true. We will need evidence to convince the council of his crimes." Buck stood. "Once this is concluded, you will take Mae your gifts. If she accepts them, she and I will plan the bride-and-groom feasts."

Buck left the room. I couldn't wrap my brain around the conversation. He hadn't given us the information we needed: a name, an address—anything. The talk of gifts and wedding feasts—well, that was just preposterous. Even in the old days, women had the right to refuse a proposal.

"I thought we agreed I would do the talking." Bryson didn't sound happy.

"What? I was trying to get you out of trouble." I stood, determined to find Buck and set him straight.

"I wasn't in trouble, Tessa. Not until you told him we were able to combine our energies. Do you know what you just did?" Bryson advanced on me, blocking my path to the door.

I set my hands on my hips and met his gaze. "If he thinks I'm going to marry you, then he is delusional."

"Tessa, it's not that simple," Bryson said. "Do you know Cherokee lore?"

"Some, I guess." My temper faded from scorching hot to a cold ball of worry.

"Tla'nuwa were a mated pair of birds. Some believe one is the bow, the other an arrow, a flaming arrow. Together, they're deadly."

"We are half-human and half-Nunnehi. How can we also be these Tla'nuwa things?" This new reality made my head hurt. The rational part of me didn't believe in old folktales and superstitions, but after I'd changed into a flaming bird, the rational side lost the battle.

"You're missing the point. We aren't Tla'nuwa in the flesh, but we are something unique in the spirit. Since we are both part spirit creatures, that means something." Bryson took my shoulders in his hands, as if he could force understanding into me by will alone.

"I don't buy any—"

Bryson cut me short with a fierce kiss. It stunned me senseless, and by the time my brain started working again, I found myself pressed against his body.

Bryson pulled his face from mine and stared at the ceiling. I couldn't tell if his pain or exasperation caused his expression. "This will all sort itself out in time. Right now, we need to find the bastard who's trying to kill you."

I followed Bryson to the car. For once, he didn't insist on scouring the area for bad guys. Somehow it didn't make me feel better. My knees shook, and I didn't trust myself behind the wheel. I tossed Bryson the keys and sank into the passenger's seat.

"So what's the plan?" I chewed the skin on the side of my thumb until I tasted blood.

"We find Marvin and somehow reconnect the bond. Once the conjurer is back inside him, we do a binding spell to keep him there, then a tracking spell to find him." Bryson didn't take his eyes off the road. His knuckles were white on the wheel.

"Great. So where do we find Marvin?" I didn't think it would be easy to find him. Never mind doing three spells in succession. How in the hell were we supposed to hold Marvin still long enough to reconnect the bond?

"You have his cell-phone number. We can start by calling him. Then we get Aaron to run his plates and get an address."

"I doubt he's going to answer my call. How are we going to get Aaron to run his plates? He'll ask a million questions. Besides, why would Marvin go back to his house if the conjurer is searching for him? Let's say we find him. How do we hold him down long enough to do the spells? What if the conjurer has moved on and has a new body? What if he figures out what we're trying to do? This is never going to work." I chewed my thumb again.

"Finished?" Bryson chuckled.

"This isn't funny. It's a crap sandwich. Just when I think I'm done, I have to take another giant bite."

"We *will* find Marvin. Don't worry." Bryson reached over and took my thumb from my mouth. "Quit chewing your fingers. It'll be all right."

I shifted in my seat. "Where are we going now?"

"To get Charlie's journal. We'll need it when we find Marvin."

"Oh no, it's at Mae's. What if Buck has already called there? We're going to be walking into a crap-storm." I brought my index finger to my mouth.

"It will go great with your crap sandwich." Bryson laughed, and hit the gas.

Thirty-Eight

"OH NO." TWO EXTRA CARS sat in the driveway. "No, no, no."

"What's wrong?" Bryson hit the "Lock" button to keep me from climbing out of the car before it stopped.

"That's my mother's, I mean, Darlene's car, and Aaron is here." I grabbed his arm. "Let's go. I don't want to do this now."

"Tessa, we have to get the journal. It will be fine." Bryson took my hand.

"Yeah, well, you don't know Darlene." I sat back in the seat, pouting. Bryson got out of the car and scanned the far side of the railroad tracks and the yard. I sprang from the car the moment he opened the door and burst through the front door with Bryson following.

"My, my, look what the cat dragged in." Darlene smiled from the kitchen table, where she sat with Aaron and Mae. "We were just talking about you."

Bryson set his hand on my shoulder. He kept me upright and prevented me from launching myself at Darlene.

"I didn't realize you weren't staying here anymore. I stopped by to thank you for your help," Aaron said, clearing his throat.

I could only imagine what Darlene had said to him.

"Yes, Aaron was telling me how you two met." Darlene slurred his name until it sounded almost singsong.

"Maybe you should call before you stop in?" I didn't mean to sound gruff, but he should have called.

"I tried several times." Aaron stood, and Darlene grabbed his hand, tugging him back down.

"Tessa Marie, that is no way to speak to a fine, upstanding member of the law." Darlene feigned horror.

Bryson stepped forward and extended his hand. "I'm Bryson. You must be Darlene."

I moved past him into my bedroom. Before I closed the door, I caught a glimpse of Darlene. She stared at Bryson like he was the tastiest cupcake in the case.

Wasting no time, I ignored the voices in the other room and stuffed the cedar box into my pillowcase. Mae would ask too many questions if she saw me taking the box out of the house.

I went back out. "Aaron," I said, "it was nice to see you, but Bryson and I have to go. Maybe we can meet up later?" I hugged the pillow, pressing the edges of the box into my chest.

"Sure, yeah. I have to get back to work anyway." He stood again, shooting Bryson and me a quizzical look.

"I'll walk you out." I smiled and blew Mae a kiss. As I turned for the door, Mae stood.

"Tessa Marie, why are you off in such a hurry?" Her tone made me feel eight years old.

"Bryson needs to be in Geneva in forty-five minutes. He's going to be late if we don't hotfoot it out of here."

Mae pursed her lips and narrowed her eyes, knowing full well I'd lied. "All right, then, you better scoot. I expect you two for dinner at six. No arguments."

"Oh, I just love a family dinner," Darlene chimed in with her saccharin-sweet smile.

"This isn't a family dinner. I need to speak with Miss Tessa Marie."

Mae's chin rose, and she nodded, telling me I had darned well better be there at six.

Darlene grinned, making no move to leave. "I better go. I don't know what's going on here, but someone is in trouble." No doubt she planned to stay and fish for information.

"Yes, ma'am." I frowned at Bryson and stepped outside. I needed some fresh air after dealing with Darlene.

Aaron on one side, Bryson on the other, I walked to my car. "Sorry about that."

"Man, you really can't lie." Aaron chuckled. "I thought she was going to send you to the corner."

I bit back my words to keep from taking my frustration out on him. This was, after all, his fault. "I'll talk to you later."

Aaron stepped in the way before I could shut the door.

"Hey, sorry. I was only teasing." He smiled. "I have news on the case. Do you have time to hear it?"

Bryson stuck the key into the ignition but didn't turn it over. I shrugged and fastened my seat belt. "Sure."

Aaron gave me the same curious look he had inside. "You're in a hurry. I'll catch you up over drinks tonight. That is, if your bodyguard will let me have you all to myself."

I nodded, thinking this situation could not possibly be more awkward. "Sounds like a plan. Call me later."

Aaron leaned in to kiss me, but I turned my head in the nick of time. His lips landed on my cheek. The situation had become even more awkward. Bryson started the car before I could think of anything to say. Aaron narrowed his eyes at the other man. "Bye, Tessa."

"Bye, Aaron." I smiled as he closed my door and slapped the top of the car.

"Well, that sucked." I pulled the box from the pillowcase.

Bryson remained stoic, his eyes on the road. "Are you going out with him tonight?"

"No, I'll tell him I have a headache when he calls." I turned my face toward the window.

"You better learn to lie between now and then." He downshifted as he pulled onto the highway.

"Are you angry with me?"

"Nope. Contrary to popular belief, we are not engaged. Hell, we aren't even dating."

I opened the box and stared at the picture of Charlie and me. What I wouldn't give to be four again, when he was the only man in my life. "We may need Aaron to find Marvin. I don't want to burn that bridge yet."

"True." Bryson nodded in my direction. "I don't have anything against him. He's a good guy, but the longer you string him along, the harder it is going to be to walk away."

"What if I don't walk away? What if we remain friends?"

"I know you have feelings for him. Can you do that?"

"I have male friends I don't sleep with."

"I'm not talking about sex. Can you keep him at arm's length and maintain a friendship?"

Could I? I didn't know.

"You know he wants more than that from you."

"I know." I turned back to the window.

Thirty-Nine

THE ENTIRE AFTERNOON TURNED INTO an exercise in patience. Marvin Hicks had disconnected his cell phone. He hadn't returned to work, and the university hadn't heard from him. Bryson followed up on a few leads and hit a wall every time. To make matters worse, he grew quiet and withdrawn, while I wanted to scream.

"I think I should call Aaron and ask him to run the plates. Do you think he can check Marvin's credit-card activity? He couldn't have vanished off the face of the earth." I paced, while Bryson banged on the keyboard.

"Sure." He leaned closer to the screen.

I threw my hands up and marched to the bedroom. I took a moment to calm down before dialing Aaron's number.

"Hey, Tessa, I was about to call you." Aaron sounded as chipper as ever.

"I thought I would call and firm up plans," I said. How many more lies would I tell before this was over?

"I should get off work by eight. Will that give you enough time to finish dinner with Mae?" He laughed.

He'd better not be laughing at *me.* I sweetened my voice. You get more flies with honey than with vinegar, and I needed a few flies. "I hope so. If not, you might have to call for backup to get me out of there. Let's say eight at Fitzpatrick's in Winter Park. Do you know the place?"

"Irish bar, near Rollins, right?"

"Yes, sir, that's the place." I swallowed back bile. Tonight I would give him the "It's not you it's me" conversation.

"Okay, see you then."

"Aaron, I have a huge favor to ask. Do you remember Dr. Hicks?"

"Yeah, he was there when you got shot."

"He's missing. He hasn't shown up for work, and no one can reach him. Is there any way you can check up on his credit cards or license plate—whatever it is you guys do to find people?"

"Sure, but someone should file a missing-person's report."

"I know, but we haven't reached any of his family. Dottie had only one number for him, and it's disconnected. It would ease our minds if we knew he was all right. With everything going on . . ." I laid it on thick, praying it would work.

"I'm on it. Marvin Hicks from UF. Anything else?"

"That's it. Thank you, Aaron." I sighed in relief. Aaron would find him. "See you at eight."

Bryson watched me as I came out of the bedroom. He turned and wrote something on a sheet of paper. The tension between us was driving me nuts. I thought we'd drawn a truce after our recent night out, but the tension returned.

"He's going to try to find Dr. Hicks. I'm meeting him at eight. I plan to tell him I need some time to deal with my loss before I jump into a relationship." I sat on the couch as Bryson pulled his boots on.

"Is that what you want?" He met my eyes.

"It's what I need to do. Hailey was right when she told me to take my time."

"Fair enough." He picked up my keys and Charlie's book. "We

need to go or we'll be late for dinner."

"Why are you so angry with me?" I'd had enough tiptoeing around. If he wouldn't talk on his own, then I'd pick a fight to get him talking.

"I'm not upset with you." Bryson folded his arms across his chest, watching me as if I were a puzzle to solve.

"Fair enough." I stood, grabbing my purse off the table.

"I'm nervous, okay?" he said.

"About what? We *will* find Marvin." If he doubted our ability to find Marvin, we were in serious trouble.

"Yes, we will."

"Then why are you nervous?"

"Mae. She was pretty quiet today. I don't know her well, but that can't be good."

I giggled, covering my mouth in an effort to hold in my laughter. The mental image of Mae beating Bryson with a rolled-up newspaper played through my head.

Bryson closed the distance between us in two strides, drew me into his arms, and half pulled me to the door. "Laugh it up, but I'm serious."

The tension in Bryson's shoulders increased with each mile. I couldn't help but grin, as he worked himself up over Mae. I didn't look forward to her lecture, but I'd faced this sort of thing before. We'd live through it. If I were a bigger person, I would have tried to calm him down. Truth be told, I enjoyed watching him squirm.

Bryson swept the yard while I waited in the car. I offered my sweetest smile when he opened my door. "Bryson, relax. She can smell fear like skunk on a dog."

He gave me a dirty look. Walking to the front door reminded me of walking in front of a firing squad. Although, this firing squad promised to be entertaining and involved food.

"You two get over here and set the table," Mae said, elbow deep in potato salad.

I winked at Bryson and pulled down four plates. He set out the forks and knives. By the time we'd set the table, Mae had the food on platters and bowls.

"It smells good, Gram," I told her.

"Of course it does. Now put the chicken on the table, and one of you needs to explain why I was asked to plan a Bride Feast." Mae dried her hands and looked between us.

"Wait, wait. Don't tell yet. I want to hear this, too." Dottie came in with a basket full of tomatoes from the garden. Unlike Mae, Dottie seemed tickled by the newest turn of events.

I decided to let Bryson explain, since every time I opened my mouth, I put my foot in it. He shook his head and took his seat at the table—of all the times for him to be a coward.

"It's all a big misunderstanding," I said.

"Tessa Marie, I'm an old woman. I don't have all night to wait for you to tell me what happened. I *know* it's a misunderstanding." Mae sat and passed the food.

I relayed the high points of our conversation with Buck. My life had more drama than one of their soap operas.

"Bryson, would you kindly tell me how old you are?" Mae never took her eyes off me.

"Ma'am?" Bryson set the bowl of carrots on the table.

"You heard me." Mae slid her eyes in his direction.

Bryson glanced between Dottie and Mae. "A little over a hundred, this August."

My jaw hit the table. He'd told me he was in his sixties when Dottie and Charlie were married, but I hadn't done the math. Mae made a disapproving noise. Dottie reached over and took Mae's hand in hers. I sat back in my chair as my world tilted.

Dottie asked, "How do you feel about this, Bryson?"

"It isn't my decision, but I do plan to bring Mae gifts once we find the one who caused all of this trouble," he said with a steady voice.

"Tessa, do you understand what he means?" Mae stared at Bryson.

"No." I slumped in my chair, trying to make myself as small as I felt.

Bryson took my hand. "It is customary for the man to bring gifts to the woman's grandmother. Mae must accept my gifts before I can ask you to be my wife. Of course, you must also accept the proposal."

I yanked my hand away and shook my head.

"Tessa, you have a lot to deal with right now. I'll wait until you're ready," Bryson said.

The defeat in his voice stole my breath. "We barely know each other. I can't believe we're even having this conversation. I don't know when I'll be ready, or if I'll *ever* be ready."

Bryson smiled. "I'm a patient man."

Mae laughed and said, "Good. You'll need to be if you're going to marry my great-granddaughter. Now that we have that settled, eat before it gets cold."

Forty

I SAT AT THE BAR ADMIRING the brass railing and shiny bar top. After some negotiation, I convinced Bryson to let me speak to Aaron alone. Despite the risks, if I had any hope of maintaining a friendship with Aaron, I needed to speak to him without a babysitter. I used to come here for happy hour once or twice a week. It felt like it had been years since I'd sat on the worn barstools and chatted with my favorite bartender.

I rehearsed what I would say to Aaron. Preoccupied, I didn't notice Hailey sidle up next to me.

"Penny for your thoughts?" Hailey leaned over, pressing her shoulder into mine.

I turned and hugged her. "I thought your rate was a hundred and twenty an hour?"

"Friends and family discount." Hailey glanced at my drink. "What I wouldn't give for a Hot Irish right about now."

I slid the drink out of Hailey's reach. "Where's Scott?"

"Parking the car. He didn't think I should walk two blocks in the rain." Hailey frowned, though I knew she loved the attention. "Are you meeting someone?"

"That detective I told you about."

"Oh, the blue-eyed Adonis?" Hailey snickered.

"What blue-eyed Adonis?" Aaron whispered in my ear and slid his arms around my waist.

Hailey laughed as I blushed. "Speak of the devil."

I eased from Aaron's grip and took a sip of my drink. "Hailey, this is Aaron, Aaron, this is Hailey, my best friend."

"Nice to meet you, Aaron. I'm going to grab a table. Tessa, call me later." She pointed and made a telephone with her fingers, mouthing "Call me" as she walked away.

"She doesn't look pregnant." Aaron claimed the stool Hailey had vacated.

"She's not showing yet." I didn't remember telling him Hailey was pregnant. I studied Aaron's face, noting the shadows under his eyes. "Are you coming down with something?"

Aaron shrugged. "I think it's lack of sleep and too much junk food. This case has me working around the clock."

"You need to take care of yourself." I sipped my drink. "Did you find out anything about Marvin?"

"Nothing yet, but I have people looking for him. Someone should have really filled out a missing-person's report before we invaded his privacy."

"I know, but I don't know how to get in touch with his family. Thanks for helping out."

"I owed you one. You were right about the computer being missing." He motioned for the bartender and ordered a Guinness.

"Did you track down the guy in the pictures?"

"Not yet. We're waiting on a court order to crack into his e-mail, but I found his Facebook page. He used the same e-mail address we had to create his account." Aaron took a drink of his beer. He then pushed it aside, looking rather green.

"Are you okay?"

"Yeah, I'm fine. So when we read Mrs. Rivera's e-mails, we figured out she was having an affair with this guy." Aaron grinned.

"That could explain him flipping out and killing her. But why would he take the kids?" While I enjoyed listening to Aaron talk about work, I couldn't help but feel uncomfortable discussing the private life of a murder victim. Sure, I discussed people's private lives every day for work, but this felt different.

"There's some discrepancy as to who fathered the children. There's no way to know what's true from reading the e-mails, but we think we've established a motive. Now, we just have to find him." Aaron swayed on his stool.

I reached out and steadied him. "You look awful. Let me drive you home."

"After you blocked my kiss, I wasn't sure you were interested." Aaron's words slurred.

"We'll talk about that later. Right now, I think you need some sleep." I stood and offered him my arm, surprised when he actually leaned most of his weight on me. Before I caught my balance, Aaron stumbled, pulling us to the floor.

Scott ran over and helped pull the passed-out Aaron off me. "Tessa, are you okay?"

"Help him." I cradled Aaron's head in my lap.

"We need an ambulance." Scott called to the bartender, "Please call 911."

"He's drunk. Give him a minute, he'll come around." The bartender laughed.

I snapped my head toward the bar. "No, he had a sip of beer and passed out. He's a cop, just got off work. Something is wrong. Call an ambulance."

The bartender picked up the phone. I put my hand on Aaron's forehead. "He's burning up."

I swallowed my panic. I had to stay in control for Aaron's sake.

Scott handed me a damp towel, and I placed it on Aaron's brow. "Help is on the way, Aaron."

He opened his eyes and smiled for a second before he drifted off again. Time slowed to a trickle. The paramedics came through the door and scooted me out of their way. I stood between Scott and Hailey, watching as they loaded Aaron on the gurney and wheeled him out of the bar.

"Wait, I'm going with him," I called to one of the paramedics.

"Are you family?" He turned and prepped Aaron's arm for an IV.

"No."

He pulled a long needle from the sterile pack. "Sorry, miss. You'll have to meet us at the emergency room. We're taking him to Winter Park. Do you know where that is?"

I nodded, and they shut the door. Scott wrapped his arm around my shoulder. "We'll drive you."

"No, thanks, I learned my lesson the last time I accepted a ride to the hospital."

"Be careful and don't speed. It will be a while before they allow you to see him." Hailey hugged me.

I sprinted to my car, left the parking lot, and dialed Bryson.

"Bryson, it's Tessa. Something is wrong with Aaron. He collapsed. I'm following the ambulance to the hospital now."

"Come pick me up. I'll go with you," Bryson replied.

"There's no time. I need to get there."

"Tessa, they won't let you go back until they have him stabilized. Come pick me up. This is not negotiable."

"Meet me in the parking lot." I hung up and tossed my phone into the passenger seat. Bryson's calmness impressed me. I felt like I was one beat away from falling apart.

The drive to my apartment went by in a blur. Bryson waited outside when I pulled up. He climbed in, and I pulled out into traffic, narrowly missing a large SUV in the process.

"Okay, slow down and tell me exactly what happened." Bryson pulled his seat belt on and gripped the dashboard as I turned a corner.

"He looked sick when he came in. He took one sip of beer, we talked for a few minutes, and then he started to go sideways. I stood to help him, and he passed out." I blew through a red light and checked in the rearview for flashing lights. I turned toward Bryson. The look in his eyes nearly stopped my heart. "Is it dark magic?"

"I don't know, maybe." Bryson set his jaw and stared straight ahead.

Forty-One

I WOKE, SURPRISED TO FIND MYSELF nestled into the curve of Bryson's chest. The clock read six. No one had come to update us on Aaron's progress. Across the waiting room, Samuels sat with his chin resting on his chest, sleeping. I eased from Bryson's embrace. "I'm going to go downstairs and get some breakfast for the three of us. Maybe some coffee will put Samuels in a better mood."

"Don't count on it." Bryson yawned and stretched his arms out in front of his body.

A doctor stepped into the room. "For Aaron Burns?"

"Yes?" Samuels stood alert, faster than I would have thought possible.

Bryson and I joined Samuels. I didn't like the concern in the doctor's expression.

"Is there any family we should call?" the doctor asked.

I blurted out. "His parents passed away."

"He has an uncle in California. Otherwise, there's no family." Samuels glanced between the doctor and me. "She's his girlfriend, and I'm his partner. He's a police detective, my partner."

I asked, "How is he? Can we see him?"

"Normally, only family members are allowed to visit the patients in ICU, but in this case we can make an exception. Two at a time, and only for five minutes. He's in critical condition. We haven't been able to find the cause of infection. We're currently giving him heavy doses of antibiotics. Has he traveled outside of the country in the past three weeks?" The doctor glanced between the three of us.

"No," Samuels replied.

"It's a good thing he was brought in when he was. His heart stopped twice in the emergency room."

Everyone drew a collective breath. I had a sinking feeling that Aaron's illness had to do with magic. My throat constricted and tears brimmed in my eyes. "It came on so fast. He was fine midday. When we met at eight, he looked worn-out, then he collapsed."

The doctor's eyes widened a fraction. "Sepsis can come on fast, but generally not that fast. Was he complaining of any pain, fever, confusion?"

Samuels and I shook our heads.

"I would try to contact the uncle in California. His situation is touch and go for the time being." The doctor clasped his hands in front of his body. "Any questions?"

I asked, "Can we see him now?"

"Of course, follow me." The doctor turned and walked toward the hall.

Samuels sat heavily in his chair. "You two go first. I need a few minutes."

Bryson set his hand on the small of my back and guided me from the room. Samuels had his elbows on his knees and his head cradled in his hands. We hustled to catch up with the doctor, but everything changed to slow motion when the door closed behind us. The doctor guided us into a small cubicle containing Aaron, and far too many machines.

I stood, unable to move, as the beeps and whirls of the machines filled the silence. Aaron had a blue-and-white tube taped to his mouth, two IVs running into his arm, and various wires connecting leads on his chest to a nearby machine. He was nude, except for a small patch of sheet across his midsection. His chest rose and fell in time with the whooshing sound.

"He's not breathing on his own," I whispered as I moved to his side and placed my hand over his. "I don't understand. What happened to him?"

Bryson held his hands a few inches over Aaron and moved them in small, slow circles. His eyes closed as he whispered something under his breath. After a moment, he pulled his hands back with a hiss.

My heart shattered into splintered pieces. I had caused this. My knees buckled as the room spun too quickly for me to catch my breath. Bryson wrapped his arms around me before I collapsed. Weeping into his chest and unable to form any intelligible thought, I gave myself over to guilt.

"We'll figure this out." Bryson stroked my back until I pulled myself together. "Leave me with him for a few minutes."

"What are you going to do?"

"Try to block the flow of magic."

"Wouldn't it be stronger if we did it together?" I grabbed Bryson's hands, desperate to do something useful. This was my fault, my mess to clean up.

"Perhaps, but you're too distraught. Let me try for now."

"No. I can do this. I can help."

He drew me to his chest and slid his hand under my hair so that his palm rested on the back of my neck. I couldn't see what he was doing, only the change in his position and the straining of muscles. I closed my eyes and focused on sending my energy through Bryson. Each syllable he spoke was sharp, yet slurred into the next until it sounded more like a whispered song.

The beeping from the machines increased in tempo, mirroring the tempo of Bryson's words. My ears burned. I expected to hear one long, steady beat—a flatline. The cadence increased until I couldn't stand it. The sound stopped with a blip and returned to a normal rhythm. Bryson pulled his hand back and kissed the top of my head.

"You were right. We are stronger together." He released me, only to take my hand and guide me from the cubicle.

We exited ICU and stood in the hall. "Will he be all right?" I asked.

"I don't know."

Samuels met us, intelligent cop eyes scanning the situation. He must not have liked what he saw because the color drained from his face. I reached my hand toward him. "Would you like me to go in with you?"

Samuels nodded.

Bryson took a step to the side. "I'll go downstairs and get us some breakfast."

Samuels squeezed my hand before releasing it. He squared his shoulders and followed as I pushed the door open and led him to Aaron. Samuels lagged behind a few feet, as if unsure he wanted to see what lay behind the curtain. When he finally saw Aaron, his reaction gutted me.

Samuels took Aaron's hand and cried against it, bargaining with God, and anyone else who'd listen, for his partner's life. I stepped from the space to give him some privacy, but he took my hand before I could retreat.

"Every officer knows ending up here is a possibility every morning when we go to work. This . . . this . . . isn't right. I could handle a bullet." He pleaded with his eyes for me to say something that would make sense of the situation.

"I'm sorry." My guilt raged through me. Watching Samuels with Aaron reminded me of my own loss and the desperation that grief brings. Wouldn't I have bargained with the devil to bring Charlie back?

Samuels stood, but kept a hold of Aaron's hand. "He's like a kid brother to me, or a son, even."

I started to speak but clamped my mouth closed. I needed to say something to help this man—all of this was my fault. "I know what's wrong with him."

Samuels turned his head and narrowed his eyes. "What?"

Why did I open my big mouth? He'd never believe me. Would it be too far of a stretch for him to believe in bad people with bad magic? "Can we talk somewhere private?"

The detective nodded and escorted me back to the waiting room. His movements held such authority that I didn't second-guess my decision to spill my guts, at least not yet. The shift from grieving friend to detective happened so fast, but how could I blame him? I understood his desperate need to understand, to do something to correct the situation.

"This is going to sound crazy. Promise to hear me out." I sat in the corner of the waiting room, and Samuels took a seat across from me. "Off the record?"

"Off the record." He leaned forward, his elbows on his knees.

"Aaron's illness is being caused by a conjurer."

Samuels shook his head and stood. "I've seen a lot of strange shit since you've been around, but this is too much."

"Listen to me, please."

He motioned for me to continue, and I explained my relationship with Dr. Hicks.

Samuels folded his arms. "Dr. Hicks? The same Dr. Hicks that Aaron is looking for?"

"Yes. Dr. Hicks is missing, and I need to find him."

Samuels pinched the bridge of his nose, hard. "So let me get this straight. You've been fighting some evil spirit, and now it's in Aaron?"

"Yes and no. It isn't an evil spirit. It's a man. A powerful man who uses dark magic to do bad things."

"The guys you shot?" Samuels looked at me like I was certifiable.

"He was a wolf when I shot him, but turned into a man."

He folded his arms and nodded. "Go on."

"I know it sounds crazy, but think about it. I was shot in the leg. There are police reports and hospital records, but I don't have as much as a scratch on me. You saw my nose broken after that spirit hit me, and now it's healed. Your men reported wolf tracks outside my aunt's house, tracks too big to be a normal wolf. Hell, I was shot in the chest. Do you believe a cast-iron skillet could stop the bullet?" Two people sat on the other side of the room. I hoped no one was listening to this conversation.

"Tessa, stop. I believe you. How do you propose we get this guy to stop hurting Aaron?"

"We have to find Dr. Hicks and try to reconnect the bond between him and the conjurer, then Bryson and I can track him down."

"Oh, yes, Bryson. How does he fit into all of this?" The skeptical look returned to his eyes. "He's not your cousin."

"No, he isn't. He's my bodyguard until this mess is sorted out. He can't know I told you this. It would only put all of us in more danger." I hadn't considered Bryson, or what he would do if he knew I'd included Samuels in tribal business. This was a bad idea, very bad. "Bryson has magic, too. He can help keep Aaron alive while we find Dr. Hicks and the conjurer."

"We?"

"I can't do it alone, and Bryson needs to stay close to Aaron. Besides, how am I going to find Dr. Hicks without police help?" It made perfect sense. I didn't like the idea of partnering with Samuels, but what choice did I have?

"I must be losing my damned mind. Yeah, okay. I'm in." Samuels sat back in his chair, staring at me as if I were a specimen under glass in a laboratory.

Forty-Two

When not visiting Aaron, I paced a path in the waiting room. The clock read six, almost supper time, and I hadn't heard anything from Samuels since he'd left that morning.

I second- and third-guessed myself, but I knew I'd done the right thing. But I wished I could convince my heart to stop pounding. Everything would work out—it had to.

"Are you hungry?" Bryson slumped in his chair. Lack of sleep and the energy expenditures of magic—which we did each time we were permitted to visit with Aaron—were taking their toll on him.

"A little. We can go downstairs for food after we see Aaron. It's almost time." I fidgeted with my phone—still no calls.

"I can't believe you talked Samuels into helping us find Marvin." Bryson folded his arms, watching me closely.

"Like I said, Aaron told him he was missing before he got sick. Maybe this is his way of helping Aaron." The more I lied, the easier it got. Bryson would lock me in my house if he knew what I was up to. "Why don't you go in and check on Aaron? I'll call Samuels to see if he's had any luck."

Bryson narrowed his eyes as he stood. "I'll be back in five minutes."

"Thanks, Bryson."

He kissed my forehead and headed out of the waiting room. My guilt took the form of a miniature Southern Baptist preacher in the back of my mind, ranting about liars burning in the pits of hell. I started to follow Bryson, to come clean about my deception, but my phone rang.

"Hello?"

"Tessa, this is Samuels. How's Aaron?" Samuels sounded as tired as I felt.

"No change."

"I have a lead on Marvin Hicks. His credit card is being used at the Motel 6 in Inverness."

"Do you have a room number?"

Samuels said, "No. He's using his credit card, so he's probably using his real name. I don't think it's a good idea for you to go alone."

"He isn't dangerous, as long as he's himself. I need to talk to him. Maybe he'll agree to help us and we won't have to force him to cooperate."

"You shouldn't go alone. I'll have someone go with you." Samuels seemed to be debating with himself. "Beecham is at the hospital. I'll have him meet you by the main entrance."

"He'll clam up if I show up with the police."

"This is nonnegotiable. If you leave without him, I will have you arrested."

"What for?"

"Obstructing justice and being an overall pain in the ass."

"I'll meet him downstairs. Bye, Samuels." I hung up. "One down, one to go," I mumbled to myself. I doubted it would be that easy to convince Bryson that I could be left on my own for a short while. Maybe I should go now, before Bryson came from visiting Aaron? No, bad idea. He'd panic if I disappeared. I needed a plan.

Bryson returned to the waiting room and sank into the chair beside me. Dark circles had formed under his eyes. Keeping Aaron alive took more of his energy than I'd realized. Part of me wanted to stay with Bryson, but I knew our best shot at saving Aaron's life was for me to hunt down Dr. Hicks.

"Bryson, Dottie called. They forgot to pick up Mae's medication today. I need to run to the pharmacy, then to Mae's. Can you stay here with Aaron? I won't even get out of the car. I'll run through the drive-through and have Dottie meet me in the driveway." I slowed my speech and hoped he didn't suspect I'd lied.

"I don't like it." Bryson glanced at the clock. "It's getting late. I'll go. Do you know the spell well enough to do it on your own?"

"Maybe, but every time I go in there, my brain goes blank. I don't think I can do it by myself." My lower lip quivered. I needed to hurry and get to Inverness or Aaron would never get better.

"Fine. Go, but be careful." Bryson drew me into a hug. "If anything happened to you, I would never forgive myself."

"I'll be fine." I felt guilty for lying, but I knew what I had to do.

It took every ounce of self-control for me to walk, instead of run, to the main entrance to find Beecham. I looked over my shoulder several times, expecting to see Bryson following me.

"Tessa Lamar?" A tall man dressed in plain clothes approached.

"Yes?"

"I'm Officer Beecham, but you can call me Greg. I'm off duty."

"Nice to meet you." I shook his hand and headed for the exit. By the time I reached my car, my hands were shaking, and I could barely get the key into the ignition. "It'll take an hour or so to drive to Inverness without traffic."

"I'm yours for as long as you need me. Samuels said it was important."

I nodded, wondering how long before Bryson would blow up my cell phone. Thankfully, Officer Beecham, Greg, remained quiet during the drive. The silence gave me a chance to think about what to say to Marvin. I figured I had one chance to get him to help, so I needed to get it right. After a lengthy mental debate, I decided to go with honesty and good old-fashioned guilt. I'd tell him Aaron was fighting for his life, and Marvin was his only hope of survival. He had to know the conjurer's name and where to find him.

My cell phone rang so many times I turned the darned thing off. I would have to face Bryson sooner or later, but there was no sense in giving myself a heart attack every time the phone rang.

"Avoiding someone?" Greg motioned to the phone.

"I don't like to be on the phone while driving, especially with a police officer in my passenger seat."

Greg chuckled. "Good point."

"There's the hotel. Do you mind waiting in the car while I go upstairs?"

"Samuels said not to let you out of my sight."

"Of course he did." I pulled into the hotel parking lot and drove around the building, hoping to find Marvin's car.

Not only did I spot his car, but I spotted him. He stood in a doorway paying a pizza man. "See, nothing to worry about. Luck is on my side. That's him." I angled into a parking spot and waited until the deliveryman pulled away.

"I'm still going with you." Greg and I went up the stairs to Marvin's room.

I knocked quickly before I could chicken out. Marvin opened the door and immediately tried to close it again. I shoved my foot into the open space and saw stars when Marvin crushed my foot between the door and the frame. "Ow! Dang it! Marvin, please let me in. I need to talk to you."

My foot smarted when I put weight on it. The move always worked in movies; never once did the hero get his foot crushed in the door. I pounded on the door. "Marvin, I think you broke my foot. Let me in. I need ice."

He opened the door a fraction and looked out as I rubbed my foot. My flip-flop hung precariously from my toes. Before Marvin could slam it shut again, Greg threw his shoulder against it and pushed his way into the room.

"Who is this? How did you find me? You need to leave." Marvin glanced outside, shut the door, and locked it.

"People are worried about you. Didn't you think someone would file a missing-person's report when you disappeared? You used your credit card to pay for the room." I sat on the edge of the bed closest to the door and inspected my foot.

"What do you want?" Marvin glanced from me to Greg to the door.

"Greg, would you please wait outside? I need to ask Marvin some questions."

"I'll be right outside." Greg frowned and stepped out.

Marvin went into the bathroom and turned the water on. I assumed he needed a minute to collect himself.

"I need the name of the conjurer and an address. One of my friends is in the hospital. His magic is making him sick. I wouldn't ask, but the guy's a cop and, well, I would hate to get his cop friends involved in all this." I looked up at the exact moment Dr. Marvin Hicks clocked me upside the head with a short, yet surprisingly heavy, glass from the bathroom.

I stood with my hand on my head. "Jesus, Mary, and Joseph! Why in the hell did you do that?" I pulled my hand away, thankful I wasn't bleeding.

Marvin darted for the door and tried to wrench it open. I tackled him before he could turn the knob. Surprised by my strength, I had him pinned to the floor, straddling him before either of us knew what happened. In the course of the struggle, Marvin split his lip, his teeth watery-red as he growled. Only then did it occur to me that he could easily shift into a giant bear and rip me in two.

I did the only thing I could think to do—I slammed my fist into his nose with everything I had. My eyes widened when I realized his nose sat more to the right than it had been before I punched him. "You stupid jerk. People are dying because of you. Tell me his name."

Greg pounded on the door. "Tessa? Are you okay?"

"I'm fine!"

Marvin struggled beneath me, and I hit him again. "Tell me or I'll shift and light you up like a campfire."

"I can't say his true name; it may summon him." Marvin stopped struggling, and the energy around him changed. He was trying to shift.

Panic rose like bile in my throat, yet words danced through my mind in a swirling pattern that reminded me of the spell Bryson had spoken over Aaron. I opened my mouth, and the syllables fell from my lips. The voice that came forth sounded nothing like my own.

Marvin stilled beneath me. If his eyes grew any wider, they'd pop out of his head. "How?"

"Tell me his English name and where to find him." I leaned closer, and the smell of blood in the air made my stomach growl.

Marvin must have gotten the hint because he started talking. "Paul Woods. His name is Paul Woods, and he lives in unincorporated Ocala."

I climbed off Marvin and shook out my hand. Punching someone in the nose actually hurt both the punchee and the puncher—who knew? Marvin rolled to his side, his fingers probing his nose. I shook my head as I stepped over him and opened the door. "I'm sorry about your nose. All you had to do was tell me his name."

I walked to the stairs with Greg close behind.

"What happened? Are you okay?" He set his hand on my shoulder.

"Other than my foot getting slammed in the door, I'm fine."

"Your knuckles are bleeding."

"It's not my blood."

Greg shook his head and didn't ask any more questions.

Part of me felt like a badass, but the saner part of me wanted to vomit. I made it to my car, willing my tears not to flow. I'd never hit someone before. My foot and hand took turns pulsing in time with the beat of my heart. The wisest thing to do was get the heck out of there, except it was a bad idea to be behind the wheel in my current state. I could ask Greg to drive, but then he'd know I was hurt.

If I didn't get us out of there, Marvin would shift into his animal form. The thought of being eaten galvanized me. I didn't dare risk using magic to stop him from shifting twice in one night. I didn't want to face the consequences if the spell didn't work.

I drove a few miles and parked in front of the Russell Stover candy factory. What I wouldn't have given for a couple of pounds of chocolate right then, but adding breaking and entering to assault and forced entry was probably not a good idea. "Would you mind driving?"

"I wondered when you'd ask. Your foot has to be killing you." Greg opened his door.

"Thanks for not insisting on driving. I needed time to cool off."

"I've been married almost twenty years. I know when to push and when to back off."

I smiled. "I appreciate it. I need to make a call."

"I need to take a leak. Be right back." He climbed out of the car and disappeared into the darkness.

I pulled my phone from my bag and called Samuels. My muscles felt like rubber. The adrenaline rush of beating the snot out of Marvin had left me exhausted. "This is Tessa. I got a name and city."

Samuels whispered, "Are you all right?"

"Oh no. Are you at the hospital?" My fatigue disappeared as another shot of adrenaline coursed through my veins.

"Yes, sir," Samuels said louder.

"Paul Woods. He's in Ocala, probably in the country somewhere. I doubt he would want neighbors." I hesitated, collecting my thoughts. "I got my foot slammed in a door and hurt my hand on Dr. Hicks's face. Otherwise, I'm safe. Beecham and I are on our way back."

"Roger that. What time is the meeting tomorrow?"

"Meeting?" It dawned on me that he was pretending to speak to someone from the office. He wasn't alone. "Uh, an hour or so? Is Bryson with you?"

"Yes, sir. I understand the situation is hot."

"Great. How's Aaron?" Tears fell to my cheeks, and for once I didn't try to stop them.

"There's no change in Detective Burns's condition. I'll keep you posted."

I hung up without saying good-bye. I sat in the parking lot as gallons of pent-up tears spilled down my face.

The screen on my phone told me I'd missed sixteen calls and had half as many voice messages, along with a handful of texts. I scrolled through several texts from Bryson, each growing in urgency. The voice mails were more of the same. Mae had left two messages. "Great." I put my forehead on the steering wheel and closed my eyes.

"Tessa, where in the hell are you?" Bryson roared through the phone.

"I'm in Wildwood."

"What are you doing in Wildwood?" His volume decreased to a more civil level. "Are you all right?"

"I found Marvin. I'm fine, just shaken up. I got the name." I listened as Bryson growled to himself or me or both.

"You lied to me?"

"I had to. You never would have let me leave. His name is Paul Woods, and he lives in Ocala—"

Bryson interrupted me, yelling again, "Get back here, now. Don't go after this guy. Do you hear me? Get back here, now!"

"I'm coming." I turned and caught movement on my left. In the distance, a wolf howled. I dropped the phone and turned the key as claws scraped down the driver's-side window. The amulet turned cold enough to hurt my chest. I could hear Bryson shouting through the phone, and I screamed, "Wolves!"

The driver's-side window burst in a shower of glass, and I hit the gas pedal. The car lurched forward instead of backward, slamming into a light pole. *Reverse.* Blackness filled my vision.

Forty-Three

THE SMELL OF LITTER BOXES pulled me from my concussion-induced sleep. My hands were bound behind my back, and my feet were tied. The concrete floor beneath me was cold. I had no idea where I was or how I'd gotten there. My nose twitched before the sneezes took control of my body. Someone stirred beside me, and I stilled, only to be taken with another round of sneezes.

A male voice whispered in the dark room. "Tessa?"

"Who's there?" I scooted away from the other person. "Greg?"

"It's Marvin. Is that you, Tessa?" His nasally voice reminded me I'd broken his nose.

"Yes." I scooted farther away, but not far enough.

Marvin kicked out in my direction and caught me in the middle of my back. "Stupid bitch."

I grunted and scooted until I reached a wall. I focused on the coil of heat in my gut, trying to shift forms and escape the bonds.

"It's no use. He bound you from shifting, like you did me." Marvin tried to kick me again, but his foot barely brushed my thigh.

"Stop kicking me." My voice sounded as nasal as his. My entire face itched. It felt as though I'd been dipped in water and rolled in cat hair. Seven sneezes, in rapid succession, left me no choice but to wipe snot on my shoulder.

Marvin whispered, "Stop sneezing. He'll hear you."

"I'm allergic to cats." I pulled on my bonds until they loosened a fraction. "Where's Greg?"

"The guy that was with you earlier?"

"Yes. Have you seen him? He got out of the car to pee before the wolves—"

"No idea where he is."

I didn't remember hearing any screams. Maybe Greg was safe. "Why are we here?"

"Why do you think? He's going to kill us." Anger thickened Marvin's voice.

"If he wanted to kill us, he would have already. Right?"

"Not if he wanted to make it as slow and painful as possible."

"Why would he do that?"

"Are you that stupid? He wants power. He planned for me to take Charlie's position, but your firebird made that impossible. Now he has access to more magic than a seat on the council. He has you."

"I don't understand." My gut clenched. "If he wants to use me, why would he kill me?"

"He doesn't want to use you. He wants your magic, and the only way to get it is through a ritual, one ending with your heart on a plate."

The mental image his words created left me disoriented and determined to break free. Until that moment, it hadn't occurred to me I should be afraid. Between sneezing and getting kicked, I hadn't thought of much. I pulled at the ties on my wrists until my skin wore thin but couldn't get enough of a gap to pull my hand out. Judging by the way the material stuck to my skin, it had to be duct tape, which meant I could chew it apart.

"Marvin. Chew the tape on my wrists. Free me, and I'll free you." I scooted toward him.

"Stay away from me." He kicked me again, this time making

contact with my arm.

I yelped and moved away. After another sneezing fit, I tried to stand. My foot ached from being slammed in the door, but now my knee throbbed as well. Whatever the cause, it took several attempts, and painful falls, before I stood.

"What are you doing?" Marvin hissed from behind me.

I ignored him and crouched down, pulling my bound hands down as far as I could. The first two times, I wobbled and nearly fell again. I managed to bring my hands under my butt. I fell back on purpose and pulled my legs through my arms. With my hands in front of my body, I chewed at the duct tape.

"I'm going to start screaming if you don't stop whatever it is you're doing," Marvin whispered.

I ignored him, knowing good and well that he didn't want Mr. Paul Woods down here anymore than I did. Another few minutes and my hands separated with a quick jerk. I felt around the tape on my ankles until I found the seam, picking at it with my fingernail. Another sneeze tickled my nose. I scrubbed my face and pulled the neck of my T-shirt up to cover the lower half of my face. Returning my attention to the tape on my ankles, I continued to pick at it. At this rate, I would never get loose. What if I took my jeans off? No, that wouldn't work. I still wouldn't get my feet loose. Not to mention, I didn't want to run around without pants.

"Are we in a basement? Are there basements in Florida?" It had to be some sort of shed or utility room—musty, with a concrete floor. I took Marvin's silence as confirmation.

I stood and hopped until I found another wall. Using it for support, I moved around the perimeter of the room until I found a basket of clothes.

"Laundry room," I whispered. I found a pair of jeans with a zipper and sat, using the zipper teeth to saw through the duct tape. It was slow, but faster than picking at it with my nails.

I nearly cried out in triumph when I freed my feet. I considered untying Marvin, but said the hell with it. No telling what he would do to me if I set him loose. Likely, he'd get us caught, and that wouldn't end well. I felt around until my fingers landed on a door frame. I hesitated to open it, unsure if it opened into a garage or a house. Judging by the complete darkness in the room, I doubted it contained a window to climb out of.

The door was the only option. I turned the knob until it clicked, and pushed it open a fraction of an inch. Everything on the outside was almost as dark as the inside. Marvin stirred when I opened the door wider. Without thinking, I slipped out and closed the door behind me. I could hear Marvin moving, but he hadn't called out.

I eased forward a few feet. Light came from under another door. I crept in the opposite direction. Using my hands to guide me, I felt along the wall, hoping to find a door or window. I came to another door and slid my fingers down the frame until I found a dead bolt. My pulse sped up; only outside doors had dead bolts.

Trying to be as quiet as possible, I turned the lock and opened the door. Footsteps echoed from somewhere behind me, and a cold rush of fear flooded my senses. I slid through the door and closed it behind me. I ran as fast as my body would move. My knee screamed as I ran, but I refused to slow down.

Once I made it to the tree line, I slowed a bit, remembering the wolves in the parking lot. Were there wolves out here, or had the conjurer sent them home after they found me? I didn't have time for an anxiety attack. I continued to move deeper into the woods. It was dark, but I could make out some of my surroundings by the light of the moon. I had to be in the middle of nowhere to be able to see so many stars.

I reached for my magic but found only a cold knot of fear where the heat had been. I'd grown accustomed to the magic inside me and missed the familiar heat. I couldn't outrun them, not without the ability to shift.

Voices carried from the direction of the house, and I stilled. Popping and tearing sounds filled my ears, but it wasn't until I heard growls that I realized they had shifted into animal form. I needed something I could use as a weapon. The thought of the wolves came back into my mind, and I started to hyperventilate. The last thing on earth I wanted to do was be torn apart and eaten alive by wolves.

I needed to get off the ground and hide. I reached for a thick, low-hanging branch, set my foot on the trunk, and hoisted myself up. Once I gained a footing on the branch, I climbed higher and higher, until the branches were too flimsy to hold my weight.

Curled against the tree trunk, I stopped and listened as the noises came closer.

Forty-Four

THE WOLVES CAME CLOSER, SNIFFING their way through the underbrush. Any closer and they'd hear my rapid breathing and the drumming of my heart. It was only a matter of time before they found me.

"Close your eyes, child," a female voice whispered in my ear.

I closed my eyes. *Close your eyes so you won't see them coming.*

"No, close your eyes so they can't see *you*," she said into my thoughts. Atsila—mother.

"They will smell me."

"Yes, but they will think you moved on. Trust me. Whisper the words with me, Tessa."

"It won't work. He bound my magic. I can't shift or—"

"He cannot bind me." She whispered the words into my spirit, and they fell from my lips.

My eyes closed, and I focused on the rustling of leaves. The men and wolves came closer and closer. They passed by my tree as I continued to allow my mother's spirit to speak through me.

I thought they'd gone until footsteps shuffled beneath me. I opened my eyes, frantically searching in the darkness. Something moved below me, though I didn't know who or what was there.

"Tessa?" Marvin's voice sounded thin with fear as he called out.

I wanted to answer, but the amulet pulsed icy-cold against my skin. It chilled when the wolves found me in the parking lot and hadn't warmed. However, this felt different. It was like wearing a pulsating cube of dry ice around my neck.

Marvin called to me a few more times, before I heard a meaty thud followed by something heavy hitting the ground.

"Tessa, daughter of Atsila, come to me now or I'll kill this man." A powerful male voice filled the air, making my skin crawl. His voice contained dark magic. Everything in me wanted to move toward his voice, wanted to obey. The need to go to him smothered my fear. I leaned forward, trying to see the one who called me. I *needed* to see his face.

"Close your eyes," Atsila whispered.

The whisper broke the compulsion. I sat back and closed my eyes. Screams of agony drifted up the tree, filling my ears. I fought the urge to cry out. I kept my eyes closed and focused on the comforting presence surrounding me—my mother. The screaming ended with a gurgled breath, the breath of dying. The conjurer walked near the bottom of the tree, chanting his spells. I wrapped my fingers around the amulet, and it warmed in my hand. The conjurer stood below. It should have been cold.

As the amulet heated, so did I. Deep inside, the coil of heat returned. Each time he cast a spell, the heat intensified. Maybe he lost power each time he used magic? Hope crept inside me. I seized the fire and tried to shift forms. When nothing happened, I rested my head against the tree and cried.

The sun broke over the horizon. Soon, he would see me in the tree. Magic was great, but I doubted it could stop a bullet. He paced below, throwing his magic at me over and over again. I hoped he burned himself out before the sun rose too high.

In the distance, something moved through the underbrush. Not something, but a group. A group of what? I turned my head toward the sound. Animals didn't make that much nose, so it had to be people. I wanted to open my eyes but didn't dare, not with Paul Woods circling below. I wanted to call out to the people. I needed to tell them to go away.

"Put your hands where I can see them."

"Hands up," another male shouted below, followed by a scream that reminded me of live lobsters being thrown into a boiling pot.

Someone called out, "Officer down. Officer down."

Gunfire rang out below, but I kept my eyes closed. After several volleys, the air around me cooled, and I could breathe deeply for the first time since the conjurer had taken me. The power inside me flared, and the heat burned deep in my gut. I peeked at the movement below.

"Tessa Lamar?" Samuels called into the woods. "Tessa?"

I covered my mouth as a sob of relief escaped me. "Up here."

When I moved, my muscles cramped. After sitting still for so long, they'd become stiff and refused to cooperate. "I'm up here."

"Can you get down?"

"I'm trying." After everything I'd been through, the idea of being hoisted down by a cherry picker seemed humiliating. I slowly made my way down the tree, branch by branch, until I could see the men standing below.

Samuels moved beneath me as I swung from a branch, trying to gain a firm hold against the trunk—trying and failing.

"Let go, I got you." He wrapped his hands around my thighs, and I let go of the branch. True to his word, he caught me before I hit the ground. He pushed my face into his shoulder and guided me away from the scene. When I tried to pull my head away, he pressed tighter. "There are some things that you can't unsee. Keep moving."

Samuels eased me into the front seat of his car, his body positioned between me and the woods. "Did he hurt you?"

"I escaped."

Samuels looked me over. His eyes lingered on the red marks on my wrists and ankles. "You are a brave woman."

"Is Officer Beecham—"

"He's at the top of my shit list, but fine. We picked him up at a gas station on Highway 40."

"Thank God."

"He said he heard wolves and the car hitting the light pole."

"I'll explain it all later. How's Aaron?"

"He scared the hell out of us last night. All of his organs shut down, almost like someone just hit a switch." Samuels ran his hand over his chin. "Then the bastard sat up and asked for food."

"What? How?" My exhausted brain refused to wrap itself around his words.

"One minute he was as good as gone, and the next he was talking to us like nothing was wrong. It was the strangest thing I've ever seen."

"You mean before you shot Paul Woods?"

"Yeah, last night."

"Huh. Well, at least he's all right." I leaned against the seat, trying to figure it out.

"I'll take you home after I call the ME. I'm curious about the details."

"Can I borrow a phone?"

Samuels grinned. "Yours is in the glove box. I confiscated it from the locals. I figured you'd want it when we found you."

"How did you know you'd find me?" I opened the glove compartment and pulled out my phone.

"Because you are the most resourceful woman I have ever met." He chuckled and walked away.

I took resourceful as a compliment, though I didn't feel resourceful at the moment.

Bryson picked up on the first ring. "Hello, Tessa?"

"Yeah, it's me." I had no idea what he knew, if anything. The sound of his voice brought tears to my eyes. I'd screwed up. Worse, I'd caused Bryson to worry.

"Thank God. Are you okay? Where are you?" He had every right to be angry, but he sounded relieved.

"I'm fine. I'm not sure where I am, somewhere in Ocala. Paul Woods is dead. I'm sorry I ran out on you. I thought I could handle it."

"We'll talk about that later, for now I'm glad you're okay. Figure out where you are so I can come get you."

"I'm with Samuels."

Bryson drew a deep breath. "I wondered what was going on when he ran out of here last night. He told me it was work. I'm not surprised. A lot of people have lied to me lately."

"I'm sorry, Bryson." Tears ran down my cheeks. "Are you still at the hospital?"

"Yes, but now that Woods is dead, I'm going to the tribal house to get some sleep."

"That's silly. Go to my apartment. It's closer. I'll meet you there." The knots in my stomach tightened. Now that the danger had passed, Bryson would leave me.

"Go home, get some rest. Go see Aaron at the hospital. I'll catch up with you tomorrow." He disconnected the call before I could protest.

I dialed Mae, and the answering machine picked up. "Hi, Gram. I'm just checking in. Everything's good. Aaron is doing better. Love you."

I stared at my phone, debating the wisdom of calling Bryson back. More than anything I wanted to make things right with him, only he didn't want to see me. Samuels paced a few feet from the car, talking on his phone. I imagined it would take quite a while for him to finish up and drive me home.

I stepped from the car, feeling like I'd been put through a meat grinder—everything hurt. Samuels hung up and walked back with a serious expression.

"What's wrong? Is it Aaron?" I braced myself for more bad news.

"No, Aaron is fine. They're moving him out of ICU this morning. It looks like I'm going to be stuck here for a while. I can send for an officer to come from Orlando to take you home."

"That will take hours." The farmhouse and forest crawled with police officers.

"I'm sorry, Tessa. It looks like you're stuck with me for a while, and they still need to get your statement." Samuels put his hand on my shoulder and eased me back into the car.

"Can you call an ambulance for me? I feel weird." I drew some of the heat from my belly into my skin.

"You do look flushed." Samuels reached in and placed his hand on my forehead. "Holy smokes, you're burning up. Stay here. I'll have someone call for an ambulance."

Samuels walked into the forest and spoke to one of the local officers. I didn't have much time or privacy; people milled about everywhere. I wrote a quick note, slipped out of the car, and crouched behind the rear bumper. My spirit animal blazed to the surface, changing my form in a heartbeat. Anyone with eyes would know this was no ordinary bird, with my feathers burning bright in the morning sun.

Samuels broke the tree line and stopped. He stared at the bright orange-and-red bird sitting next to his car with a piece of paper dangling from its beak. The human part of me chuckled several short chirps. I flew the short distance and landed at Samuels's feet, lifting my head.

Samuels glanced over his shoulder before taking the note, which read, "Samuels, I'm going to fly home. Tessa." He looked at me wide-eyed and shook his head. I launched into the air, my feathers catching fire as I soared higher and higher. In the distance, Samuels laughed.

Forty-Five

THE TIME AND THE MILES passed as I flew through the midday skies toward Geneva. Not a cloud in the sky, and the air grew hot, but I reveled in it. The aches and pains of my human form faded into memories as I stretched my wings and soared on the breeze.

I circled the tribal house. The fire pit sat empty, and only a few people milled around the grounds. The idea of walking naked through the front door made me queasy. I swooped low, over the rooftop, and cried out. With any luck, Bryson would hear me.

People heard me and came outside—several in fact, but not Bryson. I circled again and landed in a tree a few yards from the house before hopping to the ground. I shifted into my human form and held my head high as I strode through the front yard and into the building. The woman at the welcome desk nearly fell out of her chair when I walked past her.

I moved down the hall to Buck's office, relieved to find him sitting behind his desk. "I need a blanket and Bryson."

Buck shook off his surprise and pulled a cotton blanket from his chair. "Tessa, you can't walk in here naked. I heard you calling overhead. You have to be careful who sees you." He wrapped the blanket around my shoulders.

"I apologize. I'll stash some clothes in the forest before I fly in here again."

He pressed his lips together in disapproval.

"I wasn't being sarcastic. It's smart to put a bag of clothes in the forest for emergencies."

He nodded. "I agree."

"Where's Bryson?"

Buck shook his head and laughed. "You are every bit as stubborn as your grandfather. Bryson is down the hall, last door on the left."

Despite my mood, I grinned at his compliment. I felt pretty brave until I reached his door. I debated on knocking, but decided against it. Sometimes it's better to ask for forgiveness than ask for permission. He would have a harder time turning me away once I was inside.

Bryson bolted upright when I came through the door. "Tessa, what are you doing here?"

"We need to talk." I moved toward him. Sprawled on the bed, he looked sexy as hell, and I wanted to touch him, to curl up with him, and sleep the day away.

"Tomorrow. I'm going back to sleep." He started to lie down, stopping when I dropped the blanket.

"Then I'll sleep beside you." I moved toward the bed, determined not to leave until we made peace.

"You cannot shit all over someone and think sex is going to make things better."

"I didn't crap on you."

"You don't listen to a word I say. You don't respect the fact that I'm supposed to keep you safe. You're so busy running around, you don't realize when you're in over your head," Bryson folded his arms across his chest.

"I came to talk, Bryson. I flew straight here."

"Tell me what you came to say."

I snatched the blanket from the floor and wrapped it around my shoulders. My face burned with embarrassment. Never, not once, had I been so bold with a guy—his rejection hurt. I sat in a chair across from the bed and bowed my head, chewing on my thumbnail.

Bryson stared at me. "This isn't going to work."

I flinched as if he'd struck me. "What isn't going to work?"

Bryson stood and grabbed his bag.

"Wait, Bryson, don't leave. I'll go."

"The hell you will. You woke me up to talk. We're going to talk." He tossed a T-shirt and pair of sweats at me. "Put them on."

"Oh. I thought you meant—"

"I know what you thought I meant. You have a tendency to jump to the wrong conclusions." He turned his back.

I stared at his broad back as his muscles strained against his shirt. His rumpled hair hung to the middle of his back. I'd never seen it so tangled. I slid his T-shirt over my head, and it hung to my thighs. I didn't need the sweats, but pulled them on and rolled the waist. "I'm dressed."

Bryson turned around. "Before you say another word, don't lie to me again. I want the truth."

My mind went blank as I nodded. "I'm sorry."

He sat on the edge of the bed.

"I couldn't tell you where I was going because you would never have let me leave."

"Wrong. You should have told me what was going on so we could figure out how to handle it."

"I thought I could handle it. Aaron needed you at the hospital. Marvin was in Inverness. There was no other way."

Bryson drew a breath. "There's always another way."

"I should go." I stood and turned to the door.

"Sit down."

"Why? This is getting us nowhere."

Bryson shook his head and motioned to the door. "Then go."

My lips moved as if to speak, but nothing came out. Was that it? He'd send me away, dismiss me like a child. My anger rose, but I pushed it down. I came here to fix things, not make them worse. "I almost died."

"Needlessly," Bryson said.

"No, not needlessly. Paul Woods is dead." I glowered. "I did what I had to do to take care of the situation."

Bryson stood, towering over me. "Sit down."

I sat and he knelt in front of me.

"You lied to me, went off alone, put yourself in danger. You disrespected me, again, and thought only of yourself." His voice remained calm.

"I didn't go alone. Samuels sent another officer with me."

"So you endangered the life of yet another cop?"

I couldn't say anything without digging myself into a deeper hole. "I never asked you to be my guardian."

Bryson took my shoulders in his hands. "This isn't about being your guardian or asking permission. Did you ever once think of what would happen to Mae and Dottie if something happened to you? Did you think of how I felt when you didn't come back? What if you'd been killed? I wouldn't have been able to live with myself."

"I can't be killed."

"Bullshit." He released me. "A month ago, you didn't know any of this was real. You don't understand what you are or the consequences of your actions. You're not invincible. Even firebirds can be killed. Tessa, I'm falling in love with you, but I'll not allow you to run over me like I'm some whipped college boy. I realize there's an age difference between us, but I need an adult relationship."

"I'm sorry. I didn't think." I hung my head, fighting to hold back tears.

"No. You didn't." He stood. "I need to take a walk and cool off."

"I'll go. This is your room."

"Stay, think, cry, beat the pillow. Do whatever you need to do. Stop running for a damned second." Bryson stepped into the hallway and closed the door behind him.

I gasped when the door closed and I was left alone in the room. I clung to my anger, but it slipped away. Bryson was right. I'd behaved like a spoiled brat. I helped people work out their problems for a living, yet I failed miserably at handling my own.

The talk left me with more questions than answers. I decided to wait for him to come back. We would finish the conversation once we had a chance to cool off. I crawled into his bed and snuggled into the pillow, my mind racing.

Forty-Six

I WOKE IN A PANIC, STILL half-inside a nightmare and unsure of my surroundings. As the dream receded, reality rolled over me. Outside the window, crickets chirped. I didn't know how long I'd slept, but Bryson hadn't returned. I wandered down the hall past Buck's office. Everything was dark, not a soul in sight.

I hadn't thought to ask Bryson if my family knew I'd gone missing. I hadn't thought about a lot of things lately. I went back to Bryson's room, stripped, and left his clothes folded on his bed, then turned and opened the window. Shifting grew easier with practice, but closing the window in animal form was another matter altogether.

I stretched my wings and flew west toward Apopka. Without being caught up in anger or fear, my feathers remained feathers—no streaks of fire to draw unwanted attention. The quiet country gave way to city lights and traffic, but I flew high above it. From this vantage point, even the seedier side of town looked beautiful.

I landed at the bottom of the porch steps and shifted. The driveway was empty—no visitors to witness me parading around in my birthday suit. I slipped inside and walked straight to my bedroom. "Gram? Dottie? It's me."

"We're in the living room," Dottie replied.

Clothes were slim pickins at Mae's. I took most of them home, and what remained was either ratty or too small. Not that it mattered, since I wasn't trying to impress anyone. I pulled on a pair of old shorts and a tank top.

I felt like I hadn't eaten in days. "I'm going to grab dinner."

"Okay, dear," Mae called.

I tossed a leftover carton of Chinese food into the microwave. "Are they delivering Chinese out here now?"

"No, Bryson brought us supper last night." Mae's words were clipped.

"That was nice of him," I said, not wanting to think about Bryson.

"We've had quite a few visitors," Mae said.

Mae and Dottie stood in the doorway with their arms folded. They looked like a two-woman SWAT team. Dottie motioned to a bag on the kitchen table. I peeked into the bag and cringed. My dirty clothes, cell phone, and amulet were inside. I felt like a gnat drowning in a glass of sweet tea.

"You just missed Detective Samuels," Mae said as she sat. The look on her face said I'd better start talking.

I grabbed the pork lo mein, though it didn't look appetizing any longer. "I went after Marvin and ended up being taken to the conjurer's house. I got away, but Marvin didn't."

"Detective Samuels told us what happened. What he didn't tell us is how he ended up with your clothes and phone. Tessa, how could you be so foolish? Not only running after Marvin but changing near outsiders? Have you spoken to Bryson? Does he know about this?" Mae's eyes were both angry and worried at the same time.

"I messed up. I thought I could handle it, but then everything went sideways. I tried to talk to Bryson, but he was too mad to talk."

"Give him time, child," Dottie murmured as she rubbed my shoulder.

Mae shook her head. "What do you plan to do about the other one?"

"Other one? What other one?"

"Aaron. He's sweet on you." Mae went to the cupboard and pulled out her whiskey, along with two glasses.

"I was planning to break things off with him when he got sick." I eyed the bottle.

"Oh no. This isn't for you, young lady. You need to drive yourself home. I'm not going to let you hide here when you have a mess to clean up." Mae poured herself and Dottie a shot. "Bryson told us about Aaron getting sick. It would have been nice to hear it from you. I'm quite fond of the boy."

"Sorry, Gram. Everything happened so fast, I didn't have time to call."

"Next time everything is happening fast, slow down." Mae shook her head and knocked back the whiskey.

"Tessa, all of this is new to you. You can't expect to have all the answers. I know it's not your way, but lean on those who love you until you get your feet back under your fanny." Dottie sipped her whiskey.

"So, what are you going to do about Aaron?" Mae persisted.

"I need to stop it before it goes any further. If we can be friends, great, if not, then that'll be his choice, not mine."

"Tessa, Dottie and I disagree on this. I say if your heart wants Aaron, don't cut him loose just yet. Just because Buck thinks you're going to marry Bryson, it doesn't mean you're going to marry Bryson. Buck Oldham will have to get over it." Mae set her jaw.

"Follow your heart, and give yourself time, Tessa. No one can set your path for you." Dottie smiled.

"Thank you both." I sat back. Truth be told, I knew what my heart wanted—Bryson.

"Now, get your fanny out of here. The truck keys are on the visor."

Mae stood and wrapped her arms around my neck, kissed my brow, and swatted my backside.

I turned and hugged Dottie. "Good night."

"Good night, sweetheart." Dottie patted my back. "Take your time, and don't let those boys push you around."

I walked toward Charlie's truck without looking over my shoulder for bad guys, or at my feet for snakes. My personal life had turned into a hot mess, but at least no one was trying to shoot me anymore. I slid into the worn leather seat, pulled down the visor, and the keys fell into my lap. On the visor, beneath the strap, was a picture of me from my high school graduation.

"Charlie, I don't know what to do." I sat back and closed my eyes. "I can't take your position in the tribe. I'm not ready. I can't even get my life in order. Why did you leave? I miss you so much."

Old Spice drifted through the cab, mingling with the scent of old leather and sweat. Years of working out of this truck had given it its own unique smell. The aftershave scent was different, familiar, but stronger than normal. I opened my eyes, hoping to see my grandfather beside me. I was alone, only I didn't feel alone. "Charlie? Grandpa? Are you there?"

The scent faded. I shook my head and wiped my eyes. "I know you're there, and I know what I need to do."

I debated going straight to the hospital, but needed to take my time and clear my head. My bare foot pressed on the gas pedal. I needed to go home and shower first. Aaron might be feeling better, but one whiff of me right now would put him back in the ICU.

My apartment was empty—too empty. I went straight to the couch and picked up Bryson's pillow, bringing it to my face. It smelled like him, like sandalwood and fresh-cut lumber. My bed called, warm and safe, but I needed to see Aaron. Heaven knows what Samuels had told him. How would he feel about a girl who changed into a bird now and then? Not that it mattered, as I had to break things off as soon as possible.

Forty-Seven

I WALKED INTO AARON'S hospital room with a growing sense of doom. Knowing what needs done and doing it are two different things.

"Hey, there she is." Aaron grinned. He sat in the lounger next to the bed, with only one IV in his arm.

"Hi." I went to him and slid my arms around his neck for a quick hug. Aaron had other ideas. He pulled me into his lap and laid a kiss on me that would have made a sailor blush.

Samuels cleared his throat. "Tessa, where did you fly off to? A little bird told me you were in Geneva."

I cringed at his words. Did I assume Aaron knew my secret or did he just enjoy watching me squirm? "Hi, Samuels. I had to take care of something before I came here."

I eased away from Aaron. "I owe you my life, but don't expect a kiss."

"That's okay. I have a bird's-eye view over here." He chuckled.

Aaron pressed his hand to my cheek and turned my face toward his. "Samuels told me you left before giving your statement."

"I'll take care of it tomorrow. I needed to get out of there."

"Understandable. Settle something for us. We have a bet going on about how you got out of the laundry room." Aaron pulled me close, still grinning. He definitely felt better.

"I pulled my legs through my arms and chewed the tape until I could break it. Then used the zipper from a pair of jeans to—"

Aaron interrupted me with a victory shout. "I told you she did it alone." He kissed my cheek. "That's my girl."

I pulled back enough to get a breath, and turned my head toward Samuels. "Is he on pain meds?"

"Nope." Samuels chuckled as he stood. "I think I'm going to leave you two lovebirds alone. Aaron, see you tomorrow, buddy. I'll be here when they spring you."

"You're getting out tomorrow?" I asked.

"Yep, and plan on being back in the office by noon. I have some kids to find. *We* have some kids to find." He waved to Samuels.

"Have a good night, Samuels," I said.

Samuels winked and closed the door behind him.

"It's too soon for you to return to work."

"I feel great," Aaron said.

"You were in intensive care, Aaron."

"Have you talked to Bryson?" Aaron asked, pulling me against his chest again.

"Briefly." I felt guilty curled up on Aaron's lap while discussing Bryson.

"Did he tell you what happened?" Aaron ran his fingers through my hair.

"Samuels told me you almost died. Then you had a remarkable recovery," I replied, making the statement sound more like a question.

"Bryson saved my life."

"What?" I pulled back so I could see his face.

"I know you two are . . . special. He told me I was sick because of dark magic. At first I didn't believe him, then everything clicked: your quick healing, the wolf guy, your ability to talk to ghosts, and see things."

I nodded, feeling the bottom drop out from under me. Bryson had warned me not to involve outsiders, yet he'd spilled his guts to Aaron? Talk about the pot calling the kettle black.

"He used magic to heal me." Aaron pulled me close again. "He said he did it for you."

"For me?" My throat went dry.

"Because you blamed yourself for my being sick. Which, by the way, is ridiculous."

"Oh." I eased out of his lap.

Aaron frowned when I stood. "Tessa, are you okay?"

"I'm really tired."

"Is that all there is to it?"

I wanted to tell him yes, to allow him to believe everything would be fine, but I needed to be honest. "No. I'm still dealing with losing my uncle, being kidnapped, witnessing murders—the list seems endless. I have feelings for you, but I also have feelings for Bryson. With everything else going on, I don't think this is the time to start a relationship."

Aaron took a moment to process my words. "I know. Bryson and I discussed it. Do you want me to back off?"

"You what?" My face grew hot. "You two discussed it?"

Aaron nodded.

"Did you two come to any decisions? What? Did you flip a coin?"

"It wasn't like that." Aaron ran his hand over the back of his neck.

"Then how was it?"

"Come here." Aaron reached for me.

"Actually, I need to run. It's been a long day, and I have to take care of some things." I turned toward the door.

"Tessa . . ."

"Let me know if you need any help with the case." I marched out of the room and straight into Bryson's chest.

"Hey." Bryson set his hands on my upper arms to steady me, and tilted his head. "What's wrong?"

"Nothing. Everything is perfect. Just peachy." I forced a big smile and pulled away.

Aaron came to the door, dragging his IV pole behind him. He looked past me to Bryson. "We need to talk. All of us."

Bryson studied my face. "Will you sit down and talk to us?"

I dipped my chin to my chest, turned, and walked back into the room. Aaron sat on the bed, and I sat in the chair closest to the door. It may have been cowardly, but my sense of self-preservation made me stay close to the escape route.

Bryson looked between Aaron and me before moving to the lounger. "What's going on?"

"I was telling Tessa we talked after you saved my life." Aaron stared at me as he spoke.

"I see." Bryson turned to me. "Tessa?"

I shook my head. "Look, I'm tired. It's been a difficult day, and I have to drive to Ocala tomorrow to give a statement about the murders. I want to go home."

"Murders?" Bryson's eyes darkened. "I thought the cops shot Paul Woods."

"Tessa witnessed Woods killing Dr. Hicks and a Marion County deputy," Aaron replied.

The memory of the officer's strangled scream crashed into my mind. I needed to get out of there and process everything that had happened.

"You didn't tell me Hicks was dead." Bryson stared at me.

"I didn't have a chance."

"Tell me now." Bryson folded his arms. "Please."

"I was pretty high in a tree. I didn't see the actual deaths."

"Why were you in a tree?" Bryson unfolded his arms and leaned forward, his face softening.

"To get away from the wolves," I said. "After I got out of the house, I ran into the forest. I heard wolves and climbed a tree."

Bryson nodded. "Why don't you start at the beginning?"

I felt like an ant under a magnifying glass, but Bryson deserved to hear it from me. I steadied my nerves and told them what had happened, including the visit from my mother. "I had my eyes closed so he couldn't find me. I didn't see anything."

"Man, I don't think I'll ever get used to this magic stuff." Aaron shook his head.

"I didn't know, Tessa. I'm sorry." Bryson looked stricken.

"You didn't ask. Nor did you ask before you told Aaron I needed time to deal with things, or before you told him I had feelings for both of you." My anger simmered below the surface, fueling the fire in my gut. I had to learn to control my emotions.

"We're worried about you. We agreed to back off and give you some space," Bryson added.

I jerked my head toward Aaron. "You certainly didn't back off."

Aaron put his hands up. "What can I say? I fight dirty. After a near-death experience, I realized I don't have time to waste."

"Aaron." Bryson shook his head. He looked like he knew more than he said.

I stood and put my hands on my hips. "When you two figure out my life, let me know. I'm going home."

I stormed out the door, and Bryson followed. He grabbed my arm, and I ripped it away. "Leave me alone. I've heard enough."

"No, you haven't." He looked into my eyes. "He didn't have a near-death experience. He died."

My breath hitched. "What are you talking about?"

"I pulled him back, and gave him part of my spirit to bind him to this world."

I stared, my mouth hanging open.

"It would have killed you if he'd died. You never would have forgiven yourself." Bryson reached forward to touch my face, but I shrank away.

"How? What cost?" I couldn't grasp what he'd done, though it couldn't be that easy—nothing in this new life was that easy.

"We are bound in spirit."

"Right, but what does that mean?"

"I gave him part of me, and took enough of his sickness into myself to allow his body to heal."

"Are you sick? Is that why you were so tired?" My voice rose.

Bryson whispered, "I was, yes. He is so . . ." Bryson made a motion. "Energetic, because he has a small amount of my being mixing with his."

"He is rather full of energy." I rolled my eyes. "What did you tell him about us?"

"Only that we had magic."

"So, he doesn't know the shifter part?"

"No. I told him only what was necessary."

I leaned against the wall. Would Samuels tell Aaron about me shifting?

Bryson smiled. "I should get back in there before I have to peel him off the ceiling."

"I'm going home."

"Do you want me to come by later?"

"Not tonight. Maybe tomorrow, after I get back in town."

Bryson's face fell. He looked so disappointed I almost changed my mind—almost.

Forty-Eight

I BOLTED UPRIGHT, WOKE FROM YET another nightmare. My subconscious had me back in the tree with my eyes closed. Someone hammered on my front door.

"What time is it?" I murmured into the dark room. Who in the hell is knocking on my door at a quarter to six in the morning?

I tossed my singed robe around my shoulders and tiptoed to the door. Aaron stood on my doorstep with two cups of coffee, a fat folder under his arm, and a stupid grin. I opened the door and turned before I made eye contact. What was he doing here? He needed to learn to call before dropping by, especially at such an ungodly hour. I walked back toward my room.

Aaron caught my arm before I slid between the sheets. "Ah-ah-ah. We have work to do."

"It is the butt crack of dawn, Aaron. I'm tired. Call me later," I grumbled, and crawled back into bed.

"I thought you wanted to get Mr. Rivera out of jail?"

"When the sun's up, we'll talk. Go to work. Turn the bottom lock on the way out." My brain clicked on; something didn't make sense. "They discharged you from the hospital in the middle of the night?"

"Nope, I left." Aaron pulled the lid off a coffee cup and waved the steam in my direction.

The aroma of coffee hit me almost as hard as his words. "You left against medical advice?"

"I couldn't sit there until they got around to doing the paperwork. I have a case to solve. Those kids are out there somewhere."

I sat up and grabbed the coffee. It burned my tongue but tasted amazing. "You are a serious pain in my butt, Detective."

"Right back at ya, sweetheart." He sat beside me. "I did some digging this morning and came up with nothing. Samuels has a name and an address, but when he went by, the place was empty. The guy left in a hurry. Samuels is looking for next of kin and place of employment, but it's a slow process. We need to go back to the Rivera house and see if you can speak to the ghost."

"This morning? Did you sleep at all last night?"

Aaron's newfound energy worked my last nerve—no doubt a side effect from Bryson's healing. "No, and I feel great. Come on. Get dressed. Let's nail this guy." He stood and paced beside the bed.

"Fine, I'm up. Do I have time for a shower?" I frowned at the annoyed look in his eyes.

"Yes, but hurry."

I climbed out of bed for the second time and walked into the kitchen to make coffee.

"I'll make breakfast, you shower. Unless you want me to join you?" Aaron motioned toward the bathroom.

"Join me? No, I don't think that's a good idea."

"Can't blame a guy for trying."

"We have work to do." I went into the bathroom and closed the door. I needed to set Aaron straight about us, but he had more of Bryson inside him than I wanted to deal with. How long would the aftereffects of sharing his spirit last?

I showered and dressed, only to find Aaron pacing a path on my carpet. "How much coffee have you had? You're seriously high-strung."

"This is my first cup. Ready?" He snatched the case file from the counter.

"Where's breakfast?"

Aaron grinned. "I got distracted. We can get something on the way. Shall we?"

I longed for food, unable to remember the last time I'd eaten. I settled for a thermos of coffee and the promise of a drive-through. "Sure, let's go."

I had to hustle to keep up with Aaron's quick pace. Once inside the car, I buckled up and held on for dear life as Aaron drove toward the victim's house. His driving was almost as erratic as his speech. "Aaron, slow down. You're going to get a ticket."

He looked at me and laughed. "I can talk my way out of it."

"Right, cop perk." I relaxed when the car slowed to a respectable speed. "What am I supposed to ask Mrs. Rivera? If I can even reach her. There's no guarantee this will work, you know."

"Ask her about the killer. Ask her if she knows where the children are now. Maybe she can help us find them?" Aaron drummed on the steering wheel, waiting for a red light to change to green.

"Are you cleared to return to work?" The thought popped into my mind and out of my mouth.

"Not officially." Aaron smirked and turned left into the neighborhood.

I wrapped my arms around myself and sank into my thoughts. The last time I'd come face-to-face with the ghost of Mrs. Rivera, it hadn't gone well. What if the woman refused to talk to me? I didn't want to see disappointment in Aaron's eyes, not when I'd nearly cost him his life.

The car came to a stop, jarring me from my troubles. Before I could unbuckle my seat belt, Aaron pulled me toward him and pressed his lips to mine. The kiss surprised me, not because he did it, but how different it felt from our others. Aaron seemed to claim me, starting with my lips.

I released the seatbelt, and he pulled me across the console. He tangled his fingers in my hair as his lips crushed mine. The extra energy from Bryson's healing, poured through him and into me. I could almost taste Bryson on Aaron's lips. "Whoa, no, stop."

Aaron pulled back, grinned, and dove in again. I made a protesting sound and scrambled away from him.

"Sorry about that."

I fell back into my seat, breathless and more than a little confused.

Aaron hopped out of the car and walked to the front door without as much as a look back.

"What the hell?" My fingers brushed my swollen lips. I stood and slammed the door. Aaron had been through a lot, but it didn't excuse his rude behavior. I steeled my resolve to keep my distance. I stormed through the open front door. "Hello?"

"Over here." Aaron leaned against the kitchen counter with his ankles crossed and arms folded. His grin looked more like his and less like Bryson's.

"What was that about?"

"I was taking your mind off your nerves." He pushed back from the counter.

I threw my hands up with a frustrated grunt and went into the living room. He may have stilled my nerves, but my head had left the game. He'd played me, and it ticked me off.

Aaron asked, "Ready to get started?"

"Not yet. Aaron, you have to back off. I need time to figure things out."

"That's bullshit. I saw it in your eyes when you looked at Bryson. You've made your choice."

"Then why did you shove your tongue down my throat outside?"

"I couldn't help myself."

"Try."

"I am trying." He looked me over as if imagining me naked.

"Try harder."

He looked away and ran his hand through his hair. "I'm sorry. I'm not usually so aggressive. Are we good?"

"Yep, we're fine." I drew a cleansing breath and exhaled my frustration. I took my time, wandering around the room and clearing my head of Aaron's behavior.

Even though I'd been here before, I'd never get used to searching the home of a murder victim, hoping to run into a ghost. "Mrs. Rivera? Are you here? I need you to help me find your children."

I walked through the small formal dining room and into the kitchen, ignoring Aaron as I passed. I trailed my fingers over the windows, hoping to catch a glimpse of previous activity in their reflections. When no visions came, I moved upstairs into the nursery. My chest hurt as I ran my fingertips over the butter-yellow and soft-blue crib blanket. I caught movement in the corner of my eye and turned to see Aaron watching me.

"I can't find her." I wanted to give up and go home, but I could lose a little sleep if it meant saving the lives of two children. "What is her first name?"

"Amalia." Aaron's gaze lingered on the large teddy bear sitting in the rocker. "Her name was Amalia."

"Amalia? Can you hear me?" I called into the powdery-sweet room. "We need your help to find your babies."

"Only my grandmother calls me Amalia." The words came as whispers at first, increasing in volume with each anger-laced syllable.

I resisted the urge to protect my face as I searched for the source of the words. "Mrs. Rivera, my name is Tessa, and this is Detective Burns. We need your help to find the kids. Do you know where they are?"

"He took them," the spirit shouted.

Amalia Rivera sat in the rocking chair, superimposed over the white bear. She rocked the chair, staring at me.

"Who took them?"

"He took them." Her voice grew thin and shrill. "He took my children."

I lowered my voice and slowed my speech—an old therapist trick to calm a patient. "His house is empty. Do you know where else he would have taken them?"

"His mother's house. He told her they are his. She thinks they're her grandchildren." Amalia stared at the empty crib. "He's crazy. I didn't know. I thought I loved him."

"Sometimes people hide what they are from the world. Don't blame yourself for this." I wished I could reach out and hold her hand.

"I was unfaithful—"

"That doesn't mean you deserved to be hurt. Your actions don't excuse him from kidnapping your children." I inched closer and knelt at Amalia's feet. I couldn't touch her physically, but I needed to reach her emotionally. "Mrs. Rivera, we won't rest until we find your kids. I promise."

"Amy. Please call me Amy." The spirit's face softened enough for me to see behind the mask of grief, into the eyes of a beautiful young woman. A woman who was far too young to die.

Aaron stood behind me, awestruck.

I asked, "Any more questions, Detective?"

"Names, addresses. I can't hear her." Aaron's eyes never left the rocking chair.

"Miriam Warner, she lives in Mascotte, behind the elementary school." Amy faded from view.

"Thank you," I said.

"Is she gone?" Aaron took a step toward the rocker.

"Yes. Let's go."

Forty-Nine

AARON WALKED OUTSIDE AND CALLED Samuels to relay the new information. I stepped aside and dialed Bryson. The police would find the kids. Aaron and I couldn't be directly involved. A civilian, and a cop not medically cleared to return to duty, would hardly be welcome in the middle of a SWAT team, especially a team from another county. However, if I could convince Bryson to tag along, we might be able to provide an aerial view.

"Bryson, we think we know where the missing kids are. We need your help."

"Where are you?" The suspicious tone in his voice cut deep.

"At the Rivera house. I spoke with Mrs. Rivera again. Aaron and I are going to need your help. Can you meet us at the police station?"

Aaron started the car and beeped the horn. I jumped at the sound, turned, and hurried to the car. "Bryson?"

"Stay out of it, Tessa. This is beyond dangerous, going after a killer again." He sighed into the phone. "Let the police handle it."

"Bryson, what if he gets away? We can help in other ways. Please meet us at the station." The connection went silent. "I need you."

"See you there. Don't do anything stupid until I get there." Bryson disconnected.

I tucked my phone in my pocket. "He's on the way."

Aaron put the car in park and stared at me. "Are you two still arguing?"

"We aren't arguing, but it's tense."

"Why?"

I shrugged, not wanting to get into it.

"You have feelings for him."

"I do, but you knew that."

Aaron smiled and pulled onto the street. "I did, but it doesn't mean I have to like it."

"Should I apologize?"

Aaron chuckled. "No. Don't apologize for the way you feel."

I turned to the window. "What's the plan?"

"I aim to make you forget about Bryson and ride off into the sunset with me."

"Aaron . . ." I rested my head on the window and closed my eyes.

"I know. I know. So here's the plan. We go into the station together, and I'll get the address from Samuels. Our team will be assisting on this one since it's across jurisdictions. No one needs to know we're going to follow. Keep close to me and keep quiet."

"Sir, yes, sir." I smirked, imagining him giving Bryson orders. This had "bad idea" written all over it.

Local news vans and reporters mobbed the police station. Aaron failed to mention the press conference regarding the case. The brass had arranged it before the latest developments, and no one thought to cancel it.

Aaron led me to a rear entrance and ushered me into the building as discreetly as possible. Once inside, he brought me into the lobby. "What's going on?"

He gave me a firm look. "Wait here and stay quiet."

"Okay." I watched the crowd on the sidewalk outside, and called Bryson. "Hi. Listen. There are a ton of reporters outside. I'm waiting for you in the lobby."

"Great." Bryson sounded irritated again. "Why are you whispering?"

"In case someone is listening."

"Didn't Mae teach you if you're doing something you have to whisper about, you ought not to be doing it?" Bryson chuckled. "Be there in a few."

While he may have had a point, he didn't need to rub my nose in it. Bryson and Aaron needed to stop treating me like a child. I sat and folded my arms. I realized I was pouting and unfolded my arms—damn them both.

Minutes passed by, and the camera crews and reporters multiplied. Several female heads turned as Bryson walked through the glass doors. One blonde reporter had to visibly shake herself to regain her composure. The woman practically drooled after him, leaving me with a strong sense of jealousy.

Bryson narrowed his eyes. "What?"

"Nothing. Thanks for coming."

"You didn't give me much of a choice." He took my hand. "What's wrong? Why are you so upset?"

"You didn't see those women out there falling all over themselves when you came in?"

Bryson glanced out the window and shrugged. "No, not really. I was in a hurry to get inside—to you."

My irritation melted enough to manage a lopsided smile.

Bryson kissed the back of my hand. "I take it you didn't file the police report?"

"Oh, crap. No, I totally forgot."

"I'll go with you after we do whatever it is we're going to do in Mascotte."

"We're going to provide air support for the rescue," I whispered.

"That's risky—changing in broad daylight, especially with cops nearby. Oh, wait, you know all about that." He dropped my hand.

"Ha-ha. We need two cars. I'll tell Aaron we're going on to Ocala, which isn't really a lie," I added.

"Either way, he's going to notice we disappeared, and likely will find our clothes."

"Whatever. We'll think of something, even if we have to take his memory." The number of reporters outside had thinned. The press conference must be starting soon. "Speaking of Aaron, how long is he going to act like you?"

Bryson furrowed his brows. "Act like me?"

"He's been acting strange since last night. Bossy and smug."

"Are you calling me bossy and smug?" He laughed. "Bit hypocritical, no?"

"I'm serious. He's not acting like himself."

"Maybe you don't know him as well as you think you do, Tessa." Bryson leaned close, until his nose was an inch from mine.

"She knows me just fine." Aaron came back and interrupted the almost kiss, his grin broadening.

I stood, flustered. "Are we ready? Do you have the address?"

"Yeah." Aaron looked past me to the sidewalk. "Let's go out the side door."

"Good plan. Tessa and I are going to follow you to Mascotte. I'll take her to Ocala to make her statement afterward. Seems she forgot." Bryson slid his arm over my shoulder.

"We have things to discuss on the way up. She rides with me now. You can take her to Ocala." Aaron offered his hand.

"Why don't you two go in Aaron's car and I'll follow in

Bryson's?" I stepped out of Bryson's embrace.

"Ride with him. I'll be right behind you." Bryson grinned at Aaron, though he spoke to me.

Fifty

AARON WAS ALL SMILES AS we stepped out the side door. Several camera flashes stole my vision. Between our hurry to get on the road and the pissing match over whom I would accompany to Mascotte, we hadn't realized they'd moved the press conference to the side parking lot.

The police commissioner and Detective Samuels shared a small podium, surrounded by a couple of detectives in plain clothes and a handful of uniformed officers. Samuels motioned for Aaron to join them at the podium. The reporters turned to us.

The commissioner nodded toward Aaron and motioned for him to come forward. "Allow me to introduce Detective Burns, the second primary investigator on this case. It was under his direction that we brought in nontraditional resources on the case."

Aaron said something under his breath. The reporters began shouting questions at Aaron as he stepped forward. Bryson pulled me into the protection of his arm and led me to the fringe of the crowd. I turned my head and watched as Aaron stood behind the podium addressing the reporters. He reminded me of a political candidate, smiling and waving.

A reporter called out, "Inside sources tell us the nontraditional resource is a psychic? Is this true, Detective Burns?"

I held my breath, and Bryson whispered a few choice curses. Aaron's smile faltered, glancing toward me and Bryson. One or two of the cameras turned, following his line of vision, straight to me and Bryson.

"We've used every available resource to locate the Rivera children," Aaron replied a moment too late. "We won't stop searching for the children until they're found."

Another reporter shouted from the crowd, "So you believe the children are still alive?"

Bryson tightened his grip on me, tucking me against his chest as he hotfooted it out of the parking lot. Once we were on the sidewalk, he slowed his pace. "Change of plans. You're riding with me."

I nodded. "Please tell me we weren't on camera."

"I'm not sure if we were—not that it matters. They can't link you to the case, or the rumors of psychics." Bryson looked uncertain as he unlocked my door.

I left a message for Aaron as Bryson pulled onto the highway and grew quiet.

"Tessa, I'm glad you called me this morning." Bryson glanced at me and smiled. "It means a lot."

Before I could respond, my cell phone rang. "It's Mae."

"Answer it."

"Hello?" I forced a smile, hoping it would leak into my words.

"Tessa Marie, I just saw you on the TV with those two guys. I can't believe my baby girl was on the TV. Are you a police psychic?" Darlene's voice pierced my eardrum.

"No, Momma. I was visiting Aaron at the station, and we happened to be in the wrong place at the wrong time." I tried even harder to force myself to smile. The last thing I needed to do was tick off Darlene.

"Don't lie to me, little girl. You and I both know the women in this family are psychic. Just yesterday, I told Earl he was going to get a flat tire on the truck. Lo and behold, he had a flat tire this morning." Darlene said something I couldn't make out.

"Momma? Can I talk to Mae for a second?"

"Whatever you have to tell her, tell me. She's watching the news." Darlene's voice rose and grew more grating.

"Please tell her I won't be home for dinner." I hoped Mae would pick up on my code words for—I'm going to be busy for a while. After being kidnapped, I promised Dottie and Mae I wouldn't leave town without letting them know. Mascotte and Ocala were definitely out of town.

"Oh, pooh. I was hoping we could talk. I think we should open a shop to do psychic readings—"

"I have to go, Momma. We can talk later. Love you." I hung up and put my head in my hands.

Bryson asked, "Did I hear that right? Your mother, I mean, Darlene saw us on television and thinks you're the psychic?"

"Yes." I pulled my fingers down my face, stretching my eyelids and cheeks. "Let's not talk about it."

Bryson nodded. "Deal."

Ten minutes passed when my phone rang again. This time it was Dottie.

"Hello?"

"Tessa, honey, you need to hear this." The line went quiet, and then Darlene's voice filled my ear. I strained to hear what she was saying. I pressed the phone hard against my ear.

"Yes. I have information . . . missing kids . . . that detective . . . hired my daughter . . . his girlfriend. Hang on. Mae, leave me be. I'm on the phone. Yes, I'm back. That tall fellow . . . all three dating . . ." I heard bits and pieces of the conversation. Enough to give me chest pains. I put my finger in my ear, struggling to hear.

"Them three are having a ménage a twat. No wait, that's when there's two girls and one guy. What do they call it when it's two guys and a girl?" Darlene barked out a laugh. The sounds of a struggle came across the line. I feared I would stroke out, right there, in Bryson's SUV—pop an aneurism and die where I sat.

I disconnected and gently set the phone on the console. "I'm sorry, Bryson."

Before he could ask, I threw my head back and screamed—one long shrill sound erupted after the next until I disintegrated into hysterical laughter.

Bryson turned white as a sheet and eased the car off the road. He started to reach for me but stopped short. "Tessa?"

I looked at him, still laughing like a lunatic. "She told the news station we were having a ménage à trois."

"Darlene?" He seemed to have a hard time wrapping his brain around what had happened.

"Yup. Darlene told someone at the news station I was psychic and sleeping with you and Aaron." My laughter turned to tears.

Bryson made a hissing sound as he leaned over and drew me into his arms. "She's insane. No one will listen to that nonsense. It'll be all right, baby. Everything will work out."

I nodded and curled closer to Bryson. An unwelcome sense of déjà vu struck. Hadn't I been in the same position with Aaron just hours earlier? I started to pull away, when the phone rang again. This time Bryson picked it up and powered the darned thing off.

"Bryson, I kissed Aaron. I mean, he kissed me, but I kissed him back."

He tensed but continued to hold me.

"I'm sorry. He's acting so weird and I'm so freaking confused."

"Tessa, we don't have a commitment. Who you kiss is your business."

"I know, but . . ." I pulled away.

"But what?"

"I thought . . ."

He tucked a curl behind my ear and smiled. "You want me to tell you not to kiss anyone?"

Did I? Maybe? "I don't know. I guess I do."

"Don't kiss Aaron or anyone else. Consider yourself off the market from now on."

I nodded, trying to puzzle out what that meant. "Off the market."

"Feel better?" He smiled. When I nodded, he kissed the top of my head. "Let's go find those kids."

Fifty-One

AARON CAUGHT UP WITH US after being sidetracked by the press conference. He and Bryson sat in the front seat of the unmarked police car listening to the scanner while I went on a food run. We parked outside the Los Com Padres Meat Market, and lucky for us, they had a hot-dog cart. I didn't look forward to another fast-food meal, but I jumped at the chance to get out of the testosterone-filled car.

I took my time walking back, juggling three hot dogs loaded with condiments and three cans of soda. My balancing act was worthy of the Ringling Brothers.

"Any word?" I handed the food through the window before climbing in.

"No, but they don't usually use the radio to announce raids," Aaron said between bites.

"Then why are we sitting here listening to it?"

"It's more interesting than top forty?" Aaron chuckled as he turned in his seat. "So, can you two do some magic or something to find the kids?"

"Doesn't work that way." Bryson crumpled the empty foil wrapper. "It's all about intention. Since we don't know what's going on, we can't do much."

"We didn't think this through very well." I handed Bryson the remaining half of my hot dog.

Bryson inhaled it. I caught a spark of jealousy in Aaron's eyes. Was he jealous I chose to share my food with Bryson? Aaron turned away and kept quiet. Good for him, because I didn't enjoy playing the rope in their game of tug-of-war.

"I have an idea." I leaned forward. "Aaron, you can go to the scene, right?"

"Yeah." He nodded, narrowing his eyes. "No one except Samuels knows I'm not on duty."

"Good. Like Bryson said, we need to know what's happening in order to help. You can text or call us with information, and we will do what we can from here."

"Such as?" Aaron didn't seem convinced.

"If the killer tries to run, we can do something to slow him down, make him go to sleep or something. I don't know." I waited for Bryson to help me out, but he only nodded.

"Can you do that?" Aaron asked Bryson, clearly not trusting my opinion.

"Yes, that would give us an intention." Bryson finished his soda.

"I'll see what I can find out." Aaron glanced at us and started the car.

Bryson climbed out, but before I could do the same, Aaron took my hand and held me in place. He stared at me and nodded. "Thanks, Tessa."

"Be careful, Aaron." I hopped out, and Aaron drove away. When I turned, Bryson stood beside me with his arms folded over his chest. "What?"

"Just making sure he didn't try to kiss you."

I shook my head. "Thanks, I guess. I have a strange feeling about this case."

"So do I." Bryson clenched his jaw. "Let's go."

Bryson drove until both sides of the road contained nothing except orange groves. It amazed me how quickly an area could change from suburban to rural. He pulled off onto a dirt driveway and angled the SUV between two rows of trees.

"Is it safe to park here? What if it gets towed?"

Bryson held up a hand and closed his eyes. By the time he finished the chant, I felt an overwhelming desire to get out of the vehicle. One minute everything was peachy, the next my skin crawled over my bones. "What did you do?"

"No one will bother the Rover. If they notice it, they won't want to come near it." He pulled his shirt over his head.

My eyes widened, forgetting what we were there to do.

"We'll need our clothes when we shift back."

"Oh." I couldn't understand what had come over me. Bryson was an attractive guy, but I'd never felt such a physical pull to another person.

"Get your head out of the gutter, Tessa." Bryson opened his door and pulled his boots off.

"I'll wait until you're done." I couldn't look away from his muscles as he bent to remove his jeans, wiggling in his seat until he was bare.

"Tessa, I've seen you naked several times now. Quit stalling."

"Sorry. I don't know what's wrong with me."

"What's wrong?"

"I, um, I'm having impulse-control issues."

"This is unusual for you?" Bryson chuckled.

"Sexual impulse control."

"Ah. Yeah, that could be your spirit animal leaking through. I feel it, too."

"You do?"

"Yes, but we don't have time to worry about it now. Focus."

I removed my clothes, though I had no intention of opening the door and exposing myself to anyone who happened to be in the grove. I hadn't figured out how to shift inside of a vehicle. Feeling eyes on me, I turned to see Bryson watching with a look I'd only seen on his face a couple of times. He looked thirsty, but not for water—for *me.* "Get *your* head out of the gutter. You said we didn't have time for sex."

"Later. We will have time later."

I tumbled out the door, not wanting to risk him changing his mind. Not when my body reacted as it did to his expression. We would both combust if he touched me.

I shifted from human to a burst of flames before I got control of my emotions. I could have sworn I heard Bryson chuckle before his spirit animal called to me from the air.

We soared high enough to clear the sentinel pines dotting the landscape. We found the gathering of police vehicles surrounding a small house. Bryson dove low and alighted in a tree near the gathering. I landed in some brush, near where Samuels stood arguing with Aaron.

"The guy is inside with an arsenal of weapons. Right now you're a civilian. You need to go." Samuels put his finger in Aaron's chest.

"Come on. We aren't in range. I'm not going anywhere," Aaron fired back.

I caught movement through a window. Were the kids in there? I couldn't hear much from inside the house over the noise of the police. I hopped deeper into the brush and took flight, circling over the house twice, before landing on a clothesline in the backyard. Bryson landed a few feet from me on the edge of the roof. His dark, predatory eyes searched the area before turning to me.

My spirit animal called to him, reacting to Bryson stronger than I had in human form. Birds didn't go into heat like dogs, but I imagined this was darn close. He must have felt the same, given his preening each time I glanced at him. If his control slipped, we were both in trouble.

A single set of footsteps and one set of lungs working rapidly echoed from the house. They'd moved the kids. I caught Bryson's eye and shook my head. We flew in the direction of Bryson's SUV.

Bryson arrived at the car and shifted, ahead of me. I landed in a nearby tree while he dialed his cell phone. "Aaron, the kids aren't there. What kind of car does Miriam Warner drive?"

When Bryson disconnected, he turned to me. "She's in an older-model white Dodge Caravan. My guess is she's heading for the interstate. Which way? North or south?"

I cocked my head, shook out my wings, and flew north. South meant going into Orlando. People from up here avoided the city. Finding one car on any number of back roads seemed impossible, but burning off some energy might help calm my other urges.

Fifty-Two

A HAWK IN FLIGHT CAN PICK out the movement of a field mouse from a hundred feet away, and can dive at speeds of more than 150 miles per hour. A preternatural hawk and firebird can enhance their hunt with ancient magic and spells. Unfortunately, we couldn't find an old lady and two small children in an old minivan.

Bryson circled back toward the car, and I followed. We shifted back to human form and dressed. When we cooked up the plan, I thought we would find the kids and save the day. We had magic, and we could fly; I thought we were invincible.

"The police will find them, Tessa. We did the best we could." Bryson slipped his shirt over his head.

"I know, I just thought . . ." I buckled my seat belt and checked my phone. "Aaron called several times. What should I tell him?"

Bryson eased the car down the dirt path. He stopped to wait for traffic to pass before pulling out onto the main road. "Tell him we were busy trying to find the kids with magic."

I shook my head. The excuse sounded goofy even if it was true. I dialed Aaron before I chickened out. "Hey, Aaron. Did they find them?"

"Not yet. We put out an APB on the van, but they could be anywhere by now."

I shook my head at Bryson.

"Why didn't you answer my calls? What were you doing?"

"I forgot I turned the phone on 'Silent' earlier. Family drama."

"Not cool, Tessa. I was worried when you didn't answer. I can't solve this case while worrying about you. You need to be more responsible—"

I interrupted his rant. "Hey, Aaron, I need to get to Ocala today and make my statement about Woods. Since there's nothing else I can do right now—"

"Is Bryson taking you?"

"Yes, and I don't appreciate your tone."

"I'm jealous, sue me."

"Aaron, we can't do this right now. You have to find those kids, and I need to make a statement so I can put Paul Woods behind me."

"I know. Look, I'm sorry. You're right. Can I see you when you get back?"

"I don't think that's a good idea." I turned to the window.

"Okay, well. Be safe. Bye, Tessa."

"I will. Bye."

"That sounded rough." Bryson kept his eyes on the road.

"He was worried."

"He was jealous," Bryson countered.

"I know."

"It sounded like you ended it."

I nodded. "This is a disaster."

"Nah, it isn't that bad. He'll get over it." Bryson reached for my hand, and I pulled it away.

"What if I chose him, or neither of you? Would you get over it?"

Bryson seemed to consider my words. "It will hurt like hell, but yeah, I'll respect your wishes."

I snapped my mouth shut. After a moment of silence, Bryson glanced at me and shrugged. The awkward silence hung between us until I couldn't stand it another second.

"I need a pit stop." Not the most eloquent way to break the silence, but effective.

"Rest area or gas station?" Bryson grinned.

"Rest area. The sign said there's one coming up. Unless we need gas, then you can get off the highway. Either is fine with me." The words all gushed out at once, as if they'd piled up inside me and needed to get out—much like the contents of my bladder.

"Do you want to stay in Ocala tonight? We could get a room, or camp out in the National Forest . . ."

My first reaction was a resounding hell, yeah, but the newfound responsible side of me didn't think it was a good idea—not with the way the idea made me heat up. "Do you think it's a good idea? I mean—"

"If I didn't think it was a good idea, I wouldn't have asked."

"Right, but there is this weird attraction going on between us today. I'm trying to do the right thing and not rush into anything."

"It wasn't a proposition, Tessa. But if you don't think you can behave yourself, maybe we shouldn't." The car came to a stop. Relieved, I opened the door, not bothering to wait for him, and rushed to the restroom—and away from Bryson.

I wasted as much time as I could in the bathroom, trying to decide if I should tempt fate and spend the night with Bryson.

Returning, I found him standing a few yards from the car. He stared out past the busy highway toward an open prairie. He was beautiful, with his serious expression and long hair blowing in the breeze. The image belonged on the cover of a historical-romance novel, with him wearing nothing but a loincloth and a few feathers.

I slid my arms around his waist. "I'd like to camp. Do you have a tent or camping stuff?"

Bryson drew me into his arms and pressed his forehead to mine.

"I keep supplies in the Rover."

I closed my eyes and rose on tiptoes to kiss him, and my phone rang. I stepped back and checked the screen. "It's Aaron."

"Where are you? Marion County PD put out an Amber Alert on the van. We got a tip the van was on the turnpike heading north toward 75."

"We're at the last rest stop just before 75. Hang on." I turned to Bryson. "Someone saw the van traveling north toward 75."

Bryson took my hand and led me toward the SUV.

"Aaron, I need to go. We'll do what we can."

I climbed in the SUV, and Bryson pulled to the far side of the rest area.

"Be safe," Aaron said.

"I'll call you if we find them."

I turned to Bryson. "Give me a second to shift."

Bryson cracked his door open. "Catch up."

He shifted before his feet hit the ground. I leaned forward and watched him through the windshield. I ran around the Land Rover and closed the door. Bryson hadn't cast the spell over the vehicle before he left. I crawled under the SUV to stash the keys before I shed my clothes and shifted.

I followed the highway north for several miles, fighting the feeling I was heading in the wrong direction. Bryson and that minivan had to be going this way. A few more miles stretched out, and I couldn't ignore the pull to the west. Instead of following my head, I followed my instincts and let my spirit animal search for Bryson. At some point along the way, I realized I was searching for my mate. The pull was too strong to be anything less.

As I flew, I crossed several two-lane roads. I could feel Bryson nearby, but where? I doubled back and dove until I flew above the canopy of trees, searching the ground for movement. On the side of the road, well hidden under the thick boughs, sat a white minivan. Children were crying below. I landed on a low branch to get a better view.

"Are you going to sit there all day?" Bryson called from below. I chirped. Bryson wore a child's blanket around his waist. If it hadn't been for the pink-and-blue polka dots, it could easily be mistaken for a loincloth.

I landed near his feet and shifted, still giggling.

"What's so damned funny?" His upturned lips ruined his attempt to sound gruff.

"Where's Miriam?" I glanced around for the children's grandmother.

"She's sleeping, until I decide to wake her. Stay here." He walked to the van and opened the side door. He rummaged through a suitcase and pulled out something orange and flowery.

"Oh geez." I shook my head at the muumuu. Gram Mae wore similar dresses, only not in such horrid colors.

"I'll drive. See if you can calm the kids down." Bryson snickered when I pulled the dress over my head. It fit like a tent, but beggars couldn't be choosers, plus, it was better than a blanket.

"I'll drive back to the Rover; we can change and leave the van there."

"Sounds good to me." I squeezed between two car seats and looked between the screaming children. "Why didn't you make them sleep?"

"Magic on kids is tricky. It doesn't always work the way it's supposed to." Bryson watched me in the rearview mirror.

I nodded and took the little girl's hand, smiling. "My name is Tessa. Are you Lilian Rivera?"

Lilian nodded. "Mommy calls me Lilly. Are we going home?"

I blinked back tears. "Yes, sweetheart, we will get you home soon."

Fifty-Three

I CARRIED THE SLEEPING TODDLER, JONAS, into the Orange County Police Department. Lilian Rivera clung to my legs as we followed an officer into a child-friendly room. I didn't want to think about why they had a room painted with bright colors, filled with tiny chairs, and a shelf of toys and coloring books. The idea that so many children were victimized that they needed a special room for them was too much for me to bear.

A female officer stayed with us while Bryson explained how we'd come to be in the possession of two missing children and a conspirator to a kidnapping. I didn't know where they'd taken Miriam Warner, but I felt sorry for her. She believed she was protecting her grandchildren.

Jonas slept so soundly on my shoulder that he left a puddle of drool. My arms ached, but I didn't dare try to put him down.

Samuels came through the door. "Tessa Lamar. I swear, girl, you never cease to be in the middle of a big pile of . . ."

Thankfully, his internal censor went off before he finished his sentence. Lilian peeked at him from behind my legs, tugging on my shirt to get my attention. "Miss Tessa?"

"Yes, Lilly?"

"Is my daddy coming?"

"Your daddy will be here in a few minutes." Samuels smiled at the girl, then leaned close to me. "Warner is gone. Once he found out we had the kids, he gave up the standoff. Suicide by cop."

Another life lost. I adjusted Jonas on my hip as he woke. He looked around the room once, stuck his thumb into his mouth, and laid his head back on my shoulder.

"Is Aaron here yet?"

"He's finishing Mr. Rivera's paperwork." Samuels tilted his head. "You're good with them."

The comment surprised me. I never considered myself the motherly type. The door opened, and Aaron ushered a tearful Mr. Rivera into the room. The children lit up when their father knelt and held his arms open wide. I put Jonas down, and he toddled over to his father. Mr. Rivera stood with Lilian in one arm and Jonas in the other, hugging them like he'd crush them. My eyes blurred, and I looked away.

Aaron wrapped his arms around me, holding my head to his chest as he rocked back and forth. "You did it."

He released me and turned to watch the family reunite. "Bryson said you spotted them on the highway and followed them?"

I nodded, my eyes never leaving the kids.

Mr. Rivera stood and extended his hand. "Thank you. I thought I would never see them again."

I reached for his hand, only to be pulled into yet another hug. "I'm glad they're safe and back with their father."

He nodded and kissed both my cheeks as the little ones hugged my legs. I laughed and knelt, returning their hugs. Bryson stepped into the room, taking in the scene with a smile. He graciously accepted Mr. Rivera's hugs and gratitude.

I turned to Aaron and froze. He knelt, and both kids plowed into his chest. His arms wrapped around them as his eyes met mine. It was the vision I'd seen in the coffee shop.

I sank into a tiny chair before my legs went out from under me.

A look of concern crossed Bryson's face, and he knelt by my side. "Are you okay?"

I wiped my eyes on the back of my hand. "I'm fine. Just tired, I guess."

He didn't buy it. He stood and set his hands on my shoulders. "Detectives, if there's no more paperwork, we've had a long day. I'd like to take Tessa home."

"I still need to take her statement." Samuels looked between us. "It can wait until tomorrow. I'll see what I can do about bringing the Marion County guys to come to the Winter Park station. Might as well kill two birds with one stone."

I tensed at the mention of birds. Bryson looked at me with a knowing expression. The cat, it seemed, was out of the bag. I tried to communicate with my eyes, to apologize without saying the words in a roomful of people. Bryson gave my shoulder a reassuring squeeze. "Ready?"

As I stood, Lilian ran to me. "Miss Tessa, is it time to go home?"

Mr. Rivera answered, "Lilly, we have to go see a doctor first. After we make sure you and Jonas are okay, we can go home."

Tears filled the girl's eyes and fell to her cheeks. I knew better than to make promises I couldn't or wouldn't be allowed to keep. As much as I wanted to tell Lilly what she wanted to hear, I couldn't. The kid had been through enough in the previous weeks to endure any more disappointment. I knelt eye to eye with the girl. "Just a little while longer and you'll be home. I have to go to *my* home now. Okay?"

Lilly nodded and hugged me one last time.

I stood, thankful for Bryson's hand at the small of my back, guiding me forward. Had it not been for the extra support, I may have caved and never left those big brown eyes. It would be so easy to step in and play superhero for Lilly.

I understood the fear and uncertainty that accompanied loss.

Although I'd fought hard to push the pain down—ignore it, deny it, distract myself from it—I couldn't deny the hole in my heart.

Once outside the station, I crumbled. Everything I'd pushed down erupted in an explosion of emotions. I wanted to save Lilly Rivera because she was powerless to save herself. Aaron on one side, Bryson on the other, they cradled me in their embrace while I cried—not for the little girl inside the station, but for the little girl inside myself who was just as lost and scared.

Fifty-Four

"TESSA, YOUR PHONE RANG." BRYSON lifted the corner of my comforter.

"Who was it?" I opened my swollen eyes and reached for a tissue.

Bryson smoothed my hair back from my face. "Aaron."

I needed to do something, to say something to Aaron about our relationship, or lack thereof. I'd tried before, at the Rivera's', but he hadn't stopped flirting. My emotions had overtaken me at the station, and I leaned on both men. I wanted them in my life, but things couldn't go on like this—it wasn't fair to any of us.

"I need to speak to Aaron alone."

Bryson took my hand. "You've had enough to deal with. Take a day or two to think about it. I don't have a problem with him hanging around."

"Thanks, but the longer this continues, the harder it will be."

"Tessa, there are still some things we need to deal with. Do you think it's a good idea to push Aaron away before we settle things with the elders?"

I turned to face him. "What do you mean? Paul Woods is dead. The Rivera case is closed. What do the elders have to do with us?"

"You need to make a decision about Charlie's position."

"I know."

"What do you intend to do?"

"I don't know."

He squeezed my hand. "There is also the issue of our engagement. Buck wants us married."

"We aren't engaged." I couldn't understand why Buck felt he had any say in my personal life.

"We could remedy that, Tessa."

My mouth fell open. Was that some sort of offhanded marriage proposal? "I thought you said I'd been through enough for one day?"

"You have, and I was kidding. There will be no doubt about my intent when I actually propose to you."

He'd said something similar about our first kiss, and I wasn't disappointed when it finally happened. I trusted him to make it special. "Promises, promises."

Bryson chuckled.

"What did you mean about Aaron?"

"It's only a matter of time before he hits their radar. The elders won't be happy if the news runs with the psychic angle."

"Why are you borrowing trouble?"

"I'm not. I just need you to be prepared for whatever happens." He stood and handed my phone to me. "Do what you need to do with Aaron, but don't do it to save my feelings."

"Thanks." I smiled, grateful that Bryson saw past the next five minutes when I couldn't. "I need to talk to him face-to-face."

"I'll give you some time. You need to eat, and there's nothing in the fridge."

"Thanks, Bryson."

An hour later, my doorbell rang. Aaron stood on my doorstep, concerned. "Hey, Tessa."

"Hi. Thanks for coming over."

He walked inside and looked around. "Where's Bryson?"

"He went to get some groceries."

"Are you feeling better?"

After a restless night of crying and too little sleep, my image could have scared a buzzard off roadkill. "A little, I guess. We need to talk."

"I know." He sat beside me on the couch. "Let me say something first."

I nodded, though I didn't want to let him speak first. I worried that he'd say something sweet and I'd lose my nerve.

"I know you and Bryson have a bond. I get it—you share a secret."

"We do, but there's more to it—"

"Let me finish."

"I've been acting like a jackass since I woke up in the hospital. When they told me how close to death I was, it scared me. Then Bryson told me he saved my life, and I was blown away. He's a good guy, but so am I. I have feelings for you, Tessa. I don't want to lose you."

His confession hurt worse than I thought it would. They both had feelings for me, and I for them, but I realized my feelings for Bryson were different. I wondered if I'd feel so drawn to him if we weren't both Nunnehi, but I couldn't change what I was any more than I could change the color of my eyes. "You're an amazing man, Aaron."

"But?" He leaned forward and set his elbows on his knees.

"But we can't be together. I have no right to ask, but I would love to remain friends. I understand if that's not enough for you."

He hung his head. "Do you love him?"

"Yes. You're right, we share a bond that's difficult to understand."

"I won't say I'm thrilled about it, but if he makes you happy, then I'm happy for you."

"He does."

Aaron turned to me. "Friends?"

I smiled, feeling the tension leaving my body. "Friends."

"Do you want me to hang around, or should I go?"

I yawned and settled into the couch. "I'm okay, if you need to go."

"I'll stay until Bryson comes back. You were pretty upset at the station."

"Knowing those kids lost their mother, and almost lost their father, if he is their father." I drew my knees to my chest.

"Blood doesn't make someone a father."

"Or a mother." I had two mothers, though most of the time I felt like I had none.

Bryson came through the door with two armfuls of groceries. "Hey, sorry I didn't knock. My hands are full."

Aaron and I stood and each took a couple of bags. As I put the food away, Aaron and Bryson walked to the door. I thought they would go downstairs for more groceries. Aaron clamped his hand on Bryson's shoulder, speaking low. Bryson patted Aaron's back and smiled

"Have a good one, Tessa." Aaron waved as he left.

Bryson came into the kitchen. "Are you okay?"

"I'm exhausted."

"Hungry?" He took my hand and pulled me to him.

"Starving."

"Sit down and put your feet up while I cook some breakfast."

I plopped on the couch and grabbed the remote. "What did Aaron say to you?"

"He told me I'd have to deal with him and Samuels if I hurt you."

"Nice." I flipped through the channels and stopped on the morning news.

"Nothing to worry about. I don't intend to hurt you."

"Oh, crap." I leaned forward as video footage of the press conference played on the television. "Bryson, oh God. We're on the national news."

Fifty-Five

I'D BETTER CALL HAILEY." I GRABBED my phone and walked toward the bedroom.

Bryson nodded. "Do you know what you're going to do?"

"What can I do? She's going to tell me there's no job."

"You don't know that, Tessa. Talk to her."

"I do know that. Now that the story about me being a psychic has hit the national news, she'll have to fire me. My credibility as a therapist is gone." I'd spent the previous few hours searching the Internet for cases of mental-health-therapist licenses being suspended for unfavorable media coverage. Most of the cases involved the therapist committing a crime, but I was certain my career was over.

"Baby, she's your best friend. Call her back and we'll crawl into bed for the entire day if you want."

"I need ice cream and sappy movies."

"We have ice cream and cable. I'm sure it can be arranged." Bryson grinned.

I wanted to throw something at him. How could he act so casual when I was about to lose my job? "Fine. Give me five and come rescue me."

Bryson kissed my cheek. "I'll be in the living room."

Out of respect for Hailey and her family, I knew I should decline their job offer, but I needed a paycheck. My meager savings account needed life support, and without an income, I couldn't pay next month's rent.

"Hi, Hailey." I hung my head and braced myself for the worse.

"Tessa, are you okay? I've been trying to reach you for days."

"I've been better, but I think I'm on an upswing."

"I still can't believe you helped find the missing kids. You're a hero. I'm so proud of you." Hailey's tone didn't match her words. Tension or apprehension dulled her voice.

"How are you feeling? Has the morning sickness passed?"

"Ugh, no. I'm puking morning, noon, and night, but my doctor thinks it's normal." She laughed, sounding more like herself.

"Hailey, listen, I've been thinking. I don't think I should take the job in your dad's practice. I mean, I really appreciate the offer, but I loved working with the police." I wiped away my tears. As much as I needed the job, I couldn't force my best friend to fire me.

"Really? Oh, that's awesome. Dad's worried that all of the media coverage would spill over into the office." Hailey confirmed my fears.

"I figured."

"So what are you going to do? Have they offered you a position at the police station?"

I smiled to myself, hoping it would leak into my voice. "Not yet, but after finding the Rivera kids and freeing an innocent man, I'm sure they'll find something for me to do. Worst-case scenario, I'll move back with Mae and go back to school. Most forensic experts hold doctorates."

"Other than moving back home, that sounds great. How are Bryson and Aaron?"

"Aaron's back to work, and Bryson is still sleeping on my couch." I headed for the bathroom.

"Couch? I'm impressed with your willpower. If I didn't have Scott,

I'd be all over that."

"I'm trying to be an adult. You know, make good choices and all."

"Right. Well, I don't see a bad choice between Aaron and Bryson—just different degrees of yum."

"Oh no, that's not what I mean. Aaron and I are friends. He's great and all, but he's not the one for me."

"Is Bryson?"

"I think so." I frowned at my reflection. My face bore the proof of yet another day of crying fits and very little sleep.

"That's awesome, Tessa. Scott and I approve. We should get together soon. Double date?"

"Sounds good, Hailey. I need to get a shower. Can I call you later?" I leaned closer to the mirror to inspect my bloodshot eyes.

"Sure, but first promise me you won't overanalyze your relationship with Bryson and dump him before we have a chance to get to know him better?"

"I'll try. Bye, Hailey."

"See you soon, and Tessa, sex isn't always about distracting yourself from something. Sometimes it's about giving yourself permission to feel something." Hailey disconnected before I could reply.

I stepped into the shower and let the water wash away the remnants of the night before. I wondered about Hailey's last comment. She'd encouraged me to hop in the sack with Bryson. Normally, she lectured me about getting too attached and getting naked too soon.

"Tessa?" Bryson knocked on the door.

"Come in."

"How'd it go with Hailey?"

I peeked from behind the shower curtain. "I let her off the hook once I was sure she wanted to rescind the offer. It was the right thing to do."

"I agree."

I stood under the water, trying to decide if I should invite him to join me.

Bryson asked, "What will you do now?"

"I don't know. I'd like to work in criminal justice. Maybe I'll talk to Aaron and Samuels about a job. Maybe go back for my doctorate."

"You could take Charlie's position. The tribe pays a stipend, and the patrons bring gifts."

"I don't think I can pay my rent with venison and trinkets, Bryson."

He chuckled and pulled the curtain to the side. "Most people give cash, Tessa."

I resisted the instinct to cover my pink parts, and held my hand out. "Come here."

"I'm overdressed."

"So?" I turned my back and raised my face up to the water.

Bryon stepped in behind me and ran his hands over my back. I moved to the side to share the water. I'd invited him in, but with him here, my courage faded into uncertainty. He soaped my sponge and motioned for me to turn. Bryson moved my hair over my shoulder and ran the soapy sponge over my back.

"Come to the mountains with me," he whispered.

"I could use a vacation."

"Not a vacation, Tessa."

I turned and met his eyes. "You want me to live with you?"

"I do."

"I can't leave Mae and Dottie." Was this it?

"Then I'll stay in Florida with you, if you'll have me."

"I can't ask you to move here for me." I rinsed my back and reached for a towel.

Bryson grabbed my hand and pulled me against his chest. "You aren't. I'm offering. Do you want me to stay?"

"Yes." I tilted my face toward his, and he leaned in to kiss me.

He cupped my face as he explored my mouth, drawing me in until I wrapped myself around his body.

Bryson moved his hands down my sides to my hips, and lower still. I rolled my hips forward, desperate for him. He turned my back to the wall and dipped his head to my chest, circling my nipple with his tongue. I curled my fingers in his hair, holding on to him for support.

The doorbell rang. Bryson glanced at me, his mouth still fastened to my breast.

"Ignore it." I tugged his hair.

On the third ring, Bryson stepped out of the shower and wrapped a towel around his waist. I dried myself and slipped into my singed robe. Voices rose in the front room. Oh God, was that Darlene?

"Bryson, will you give us a minute," I said as I walked into the room.

"Of course." He turned and went into the bedroom, closing the door behind him.

Darlene grinned at me, quite proud of herself. "Am I interrupting something?"

"Please sit." I refused to defend myself, or what I may or may not have done in the shower.

Darlene sank into a chair. "I knew you were lying to me when you said there was nothing going on."

"Why are you here?"

"I've been calling, and you haven't returned my calls." She looked around the room and back to me. "We need to get to work on the psychic business. We can use Dottie's house. I think we—"

"Did you ever love me?" I'd always wanted to ask but had never had the guts.

"Of course I loved you. Now, as I was saying . . ."

"Why did you leave me with Mae all those times?"

"Tessa, honey, I was a baby myself when I had you. I didn't know how to raise a child."

She continued to talk about capitalizing on my publicity. I imagined being a teen mother, poor, with no education. I tried to see the logic in bouncing in and out of a child's life, but couldn't. I wasn't her daughter, but she didn't know that. "Do you want to know what I think?"

"Yes. Dammit, Tessa, why do you think I've been trying to reach you?"

"I think you're jealous and always have been. You're jealous that I made something of myself, that Mae, Dottie, and Charlie love me, and I think you're angry that I'm not like you."

Darlene laughed, but her eyes narrowed. "Is that so?"

I nodded.

"I loved you. Hell, I still do, even if you're an ungrateful little bitch. I did the best I could by you. If I were such a monster, why would I leave you with Mae? I knew she could do a better job of mothering you than I could. I wanted the best for you, and I wasn't it." She turned her head as tears spilled to her cheeks.

"I'm sorry, Momma. I just can't understand why you're so hateful to me. Why did you call the news station? Do you have any idea how much trouble you've caused?"

"Trouble? What trouble? I told the truth. You saved those kids with your God-given gifts."

"People either don't believe or are afraid of anything different than themselves. This was a high-profile case. When the reports said a psychic was involved it raised red flags." I waved my hand. "It doesn't matter. I lost my job and will probably lose my counseling license."

"Which is why we need to open a psychic shop." Darlene punctuated each word with a pause.

"I can't open a psychic shop."

"Why not?"

Bryson walked into the room and sat beside me. "Because she's not the psychic. I am."

Darlene's eyebrows crawled into her forehead. "You are?"

"Yes, ma'am, and I can't go into business with you. I don't believe in profiting from my God-given gifts." Bryson stood and offered her his hand. "I hate to be rude, but Tessa and I have an appointment."

I stood as Darlene took Bryson's hand. Her cheeks flushed, and for once in her life, she didn't argue. "Thanks for settling that, Bryson."

"No problem." He smiled and ushered her toward the door.

I stepped forward and hugged her. "I love you, Momma. Thanks for answering my questions. I hope one day we can be close."

Darlene pulled back and looked at me. Her lower lip trembled as she nodded. "I'd like that, too, Tessa. I really would."

Fifty-Six

"I WOULD EXPECT THIS FROM THE girl. She's green as a leaf in spring, but you, Bryson? Do you know what you've done?" Buck Oldham could have chewed iron and spit nails.

Bryson hung his head.

"He doesn't know we're shifters," I interjected.

"Not yet. How do you intend to keep such secrets from a detective?" Buck glared at me. "This is not acceptable. You both must sever all ties with Detective Burns or he'll be taken care of."

I shook my head and walked to the window. Two months after we'd rescued Lilly and Jonas, the full Council of Elders summoned Bryson and me. That it had taken two months surprised us.

The council's accusations and demands didn't come as a shock, though how casually they spoke of killing another human surprised me. I wouldn't turn my back on Aaron or Bryson. I decided to play our trump cards.

I stood and moved behind Bryson. *Here goes everything.* I placed my hand on Bryson's shoulders. "With all due respect, Detective Burns is not the concern of the council. I claim Aaron Burns under my protection, just as the Nunnehi, my people, protected your people before the resettlement."

"You cannot claim him. You can barely protect yourself, girl." A chief from the Southern District stood, breaking protocol with his outburst. Several others shouted in agreement.

Bryson stood and took my hand. "I am Tla'nuwa, and she is my mate. We are Nunnehi. We are separate, yet we are a part of the First People."

A collective gasp rose through the gathering, followed by more shouting. Not all the elders gathered had witnessed my first appearance as a firebird. Rumors, like flies, buzzed in a frenzy one moment and were forgotten the next. Even the fact that I'd survived numerous attacks by a skinwalker hadn't impressed the group. They needed to see it with their own eyes, and even then, some still wouldn't believe.

Hand in hand, Bryson and I stood in the center of the gathering and slipped from our human forms. I burned as bright as the ceremonial fire that blazed a few feet away, yet Bryson was unharmed by my flames licking along his wings. We sprang into the air and soared upward into the night sky. When we were nothing more than a red glowing star in the eyes of those below, we turned and dove back toward the earth, only to rise again. The second descent ended with us in human form. My hair flamed at the ends, as my feathers had moments before.

"We are Tla'nuwa. We are the last known Nunnehi. We are separate, and we are part of the First People. We claim the position of shaman, as the blood of Cheasequah, or we will remain as our ancestors once were, separate from the First People." Our voices formed each word in unison.

Buck spoke first. "We will discuss your words."

"No, you won't discuss it. You will do it," I said.

Buck stared at me, his mouth gaping. I doubted anyone had ever back-talked him, or the council. He turned and walked away, with the others following.

Bryson nodded and led me away from the gathering as the men debated the future. He guided me to the river. We stepped into the warm water side by side. He faced me and set his hands on my cheeks, staring into my eyes. "You did great. Though, you shouldn't have disrespected Buck."

"I'm tired of being pushed around."

"Me, too."

"What if they refuse?" My knees trembled, and I didn't know how they kept me upright. We'd gambled with Aaron's life.

"It won't come to that."

Before I could say another word, Bryson pressed his lips to mine. My body melted against his as I parted my lips to accept his tongue. I ran my hands up his back as I drew his lower lip into my teeth, biting until he made a sound of protest. I released it, and his lips curled into a hint of a smile. A small reprieve before he claimed my mouth, leaving me breathless.

Bryson broke the kiss and rested his chin on top of my head. "Someone's coming."

"We can never finish what we start." I eased from his embrace. The decision to wait to get physical until things settled seemed like a good idea at the time; however, I was growing to regret it. It was like waiting until the wedding night to have sex when you're already living with the person. It did nothing but fan the flames, and inspired way too many cold showers.

"Please return to the meeting." The boy who approached us looked scared.

Bryson took my hand, and we returned to the center of the gathering, the same way we'd left it—naked, hand in hand. I held my head high and my shoulders back, feigning self-confidence—easy to do when standing next to Bryson.

Buck stood and faced us. "The council will honor your claim to the position of shaman, after you are joined as husband and wife. The council will not honor protection of Aaron Burns by Tessa, daughter of Atsila."

The words hit me like a punch in the stomach, though I refused to let the air leave my lungs. I stood as still and stoic as Bryson while Buck announced the decisions of the council.

"Should you, together, claim the man, the council will honor the request." Buck looked between us.

"We claim him together," Bryson and I replied. While I hated the politics of the situation, I understood. I was young and still unknown to many of them.

Buck asked Bryson. "Have you given the gifts to Mae, heart mother of Cheasequah?"

"I have not."

Buck grinned. "Did you not take both Mae and Dottie pork and noodles?"

Bryson flinched, and I felt the earth tilt on its axis. We stared at each other for a beat. I turned back to Buck. The darned lo mein would cause me more trouble than heartburn.

"I did." Bryson didn't sound as upset as I would have liked.

"Did Mae accept the gifts?"

Bryson nodded.

Buck had the nerve to grin when he met my eyes. "Did you accept the gifts?"

"I ate the leftovers, if that's what you mean," I shot back, as Bryson squeezed my hand hard enough for it to hurt.

Buck turned to Mae and Dottie. "Did you accept the gifts?"

Dottie bowed her head, and Mae narrowed her eyes. "What are you doing, Buck?"

"Answer my question."

"Charlie would have your hide for this." Mae shook her head. "Yes, we ate the food."

"So you had the bridal feast with the women of your family?" He made the question a statement. "Bryson, while you were here, you shared a feast with the men before your intended came into your room wearing nothing but a blanket."

Bryson nodded. I had no idea what my going to his room had to do with the situation, other than to imply we'd had sex.

"Nothing happened in his room," I said.

"What happened or did not happen behind closed doors is not our concern. The matter is settled." Buck smiled and motioned to someone in the crowd. Three women approached with blue blankets. One draped a blanket over my shoulders, and another draped one over Bryson.

Bryson turned to face me and leaned to whisper, "If you don't want this, now is the time to speak your mind."

I didn't not want this. Did I? The logical part of my brain said this would save Aaron, but I knew it was a lie. I could walk away from all of it—Aaron, Bryson, the tribe—and forget the entire ordeal and get on with my life. No, I couldn't do that, not when I looked into Bryson's eyes and felt nothing except peace.

"I want to marry him one day, but not like this." I turned to Bryson. "I'm sorry."

"I would rather honor you and our marriage with a proper ritual. You deserve more than this."

"We agree to broker peace and to protect our friend, but we will marry when we're ready." I took Bryson's hand.

Bryson spoke to the elders. "I will not dishonor this woman or myself by allowing you to force our hands."

Buck asked, "You are refusing the position within the tribe?"

Bryson and I shared a glance, then answered, "Yes."

"And will sever ties with Detective Burns?" Buck persisted.

"No. We claimed him together, as the council demanded. Our claim of protection has nothing to do with the matter of the position of shaman." I squeezed Bryson's hand tighter.

Buck narrowed his eyes, knowing he'd been played.

Mae chuckled and slapped Buck on the shoulder. "You should have known better than to try to govern Nunnehi. They never have and never will bend to the laws of the council."

Fifty-Seven

DOTTIE AND I SAT IN lawn chairs, soaking up as much of the Florida sun as our fair skin would allow. The days were growing shorter, and the humidity had fallen to a comfortable level. Winter in Florida was pure bliss—there were fewer bugs, and the skies brightened.

Bryson busied himself tending to the new barbecue grill, which he'd bought for Mae on her eighty-seventh birthday. A mischievous chocolate Labrador retriever sat by Bryson's feet, supervising the meat preparation. Maddie, the other woman in Bryson's life, had become a furry member of the family—so much so that Mae allowed the dog in the house and on the furniture—one of many firsts.

Aaron and Mae emerged from the house carrying a pitcher of sweet tea, two bottles of beer, and a bowl of potato salad. "The baked beans will be ready in a few minutes," Mae called to anyone with ears.

Aaron handed Bryson a fresh beer and brought Dottie and me a cup of sweet tea. "Do you ladies need anything else?"

"No, thanks, we're enjoying watching the show." I winked.

"I need to see to the beans." He turned and headed back into the house.

Dottie whispered, "I don't care what you say. That boy is still sweet on you."

"We're just good friends. Besides, I don't think Bryson is willing to share." I giggled at Dottie's expression. Everyone assumed the three of us had had wild threesomes, but the sad truth was that I hadn't had sex since the day Charlie died. I promised myself time to heal without romantic entanglements. Unfortunately, I was up to my eyeballs in romance, and it was high time I ended the celibate streak.

Bryson's cell phone rang, and I listened to half the conversation. I hoped one of the tribe didn't need healing or a love charm today, our only day off. Dottie was renting her house to Bryson, who'd turned it into a part-time art studio and part-time medicine shop. He used Charlie's old office as a bedroom, though most nights he slept at my apartment. Once word got around we were open for business, a steady flow of people came by seeking all sorts of requests and favors. I helped out between working murder cases.

I'd accepted a position with the Orange County Police Department as a victim's advocate. My new job put me in the perfect position to use my gifts to help solve crimes. The best part of the job was working with Aaron and Samuels. Life was pretty darned good.

"Another appointment?" I called out as Bryson put the phone back in his pocket.

"For Tuesday." He jogged over to me and stole a quick kiss. A screech interrupted our face time.

Mae swatted at Maddie, who'd managed to steal one of the bigger steaks off the grill. The dog hightailed it to the other side of the yard to enjoy her prize. Mae fumed, as close to cursing as she could be without needing a mouthful of soap.

Bryson pressed his forehead to mine. "Do you think we'll ever get an uninterrupted kiss?”

“Mmm-hmm, tonight, my place.” I laughed when he kissed the tip of my nose, and ran off to reassure Mae. We had enough steak to feed a small army.

“Too bad,” Dottie mumbled under her breath.

“Too bad, what?”

“Too bad they wouldn’t share you.” Dottie laughed deep in her belly as I blushed from my hairline to my chest.

“Aunt Dottie.” I shook my head, giggling.

“What? People do it. I’ve even seen it on the soaps.” Dottie smiled with a wicked gleam in her eye.

None of us could recall the moment it happened, the moment when grief gave way to a new sort of normal that brought peace and bits of pure joy. Yet, here we were, a family with a couple of new members and a pain-in-the-butt dog to top it off.

“I love this.” The breeze picked up, and the cobalt-blue and clear bottles in the bottle tree clanked together, reminding me of Charlie.

“Do you hear it?” Dottie turned her head toward the tree, smiling as she closed her eyes.

“Yes, ma’am.” The breeze carried the sweet whistled tune from the tree to the garden. The rustle of leaves and the clanking of bottles mingled perfectly into the song. “Yes, I do.”

About the Author

Kathryn M. Hearst is a southern girl with a love of the dark and strange. She has been a story teller her entire life, as a child she took people watching to new heights by creating back stories of complete strangers. Besides writing, she has a passion for shoes, vintage clothing, antique British cars, music, musicians and all things musical (including theatre). Kate lives in central Florida with her chocolate lab, Jolene; and two rescue pups, Jagger and Roxanne. She is a self-proclaimed nerd, raising a nerdling.

Find more books by Kathryn:
https://www.facebook.com/kathrynmhearst
https://www.kathrynmhearst.com

People are sustained by eating food. Authors live on reviews. Please consider leaving a review for The Spirit Tree on Amazon, Goodreads, or social media.

Made in the USA
Charleston, SC
19 July 2016